Craft

Gibson Boys Series, Book #2

Adriana Locke

UMBRELLA
PUBLISHING INC.

Books by Adriana Locke

My Amazon Store
Signed Copies

Brewer Family Series

The Proposal | The Arrangement | The Invitation | The Merger | The Situation

Carmichael Family Series

Flirt | Fling | Fluke | Flaunt | Flame

Landry Family Series

Sway | Swing | Switch | Swear | Swink | Sweet

Landry Family Security Series

Pulse

Gibson Boys Series

Crank | Craft | Cross | Crave | Crazy

The Mason Family Series

Restraint | The Relationship Pact | Reputation | Reckless | Relentless | Resolution

The Marshall Family Series

More Than I Could | This Much Is True

The Exception Series

The Exception | The Perception

Chapter 1

Lance

One hand working the tie around my neck, I lift the phone with the other. No picture, not even a real name, just a silver-grey profile picture with a bright pink set of lips pressed into a kiss. Why this generic image representing a woman I've never met makes me smile, I'll never know. But, in my thirty-some years of life, I'm learned not to question every reaction. There's no fun in that.

My fingers swipe across the screen, the upturn of my lips firmly in place.

> Me: Only when excellence calls for it.

> Nerdy Nurse: Now you're making me regret this thing that came up.

My fingers stall. Hovered over the keys, I re-read her words.

This is the most bizarre thing I've ever done. Carrying on this little conversation-ship with Nerdy Nurse isn't, on the surface, my idea of a good time. I downloaded this dating app to keep from having any words ending in -ship. Yet, our back-and-forth is something I look forward to. Her wit and curiosity, her intelligence, is something that I crave. Even when we make plans to meet nearly every week, one of us will inevitably cancel. I'm okay with that because it means a continuation of this little thing we have going on.

Do I want to meet her? Abso-freaking-lutely. I want to fuck her so hard, so soft, so thoroughly that she's ruined for anyone else. Until then, I'm good with this messaging thing. Strangely.

Adjusting my cock inside my khaki's, I grab my briefcase and head into the kitchen. The coffee pot has one last cup left in the bottom and I pour it into a travel mug before flipping off the switch.

The clock on the stove shines the time my way in a bright, red warning that I'm going to be late. With a nod that way, I place my things on the counter and pull out my phone again.

> Me: I bet it's going to be harder for me to get it down than you, if you catch my drift.

> Nerdy Nurse: The pitfalls of being a man. 😌

> Me: Reschedule?

I can't even type the words without a chuckle.

> Nerdy Nurse: What would we be if we weren't rescheduling? Ha! I'm not sure what shift I'll be on after tonight, so I better not commit quite yet.

> Me: A woman after my heart.

> Nerdy Nurse: Not exactly what I'm after. Hearts make me squeamish.

> Me: Keep talking dirty to me. 😉

Grabbing my things, I manage to get to the car and into the driver's seat as her chat bubble flickers as she types on her end. Just before I pull out, her words pop up.

> Nerdy Nurse: Blood is pouring onto the floor as we speak. Dirty enough?

> Me: Blood makes me squeamish.

> Nerdy Nurse: The guy before this had gangrene. Should we try that?

> Me: You're twisted.

> Nerdy Nurse: I really need to go now.

> Me: You know where to find me. At the top of your matches.

Nerdy Nurse: And to think you started at the bottom. If I hadn't changed my preference from biographies to historical reads, you might've stayed there.

Me: Is that where you like it? The bottom?

A quiet groan passes my lips as I imagine her sprawled out under me. I wonder what she looks like, tastes like, what her voice sounds like as it moans my name. The scent of her sweat as he drips down her chest, the feel of her skin damp from her arousal.

Flicking on the car, the clock blazes the time and I know I'm already a few minutes behind. I need to get out of the garage, but her chat bubble bounces again and my mind imagines her tits, round and firm, bouncing in front of my face.

Good god. Get a grip.

Nerdy Nurse: Taking notes?

Me: Every good student takes notes.

Nerdy Nurse: And here I thought you told me you were a teacher.

Me: You can't teach what you don't know and I never stop learning.

Nerdy Nurse: Such a nerd answer.

Me: Looks like we're a match then.

Nerdy Nurse: I was hoping for more … alpha.

> Me: I hate that modern society thinks nerds can't be alphas. Who runs the word? Who has the true power in the universe? Nerds. We just don't go flexing around about it.

> Nerdy Nurse: Sounds like the start of a syndrome …

Foot on the brake, I move the shifter to reverse but still don't back out.

> Me: Are you talking medical to me now? Let's go back to the dirty part. I liked that better.

> Nerdy Nurse: Bye.

> Me: Don't get cold feet on me now. I was just getting going.

> Nerdy Nurse: You're exhausting.

> Me: You're still responding.

> Nerdy Nurse: You're so full of yourself.

> Me: Bet you wish you were full of me.

Nerdy Nurse offline

My phone hits the leather seat beside me with a thud.

As I wait on the garage door to open, thoughts of Nerdy Nurse begin to fade away. They're replaced with thoughts of work and, most importantly, what I'm doing on my lunch break.

I just hope there's peanut butter icing involved.

Chapter 2

Mariah

"Let me be clear about one thing ..."

"No, let me be clear about one thing," I say, whirling through the doors of my office, my voice leading the way. "Get out of my office, Lance. Now."

Shoulders thrown back, lips pressed together just as firmly as my arms clench across my breasts, I say a silent prayer my demonstration is enough to convince him I mean business. Then, I do what I always do: brace for his attack.

His free hand clasps the back of his neck, toying with the edges of his hairline, which is sharp from a fresh cut at the barber shop. He runs his palm around the side of his throat as he releases a low, amused chuckle. "Jessa, I'm going to have to call you back."

"You don't have to call her back," I say, aware my voice is projecting a few octaves louder than usual or necessary. "You just have to take it somewhere else."

Three.

Two.

One.

The bastard turns to face me, his full lips twisted into an undeniable smirk.

Bingo.

His shot is fired.

"I'm at work," he says into the phone. He may be talking to her, but there's no doubt his attention is set on me. Gaze searing into mine, the heaviness making it hard to breathe, he swipes his bottom lip with a slow, single stroke of his tongue. The wetness left in its wake seems to somehow make its way between my thighs.

Damn it.

Every morning when I pull into the staff parking lot, I tell myself it'll be different. This is the day I won't let Lance Gibson's patented way of getting to me work. That he won't quiet me with his smirk, immobilize me with his big green eyes, and twist me into a knot with his crude words delivered with the punch of a professional.

Of course, I'm also saying these things while balancing a tray of baked goodies I think he'll love. I hate myself for that almost as much as I hate that I'll be stripping myself of my panties in the ladies' room between study halls because he's so goddamn sexy and I can't bear to feel them soaked between my thighs for the rest of the day.

Needless to say, I fail before I even walk in the door. I'm only a mortal. Silver lining? I'm a smarter mortal than I used to be. Nowadays, I can see what Lance is and ascertain what a disaster this intelligent, beautiful, smoldering book loving man would bestow upon me. After I spend the walk from my car to the high school library's doors imagining every way he'd touch me, I also visualize the heartbreak that would coincide with the ache elsewhere.

No, thank you.

"Do you think I fuck women while I'm working, Jessa?" he continues, amusement laced in his tone as he watches me with a perfectly quirked brow. "What kind of an animal do you think I am?"

"Oh, for the love of God," I mutter.

Setting my refrigerated lunch bag down, I cast him a narrowed glare as I make my way around my desk. The water in my purple

Librarians Are Cool cup is room temperature, but I take a sip anyway. It's a futile attempt to redirect my attention away from Lance and the vivid imagery of him with his fist in my hair as he bends me over this desk. This vision will be useful later, but not right now.

His games are frustrating. Listening to him make plans with his bevvy of bimbos is more than annoying, even if I'm conscious they may not be bimbos. It's possible they're just sexually satisfied and able to separate love from sex. Good for freaking them. I hate them.

As I watch him lean against the wall and his tongue sneak out between his perfectly straight teeth, I realize: I can't blame him. At least he owns his philandering. Unlike my good-for-nothing, no-balls-having ex, Eric—Lance owns it. I can respect that.

I wish I could hate him. But how do you hate something that aesthetically pleasing, especially when he dampens his crass with just enough charm to soften you up? You can't. I can't, anyway. I can only remind myself to look through the smolder well enough to see the Y-chromosome. That specific chromosome, after all, carries the "master switch" gene, SRY, which decides whether an embryo will be a male or a female. It's like men are apologizing from the start.

"Eight o'clock. See you then." With a flourish, he drops his phone into the pockets of his pants. "How are you today, Ms. Malarkey?"

"My office is not a phone booth for your ... whatever that was." My cup hits the desktop with a thud, the chair beneath me squeaking as I relax onto its leather cushion. He leans forward, hands planted on a stack of papers, a grin digging deep against his chiseled cheeks.

There's nowhere to go, no way to put any distance between us, but that's not the problem. The problem is that I like it. And he knows it.

"Would you like to know what that was?" he teases.

"No." Heat radiating from my face like it's spent a long day in the sun, I stare back in hopes it'll distract him from my blush.

"I can give you all sorts of details. Bet some of them will make you blush more than you are right now."

My lips part to respond, to tell him he's dreaming, but the twinkle in his eye stops me. He'd enjoy calling me out if I were to say anything. It's happened more times than I care to admit. Instead, I deflect.

"You can't keep coming in here," I tell him half-heartedly. "It's an invasion of my privacy."

"That's what this is about, isn't it?"

"Of course it is. We have this conversation every week."

And we've had it for so many weeks you could measure it in months. The exact date this began is lost to time, but it seems like it's always been this way—him working to irritate me, me working to be irritated by him.

Biting the inside of his cheek, he fights a grin. "You're just mad that's all I'm invading."

"You wish." *I wish.*

"Not denying that," he says, a flicker of something I don't want to name ghosting across his face. "Is that a roundabout offer?"

"Hardly," I scoff. *Totally.*

His burst of laughter sounds through the room just like his cologne spices the air as he moves.

"How many women do you talk to? In here alone? Since the beginning of the year, I'm guessing twenty? Thirty? More?"

He cocks his head to the side. "Just talking?"

"Oh my God ..."

"Fine. While I find it extremely satisfying you estimate my numbers that high, I would have to disagree with your figures. There are repeats."

"You do see some of them more than once?" I balk. "That's surprising."

"Why is that surprising?"

"I don't know," I shrug. "I just figured you for a one-and-done kind of guy. Maybe that's because I figured some of those women would be smart enough to not take your shit a second time, but I could be wrong."

"For the record, smartass, they're more than willing to take my shit multiple times," he winks.

Scoffing, I turn away.

The afternoon sun is poised almost directly across from my office, the streaks of light warming my skin as I face it. Lance moves around behind me, the energy exuding off him and tugging at me from different angles.

Despite my exasperation with his man-whoring, selfish ways, this part of my day is always my favorite. It's the routine of it all, the mere predictability of his insolence, the sureness of his presence. There's something steadying about him that I can't quite put my finger on and don't try to. Putting my finger on something about Lance, even if it's in theory, feels like opening a can of worms I can't afford to unlock.

"What can I say?" he asks. When I turn back around, he's shoving his phone back into his pocket. "I'm a hot commodity."

"So I've heard."

"Ah, so you admit you eavesdrop?"

I stare at him blank-faced as I stand. "It's not hard when I walk in here and you're giving aural."

His laugh permeates the space between us. The blend of rugged and smooth creates a sensation in the room that I couldn't ignore if I tried.

"Giving aural?" he chuckles. "Is that a partial Freudian Slip?"

"No." Sighing, I fall back into my chair again. My shoulder bumps my computer and bring the screen to life. "Will you just go?"

"Let me ask you a question."

"No."

"When is the last time you went out on a date?"

"Recently enough," I reply, not looking up from the computer screen.

There's no way I'm telling him my last real date was six weeks ago and that I've been in a dry spell for almost six months. Someone like him, someone who doesn't bother with liking, feeling, or loving doesn't get hurt. People like me, who get our emotions twisted up in a half a second flat, have to guard ourselves constantly. It complicates everything.

Half-sitting on my desk, he stills. "Really? With who?"

"What's it to you?"

"It's nothing to me. I'm just curious," he says, his tone a touch softer than before.

This is what kills me with this man. This is the final move in his little game of chess, the one that captures the king. Or, in this case, the librarian.

It's his ability to switch from smolder to sweet, from crass to charismatic, that, as much as I would never admit it out loud, intrigues me. I hate that I notice and I wish with every book on the shelves in this library I didn't, but he makes it impossible.

He's impossible.

I face him again. This time, folding my hands in front of me only inches from his thigh, I lean forward. He bites; he's leaning closer to me like I'm about to tell him a secret.

"Lance?" I whisper.

"Yeah?"

"Take your curiosity out of my office."

A low rumble courses from his throat as he twists his lips in amusement. "I'm about to take—"

We both jump, Lance clamoring to his feet as I shove away from my desk at the sound of a knock. The door is semi-closed, but Tish's head pokes through the small opening. "Am I interrupting something here?"

"No," I say, running a hand through the air. "Mr. Gibson was just leaving."

"Uh-huh," Tisha grins. "Looked like it to me."

"I wasn't, but guess I will now." Lance sweeps his gaze across the room, stalling briefly on me, before settling on a plastic-covered bin on the corner of my desk. "Have you had one of these, Tish?" He pulls back the plastic and exposes the chocolate cupcakes with peanut butter frosting I made last night. "Damn, they're good."

"Hey! Those aren't for you," I tell him, jerking the plastic back over the dessert.

"Your fault," he says, grabbing one and pulling back the yellow paper liner. "You left them unattended."

"In my office."

"Unattended." He breaks his smile only long enough to insert half the cupcake. "So good." Crumbs fall from his mouth along with the words, a dollop of icing is left in the corner of his mouth as he swallows.

"Missed some." Tish points to his face. "I could lick it off, if ya want."

"Why aren't you this helpful?" Lance asks, looking pointedly at me.

Tish giggles. "Because I don't have a boyfriend."

"And you do?" he asks, his brows pulled together.

"You were leaving. Remember?" I ask, crossing my arms in front of me.

"I think you missed the part where I said *I* don't have a boyfriend," Tish interjects. "That was the focal point of the sentence. Me. Unattended, if you will."

Lance laughs, licking his lips. "You'd break me in half."

"Oh, you have no idea," Tish purrs.

He starts to leave but turns back and grabs another cupcake.

"Are you serious right now?" I ask, jerking the dish toward me. "Get out of here."

"I'm going. I'm going," he chuckles, heading for the door. "Good-bye, ladies."

"I have Prep sixth period," Tish calls after him. "I'm happy to chat. I'll bring brownies tomorrow."

Knowing there's no chance Tish isn't watching him, I don't bother pretending I'm not.

As he reaches for the door, his back muscles shift beneath his shirt and I'm taken back to the day in the spring when I stayed late to shelve books. The doors were locked so I had to exit through the gymnasium. The sound of squeaking tennis shoes and shouts from the basketball team met me in the hallway, so I was prepared for that. What I wasn't prepared for, not in the least, was to see Lance shirtless, sweaty, and mid-layup. That V-cut of his groin is imprinted, permanently, I fear, in my brain.

"Is it wrong that I requested my classroom be moved across the hall from his?" Tish asks. "Principal Kelly just laughed, but I don't think it's a coincidence he's positioned in the middle of a bunch of male teachers."

"What are you getting at?"

"She wants him for herself! Obviously," she groans.

"She's married," I laugh. "And so are you."

"And what point is that supposed to make?" she sighs. "I'm fifty percent sure my husband is screwing his secretary, which is fine by me but I wish he'd just leave me for her. Damn. Let her do his laundry."

"Tish!"

"What? My God-fearing soul can't file for divorce."

"But you can have an affair?"

"What is this? Morality hour?" she laughs, taking a cupcake from the tray. "Besides, I don't know how any woman could have restraint around him." Watching me expectantly, she waits for my reaction as she peels the wrapper from the dessert.

I look down, cheeks hot. Again.

"Do you?" she asks.

"Do I what?"

"Come on, Mariah. Don't you find that boy attractive?"

Gulping, I pucker my lips together. "I find him ... frustrating."

"All the good-looking ones are, honey," she says, biting into a cupcake. "These are good."

"Thanks. You have some icing on the corner of your mouth," I laugh.

She grabs a tissue and dots her lips. "Every day I come in here and every day he's in here. That wouldn't be true if all you found him was frustrating."

"Look," I say, gathering my pride, "he's cute. For sure. But I've had cute. Eric was cute. He was smart on paper. He could be funny. And the only good screwing I got out of him was out of the sheets."

Ignoring my shiver, Tish pushes on. "You need to forget about him. It's been, what? Two years?"

"Ish," I sigh. "And I have forgotten about him. I just remembered him to make a point."

Her laugh fills the room as she brushes her hands off over the trashcan. "What about the guy you've been seeing? How's that going?"

"I haven't been seeing anyone," I mutter.

Picking up a paper, I try to be interested in the numbers. Truth is, I have no idea what I'm even looking at. Saying Eric's name out loud, something I never do, ushered in a tenderness in my heart I can't just brush off. It hurts. It stings. I wonder if it always will.

The bell rings, breaking me out of my reverie.

"I gotta get back to my classroom," Tish says. "The freshmen are in there and they're the worst class I've had in the twenty years I've been teaching."

"Good luck with that," I say.

"See ya tomorrow."

She disappears into the library. I turn towards my computer when I spy the cupcake container. The plastic is dropping into the icing, the pieces missing from Tish and Lance.

As I fix the covering, a warmth washes over me like a warm summer rain. I settle back in my chair and try to get back to work. Yet, as my fingers hover over the keyboard, they don't move. Instead, I glance at the cupcakes again.

Memories sweep through my mind of baking with my grandmother. She taught me the peanut butter icing recipe that Lance loves so much. Gran taught me how to bake, crochet, and even let me read the romance novels I craved though my mom said they were trash.

Everything was trash to her unless she could garner a social benefit. Me included.

One day, I tell myself, swiping up a dab of icing on my finger. One day I'll have a family of my own and won't rely on acceptance from co-workers to prove my mettle.

Chapter 3

Lance

The bell blares its final warning for students to be seated.

Hopping onto the edge of my desk, I face a room full of animated juniors. It never ceases to amaze me that the human population doesn't die off at age seventeen. At that point in our lives, we think with our genitals, smell like shit from either perspiration or too much cheap cologne, and have virtually no idea what we're doing. Yet, we make it. Somehow.

With no regard for his classmates or my classroom, the captain of the football team elbows a girl a third of his size out of his way and takes her seat.

He may be the one who doesn't make it.

"Brandon!" I shout over the ruckus in the room. "To the office."

The students quiet, settling into their desks. They look from me to Brandon.

"Are you fucking kidding me?" he asks, scrambling to his feet. "What's up your ass?"

My foot if you don't get out of here.

"Class," I say, my eyes still pinned to Brandon. "What's the first rule of history?"

"It repeats itself," they respond in unison.

"It repeats itself. That's right." I mosey toward the door and yank it open. "Last week, you accidentally bumped Mr. Greyson and knocked him into the wall. Do you remember that?"

His jaw sets.

"There was plenty of room for you to walk around but you found it acceptable to plow through him instead. I removed you."

His eyes narrow.

"You just took Ms. Cambria's books off her desk and kicked her out of her spot. The first rule of history applies: you will be leaving us once again. Only this time, the second rule of history applies too."

"The second rule?" Stacy asks from the front row.

"You never get the war you want." Flipping my gaze back to Brandon, I nod toward the hallway. "Get out."

"But—"

"You want to flex your muscles? Do it in the principal's office."

"But—"

"What?" I ask, lifting a brow. "That's not the fight you're after? Suddenly it's not fair for someone with more power to exert control?"

"Fuck this," he snaps, storming by me.

"I refuse to believe you're the dumb jock you try so hard to make us all believe."

This catches his attention. He stills, his fingers re-gripping the edge of his books, as he stops on the second landing leading to the office. I step into the hallway and partially shut the door behind me.

"Pushing people around and using language any idiot can use isn't doing you any favors, Brandon," I say, just loud enough for him to hear.

He doesn't look back, but doesn't move forward either. I take this as a win.

"You might get away with that at home and in your other classes, but you won't in mine. I expect you to work to your ability and behave the same. Is that clear?"

There's no answer, and I don't expect one. He heads down the steps with a little less flare than before.

I head back inside my classroom. "Cause and effect, boys and girls," I say, hopping back onto my desk. "Act like a fool, get treated like one."

"You sound like my dad," Kyler laughs.

"Your dad must be a genius. But is he as good looking as me?"

"That would be a no," Stacy giggles.

The entire room bursts into laughter and I kick myself for walking right into that one. "Okay. Settle down. I want you to write a paper ..." Standing and walking around my desk to the dry erase board as their moans ring out behind me, I write out the topic in black marker. "Write a minimum of one thousand words about a historical event of your choice and what caused it and its effects on the world."

"Can I write about Kim—"

"No." Looking at Stacy over my shoulder, I shake my head.

"But—"

"No."

"But she—"

"All events must have taken place before you were born." I look at the fairly young faces of my students. "That should eliminate a lot of popular topics," I say pointedly at Stacy.

"Fine," she grumbles.

They busy themselves writing down the assignment, whispering amongst each other about potential subjects. Everyone, that is, but Ollie.

Ollie's head is down on his desk, his arms stretched out and dangling over the edge. The mop of hair that used to be kept cut short is a wild array that somewhat resembles a broom.

Last spring, he was one of my best students. Bright as fuck. Engaging. A charisma that reminded me of my cousin Peck. As the year went on, his clothes became wrinkled. His face more blemished. The edges of his papers more frayed.

"We have a game tonight, Mr. Gibson," Lottie says from her chair. "Can we work on this today in class? Please?"

"How are your extracurricular activities any fault of mine?" I scoff playfully, snapping the cap back on the marker. Glancing down at the stack of papers needing grading, I decide to give in ... eventually. After all, I can't let them think I'm easy. They aren't the right demographic for that.

"I'll dedicate my first goal to you tonight," Lottie offers, smiling a mega-watt grin.

Sighing for effect, I slip into my chair and kick my feet up onto my desk. "You need to do better than that."

"We won't try to negotiate a lower word count," Kyler offers.

I pretend to consider this.

"I won't tell Ms. Malarkey you stole a cupcake from her office." Stacy raises a brow, her lips pursed together. "I saw it on your desk."

"She gave that to me, thank you very much." My voice is smug, as is the look on my face. "She gave me two, actually."

"You two have a thing going on? She's single, you know. And freaking pretty," Stacy shrugs. "Just saying."

I begin to object, to point out Mariah just told me she wasn't single. Before the words can escape my lips, I stop.

"I'm just saying," I say, pulling my feet to the floor, confusion wracking my brain, "which staff members are single is none of your business."

"Since you're too old for me, at least for another couple of years, you should consider—"

"Enough," I say over top of her.

The room breaks out into a fit of giggles and I give up.

"Fine. You win." My hands thrown up in the air in defeat. "Work on your papers now. But if any of you start talking, I'll lecture. I can talk all day about the Revolutionary War, kids."

Much to my surprise, they pull out their notepads. I refrain from pacing around the room and making sure they're writing what they're supposed to because I'm certain they aren't and I don't have it in me to argue with them today. I'm just happy they didn't press their luck because my brain is stuck solidly on Mariah's dating life and not a war that took place in the seventeen hundreds.

With a final glance at Ollie's napping frame, I move to grab a paper off the pile. My arm hits the discarded cupcake wrapper.

A soft, half-laugh finds it way past my lips as I grab the wrapper and toss it into the trash. Mariah is too easy to mess with, too easy to rile up. Her predecessor in the library was a senile old woman who never used the office. The first day Mariah walked in and caught me in a conversation that straddled the line of acceptable in a high school building, she ripped my ass. I, in turn, wanted hers. Beneath me. My hands cupping each round globe of her ass cheeks.

"Shit," I mutter, adjusting my cock as discreetly as I can and forcing all thoughts of a naked Mariah Malarkey out of my mind.

The bell rings, assisting my efforts for once. "Have a good night, everyone. Stay out of trouble." The kids leap to their feet, grabbing book bags and making plans for the weekend; it's a scene of complete chaos. "Ollie, can you stay for a minute?"

He gathers his things and waits for the room to clear out. Once it's just the two of us, I sink back against my desk. "How are things?" I ask.

His shoulders rise and fall. "Good. Fine. Why?"

There's a hesitation in his voice that causes me to hesitate too. If I push, he'll close up. It's the code of teenagers.

"I have a younger sister and two younger brothers. It's a thing when you're the oldest kid in a big family—you notice things. And I've noticed you sleeping a lot in class lately." Ignoring the rest of what I've observed, I tread a little deeper. "Things okay at home?"

"Yeah. It's all good." He shuffles his feet, his t-shirt hanging loose around his middle. "I appreciate you checking on me, Mr. Gibson, but I'm just tired. I can't miss the bus."

"Sure. Yes, go ahead." There's something that gnaws at me as I watch him leave. The sensation grows with each step he takes towards the door. He's almost passed me before I speak again. "Hey, Ollie?"

"Yes, sir?"

"Just going to toss this out there—if you ever need help with something, don't hesitate to reach out, okay?"

Shuffling his sneaker against the linoleum, he nods his head. "Sure. Thanks, Mr. Gibson."

With a little wave, I watch him join the masses in the hallway and disappear from sight. Then, just as quickly as the hallway filled with students, it empties.

Taking my time, I grade a few papers on the history of Latin America. Placing Brandon's essay on top, I make a few remarks that the laziness used to put together this project won't cut it. This kid is capable of so much more. His parents don't push him. His other teachers let him get away with half-assed work. Everyone seems to walk on eggshells around this kid just because he can play football and a few big schools are rumored to be looking at him.

Fuck that.

I'm all for following your dreams, but I'm also for following logic. Logic says you aren't going to make it in professional ball, so you better have something to fall back on. Like a work ethic. A useful mind. Good habits.

While I'm straightening the stack of papers, movement in the hallway catches my eye. I'd know that ass anywhere.

My briefcase is on the floor and I grab it on the way out. After switching off the light, I head down the corridor littered with gum wrappers and wadded up paper. My steps increase so I can jet by the teacher's lounge as Principal Kelly's voice rings through the partially opened door. By the time I hit the double doors leading to the parking lot, I'm nearly jogging.

Then I stop.

I don't time this perfectly every day. Not that I don't try, it's just Mariah is erratic. Sometimes she leaves at the bell, sometimes she's here well past dark.

"Well, imagine seeing you out here," I say, closing the distance between us. She stutter-steps, not looking back, as I approach. "How was your day?"

The wind ripples through the empty parking lot. Her long, dark hair that I'm one-hundred percent sure would look perfect wrapped around my hand as I pull her head back and plant kisses down the side of her neck before burying myself in her sweet little body, billows in the air.

"It was a good day," she says, stepping up on the curb. "How was yours?"

"After the sugar high from the cupcakes?" I grin. "Those were great, by the way."

"Those weren't for you."

"Eh. I think maybe they were."

"Oh, really?" she laughs. "How do you figure?"

Our steps stop at the same time. We stand at the front of our cars, parked side-by-side by no accident. Her cheekbones are high, framing the pink-hued cheeks that have been kissed by the cool breeze.

"You know I use your office as my personal phone booth. When you leave little treats laying around, it certainly feels like you're training me. Like Pavlov's dog. I use your office—I get a treat." Holding my hands to the side, I shrug. "I can't help it you've trained me to come see you every day."

Her eyes roll as she uses her key chain to unlock her car with the press of a button. "I'm going to get a lock installed."

"You are not or you would've done it way before now."

Her lips part, as if she's about to argue, but nothing comes out. She opens the back door and tosses her bag into the seat.

"I heard a nasty rumor about you today," I say, leaning on the side of my car.

"This should be interesting."

"Seems a girl in one of my classes thinks you're single."

Her laugh is light as she leans against her car. We face each other, our stances mirrored. "I'm glad the student body is spending their energy concerned about my dating life."

"It was an offhanded comment," I admit.

"And we wonder why their grades are plummeting."

"Is it true?"

"Yes, their grades are plummeting," she winks.

Tucking my hands in my pockets, my goal is to appear casual. "Not what I meant."

"Um ..." She tucks a strand of hair behind her ear. "I'm not sure why that matters."

"It doesn't," I say. "But is it true?"

"Kind of?" she laughs. "I hate labels."

"If I were the guy you were seeing, I'd hate to think you were 'kind of' single."

Shoving off the car, she laughs again. "Oh, I bet you would. You make that completely clear with your girls, don't you? You're like, 'Now, remember. I'll be sleeping with Gloria tomorrow so you are absolutely single.'"

"That's not what I mean," I say, standing straight too. Although she's right. But this isn't me. This is her. It's different. "I mean, doesn't the guy you're seeing find offense in that?"

Her arms cross in front of her and it's clear she's not about to answer my questions. I voluntarily change the subject.

"Do you ever make red velvet cupcakes?" I ask. I don't even know what the hell those are, but I heard my brother's girlfriend talk about them the other day at Sunday dinner.

"I have," she says, obviously confused. "I make them sometimes for the Senior Center."

"The nursing home over by the church?"

"Yeah. Long story, but I knew a girl who worked there. She would tell stories about some of the residents and how they didn't have family and it broke my heart. So I bake for them sometimes." A small smile slips across her face. "There's this old man there. They call him The Mayor, but I'm not sure he ever was the mayor," she laughs.

"Anyway, Red Velvet is his favorite. I make sure there's some in every batch I deliver."

There's something different about her, a gentleness I don't see often. She's usually raring to go with me, a sharp tongue ready and waiting.

"Lance?"

"Sorry," I say, clearing my throat. "That sounds like a nice thing to do."

"It gives me purpose." She no sooner than finishes the sentence before she sticks a finger my way. "Don't even."

"Don't even what?" I laugh.

"Don't make fun of me for saying that."

"I ..." Cocking my head to the side, I reconsider. "We all need a purpose. We just get them from different places. You get yours from cake ... well, I kind of get mine from your cake too."

Rolling her eyes, she pops open the driver's door. "Big plans tonight?" she asks, changing the subject.

I want to back up to a few moments ago. To the moment where she looked a little vulnerable, like she was almost ready to tell me something real about herself, but I let it go. No sense in playing in a sandbox when I have no intention of staying there.

"I'm going to give some excellent aural in a minute," I tease, "then possibly some oral, depending on how it goes."

"I can't with you," she laughs.

"You can. There's a standing invitation. Have I not made that clear?"

Her laughter grows. "You have. Thank you."

"And ..." I coax.

"And ..." She mocks. "And what?"

"And you are taking me up on that when?"

"Good night, Mr. Gibson."

It's totally unprofessional of me to watch the hemline of her dress ride up her thigh as she gets into the seat. It's even more unprofessional to look at her and wink when she catches me in action, but hell

—that's nothing compared to the vision of her naked in the backseat of the car that I'm imagining right now.

"You're a cad." The engine fires but her door stays open.

"You love it."

"I have no idea why you'd think that."

"You've trained me, remember?"

"I'll have to work on reprogramming you." Before I can respond, she pulls out of the parking lot with a coy little smile.

With the wind at my back, and her flowery perfume still lingering in the air, I watch her pull away. There's a weird-ass feeling I get around her that I kind of both hate and love. It's a complete raging hard-on coupled with a comfort level I've never had with a woman in-person before. Probably because she's the first woman who's given me blue balls on a regular basis that I've not fucked.

That's the part I hate: I haven't fucked her.

Then again, that's kind of the part I love: I haven't fucked her.

So weird.

A vibration in my pocket shakes me out of my thoughts, and I pull my phone out to see a message from my dating app. My stomach churns.

Glancing up as the taillights of Mariah's car takes the corner towards Goodman's Gas Station, I almost feel ... guilty.

Stop it. Fucking is freeing. Clear. Uncomplicated. Don't be dumb.

Her message pings again.

> Nerdy Nurse: I'm a little flu-ish tonight.
> Happy to chat later but can't meet up.

> Me: I think you're suffering from a lack of Vitamin Me.

Laughing as I type out the line, the acid in my gut evaporates and everything feels normal again.

Nerdy Nurse: Every. Time.

Me: You'd think you'd expect it by now. We've been exchanging these messages for how long?

Nerdy Nurse: You sent your first dick pic two months ago.

Me: It wasn't my dick.

Nerdy Nurse: Those weren't my legs either.

Me: Such a letdown.

Climbing into my car, I get situated as her text bubble bounces on the bottom of the app.

Nerdy Nurse: Is that a deal breaker?

Me: We have a deal?

Nerdy Nurse: Two months and we haven't managed to meet up yet …

Me: That's why I like nurses. You're busy. You can't be too attached. 😉

Nerdy Nurse: We're also well-versed in needles and serums. 😉

A quick glance up has me looking into the window of Principal Kelly's car. She gives me a dainty wave full of unspoken innuendo. I return her a two-finger salute before dropping my attention back on my conversation.

Me: You're right. I need to reconsider this arrangement.

Nerdy Nurse: If that wasn't your dick, I'm in the same boat.

Me: You only wanted me for what I was packing?

Nerdy Nurse: It's a dating app. Did you think I wanted to marry you?

Me: Most women do, yes.

Nerdy Nurse: Patient coming in. Try not to miss me.

Me: K.

Nerdy Nurse: Bye, Potassium.

Nerdy Nurse offline

Chapter 4

Mariah

"I love how you just make yourself at home." Dropping my bag on the sofa as I go by, I kick off my shoes. "You could at least make me dinner after a hard day's work."

My best friend, Whitney, glances at me over her shoulder. "I don't cook. I'll order something for you though."

"I thought you worked today?"

"I thought I did too. I hate this floating schedule crap," she sighs, peering up at me with a set of big, blue eyes. "I actually showed up at the hospital to find out it's not my day. Who does that?"

"You."

She turns back to the book she was reading. Filling a glass with ice, I find a Coke hidden behind a head of broccoli. "So, why are you here?"

"Your house is closer to the hospital than mine and I needed a nap."

Looking at her over the brim of the glass, I wait for more of an explanation. I don't get one. In fact, she doesn't even glance up at me.

Whitney operates on her own wavelength. I stopped trying to figure her out years ago. She's smart, fun, and as loyal as they come, but you have to let some things go where she's concerned. She doesn't always make sense.

"How was school today?" she asks, closing the paperback. "I feel like my mother when I say that."

"That's sweet. My mother used to say, 'What did you do today, Mariah, so I can compare it to what your sister did and tell you how you fail to measure up.'"

Whitney scowls. "Well, your mother is an asshole and I'm not even sorry for saying that."

Just the mere mention of the woman who brought me into the world sends my spirits sinking. "Let's not go there," I sigh, rubbing my temples. "I came home with a headache anyway. The last hour study hall doesn't comprehend the idea of being quiet in a library."

"I remember being that age. Friday nights held so much promise." She picks up her drink and follows me into the living room. "It's so sad, isn't it?" Her bottom lip protrudes almost to her chin. "I used to have such a social life. Who would've thought I would be the one sitting around bored on a Friday night. I'm slowly turning into ... you."

"You say that like it's a bad thing." Curling up on the sofa, I watch her nestle into the chair across from me.

"You're a librarian. It is a bad thing," she laughs.

"It's the best job ever."

"Sure it is. That's why you're practically a hermit. Every time I come over, I expect to be met with a flock of cats."

"A flock of cats?" I laugh. "That's not even a thing. What's wrong with cats, anyway?"

"Nothing is wrong with one cat. One cat is perfectly normal. Two cats are a sign something's amiss. If you have two cats, you spend way too much time alone. Three cats? That's a flock and that means you have no people skills and will spend the rest of your life on your hairball-filled couch surrounded by fictional people."

Lifting a brow, I ponder this for her amusement. "There are

gadgets to clean hairballs these days. I really can't see anything wrong with this scenario. It's kind of appealing."

"No, it's not," she says, placing her phone on the table next to a framed photo of us at Lake Michigan a few summers ago. "It's unhealthy."

"It's healthier than going into public and ending up losing my sanity from all the people-ing!"

Biting her lip, her eyes narrow ever-so-slightly. It's just enough of a warning.

Sighing, I close my eyes and wait for it. She doesn't make me wait long.

"Speaking of people ..." she says, her voice trailing off.

"No."

"But he's so cute!" Her tone is almost giddy. "He's a resident, which means he's super smart and will be making big bucks soon."

"Whit. No."

"Why? A date won't kill you."

"It happens. I watch those shows on television. Blind dates aren't what they used to be, pal."

Rolling her eyes, she leans forward. "It's not a blind date. I know him. Kind of, but that's not the point. The point is it kills me to see you wasting your life away in this little house. You're young, Mare. Gorgeous. You have a great personality when you're not being a dick on purpose."

"Gee, thanks," I giggle.

She smiles, but it fades slowly. "I want you to live your best life. Jonah could be your best life. Or a one-night stand ..."

I try to look at the ceiling while her stare almost drills a hole in my face. My best life is something I desperately want—a life filled with respect and love and two or three babies at some point. The life I've never had and craved so badly from as far back as I can remember.

I counter to myself. My life isn't bad. I have Whitney and Tish who like me and make me happy, even if I never see Tish outside of work. But that's not the point. I'm fulfilled by baking and have thought about getting a kitten at the shelter for companionship, but Whitney's comments about the whole cat lady thing make me a little leery of jumping into that too soon.

Still, my life isn't bad. It's just not great.

When I look at her again, it's like she can read my mind.

"You deserve a great life. One filled with laughs and love and orgasms," she winks.

I don't disagree. It sounds heavenly. It also sounds virtually impossible and, on the off-chance it is possible, the process sounds very, very people-filled.

"His name is Jonah," she repeats, a little softer and less enthusiastic this time. "He was top of his class at Northwestern. He has a great smile, blue eyes that match his scrubs in the weirdest way but it's a total turn on," she rambles. "Plus, I might've viewed his abs on accident and they. Are. Killer."

The vision she's painting is vivid, but I don't think it's the one she's aiming for.

At the mention of killer abs, my mind goes where it always goes. I used to fight it, to chastise myself for allowing him to affect me even when he's not in my office, but I gave up on that around Christmas of last year. I've accepted it as my dirty little secret: I fantasize about Lance Gibson.

Sweat rolling down his muscled back, the dips and curves not too bulky like he spends his free time in a weight room, but sexier. Like he might throw down some push-ups here and there. The way his hips twist and flex, the cut pointing down to his groin—

"Where did you just go?"

My head snaps to Whitney. She's got that 'gotcha' look painted on her face.

"What are you talking about?" I ask, feeling my face rat me out. I can't wipe the smile from my lips, nor can I cool down the heat caused by the memory of the sight of his sweaty skin.

"What were you thinking about?"

Filling my lungs with oxygen, I blow it out as slowly and as time-consumingly as I can.

Maybe I should act on this. Maybe she's right. Maybe I am going to turn into an old cat lady if I don't get out. But just as I'm about to agree with Whitney, images of Eric's dumbass smile rip through me, Chrissy tucked under his arm, and my mother's voice rings through my ears—

Snap! Whitney's fingers whip against each other before she starts wagging one my direction. "Stop it."

"I—"

"No." She clamors to her feet, her hands going into her hair and drawing it back into a high ponytail. "I love you to pieces but I'll love you a lot more when you stop playing that stupid spiel through your head."

"I don't know what you're talking about," I gulp.

"Yes, you do. You start to come around and then let them win."

"No one is winning," I protest.

I don't know whether it's worth it to defend myself or not. Her stance is always the same. So is mine. It's an impasse in our friendship.

"Every day you sit here miserable is a day they win," she says matter-of-factly.

"What do you want me to do, huh?" My hands flail in the air. "This is fucking hard, all right? It stings." It feels cathartic to just let it out. "My sister, the perfect daughter according to my mother, just had a baby with my ex-boyfriend. You know the one. The one I thought I was going to marry."

I expect to see a dose of sympathy. I get a blank face instead.

"Your sister did you the first favor she's ever done. Be glad," she deadpans.

"Ugh."

Whitney chooses her words carefully. She wants to pick apart Eric, listing his various flaws and telling me why I'm better off without him, but the birth of the baby last week has her reconsidering her flamboyant response.

Falling back onto the sofa, I pick up a pink embroidered pillow and hold it against me. I finally broke down a couple of nights ago and trolled Chrissy's social media. The baby is absolutely beautiful with Chrissy's long eyelashes and Eric's olive skin. She has a birthmark on her cupid's bow, just like me.

The tears I blink away aren't for Eric, although that's probably what Whitney thinks as she watches me. It's for the little girl I'll never know because her mother and I have been at odds since we were kids. Nothing I've ever done, no choice I've ever made, no clothes I've ever worn or way I've styled my hair has ever been good enough for Chrissy. Or my mother. There's got to be some irony in the fact Eric was good enough for them.

"I saw the birth announcement in the paper," Whitney says from behind me. "I know this sucks for you and I hate it. I'm sorry."

My body sags with the weight of a broken heart. I loved Eric. I looked in his face and thought I saw my future. Then came the night he broke up with me with the generic line, "It's not you, it's me." I knew it was bullshit. I knew there was something more. I just didn't dream how bad it was.

"What is this?" I glance around my mother's living room. Nothing appears out of the ordinary except for the two people sitting on the love seat. "Why is Eric here?"

My older sister, the one person in the world I've forgiven so many times, prayed for her friendship over and over, even idolized in the early parts of my life, reaches over and takes my ex-boyfriend's hand in hers.

"We have something to tell you," Chrissy says sweetly.

I didn't listen to the rest. It may have been six weeks since Eric and I had broken up, but it still stung like a million beestings that he was with my sister. And my mother, standing by the doorway in a silent approval of this debauchery, knew it.

But that's not the source of my heartbreak. Not really. The heartbreak lies in the answer to the questions I've always asked: will I ever be enough for my family? Will they ever take my side?

The answer is a resounding no.

The backs of my hands are streaked black with mascara as I wipe my eyes dry. "You're right." The flame in my chest starts to putter out; the smoke clears from my lungs. "If I sit here all weekend, I'm going to keep thinking about this and I refuse to do that to myself. I'll go out. Want to be my dinner date?"

Her lips twist in a way that makes my stomach turn.

"What did you do?" I ask.

She grabs her jacket off the back of the chair and walks backwards to the front door. "You have a date with—"

"Whitney. You didn't."

"I did," she winces. "He's picking you up on Saturday night but he has a rotation earlier in the evening, so if he's a few minutes late, cut him some slack. Wear something low-cut. He's a breast man."

I whirl a magazine in her direction, but it hits the door just as she shuts it behind her. The pages of the magazine shuffle as they hit the floor, my pride falling along with it.

She means well. She always does. But I don't want to force myself through a conversation with a stranger and pretend to be interested in medical implements when I just want to grab a book and a mug of hot chocolate and not talk to anyone at all.

I wonder if I'd be more of a people person had I felt more self-assured growing up. It would be an interesting experiment. It took me a long time to find myself, to know I'm not everything my mother said I was. To understand that it's okay I prefer country music over opera and drugstore over luxury brand cosmetics. I'm good with who I am. I just can't help wishing my family were too.

Closing my eyes, I try to get comfortable with the idea of going on a blind date. The longer I think about it, the more awkward it feels. Having a conversation with a man I already know is hard enough. How do you have one with someone you've never met?

Lance's face pops into my mind, his shit-eating grin tugging up the sides of my lips. He would say this is why you just sleep with them. There's no talking involved.

Laughing out loud, I wonder who he's with tonight. If it's the girl he was speaking to in my office or another one. Maybe both.

He's such a scoundrel but the difference between Lance and Eric is that Lance doesn't hide it. Why that's almost refreshing, I'm not sure. Either way, one thing is for sure: if Eric could inflict this much pain, a guy like Lance would destroy me.

Chapter 5

Lance

Sitting in my car just outside Crave, the local watering hole owned by my youngest brother, Machlan, I listen to the rain drip against the windshield. The texts are still coming in from my sister as she rails my ass for using a dating app to meet women.

According to Blaire, I should value my own worth as well as the worth of women more by doing it the old-fashioned way. When I explained that the *worth* we are going for involved lube and cock rings, she lost it. I think she was joking when she said I needed my head examined, but if a doctor calls with an appointment next week, I won't be shocked.

. . .

Nerdy Nurse: Bad hook-up tonight? LOL

Me: Strangely, my sister.

Nerdy Nurse: You hooked-up with your sister? I'm out.

Laughing, I flip off the engine but don't get out of the car.

Me: Very funny.

Nerdy Nurse: Here's my fun fact for you for the night—don't stick things where they don't belong.

Me: Is that some kind of sexual warning? Not into anal? That kind of thing?

Nerdy Nurse: Speaking of anal …

Me: That's my girl!

Nerdy Nurse: … I just watched a man have a candle removed from his anus.

Squirming in my seat, I try to imagine this and then decide I don't want to.

Me: Sorry. Took me a minute to make sure I read that right. Can I ask why?

> Nerdy Nurse: Apparently if you insert it and light the wick end (that you leave outside your anus), the wax provides some sort of erotic stimulation. I think the removal of the broken piece did not.

> Me: You scare me.

> Nerdy Nurse: Ha.

Glancing at the door to the bar, I contemplate just starting the car and going back home. Initially, I thought I could see if Megan McCarter was around and at least score a blow job, but the more I think about it, the more it feels meh.

Still, going home alone feels even less appetizing.

> Me: Gotta go. Good luck with all that anal play.

> Nerdy Nurse: You know it. 😉

> Me: I'm glad we had this little convo.

> Nerdy Nurse: Don't get too excited.

As my laughter fills the car, I think it's already a little too late for that.

Closing the app, I lock up and make my way down the sidewalk and into the bar. The lights are dim and the music quiet. Not what I hoped for or expected.

"Didn't expect to see you tonight." My brother Machlan looks at me from the other side of the bar, already reaching for the whiskey. He's younger than me, the youngest in our family.

It's pretty empty inside Crave, especially for a Friday night. I slide onto a stool toward the cash register and watch him make my Old Fashioned. I'm not much of a drinker, especially when I have a boatload of work to do at home. I just don't feel like reading essays on Latin America tonight and I definitely can't concentrate on them.

My brain is a clusterfuck of randomness. That is never a good thing.

"Bored, I guess," I say, shrugging. "Do I need a reason to come in here?"

"Everybody has a reason to walk into a bar," he laughs. "Some accept that reason and some don't."

"Look at you getting all philosophical."

He slides the drink down the bar. It stops almost perfectly centered in front of me.

"Impressive," I laugh, picking it up.

Machlan makes a face. "I learned it from Peck. It's one of his weird parlor tricks."

This isn't hard to imagine. Peck, our cousin, is the resident joke-ster. He's full of weird facts and unusual knowledge and can link toothpicks together with his mind. I've seen it done. Strange shit.

Still, he's one of my favorite people in the world. Heart of gold, straight shooter, and he can talk his way out of, or into, anything.

"Glad to know he's putting his time to good use," I say, taking a sip of my drink.

"Who's putting their time to good use?" Peck asks, hopping on the stool beside me. "Hey, Machlan. Can I get a beer?"

"No, fucker, you can't. Your tab hasn't been paid in a month."

Peck throws his head back and sighs. "I don't have my wallet and your brother almost killed me today. Cut me some slack, will ya?"

"What did Walker do?" I ask, wondering if Peck is exaggerating or if something happened. He works for Walker—the middle child out of us three Gibson boys—at his repair shop, Crank. My mother once had a recurring nightmare something happened to Walker in that shop.

"Nothing. He did nothing. That's the problem," Peck moans.

"Sienna, God knows I love her, but when she's around Walker is about as useful as tits on a nun."

"Yeah, well, I can't say I blame him," I say, taking a longer swig this time. "Is it wrong to wish she'd have beat the hell out of my car just so I could've called dibs?"

"You better not be talking about what I think you're talking about." A large hand makes contact with the back of my head, sending me rocking forward. Just as I'm about to turn around and go toe-to-toe with whomever just smacked me, Walker sits on the other side of me. He eyes me with a seriousness that only Sienna can bring out in him. "Why are you talking about my lady?"

"It was your sidekick over here bringing her up." I nod to Peck, rubbing the back of my head. "Touch me again and I'll whip the shit out of you."

He laughs, taking a beer from Machlan. "I'd love to see you try."

"Watch this." Machlan ambles to the other end of the bar and slides a beer down the wooden slats. It lands perfectly in front of Peck. "Nailed it."

"I told you. It's all in the wrists," Peck laughs, tipping the bottle Machlan's way. "Thanks."

"Yeah, yeah, yeah."

"If you put this much energy into work every day—" Walker starts, but Peck promptly cuts him off.

"As much as you eye-fucked Sienna today while I was working—"

"Don't start with your shit, Peck," Walker says.

Peck rolls his eyes and plops his bottle back on the bar. "I will start my shit because I'm exhausted. You better show up tomorrow ready to do some actual labor."

"Take it easy on him," I tease, scooting in my seat towards Peck. "I'd have a hard time working too if I had that to go home to. Hell, I'd probably never get out of bed."

Anticipating the punch before it comes, I duck. His hand dusts the edge of my jacket and misses me entirely.

Machlan laughs. "Getting slow there, Walk."

"If he gets too slow to—"

I don't anticipate the second punch. His fist plows into my bicep at about a quarter of the power he could've used, jolting me into my cousin. Peck's beer sloshes out of the neck and splatters the front of his shirt.

"That hurt a little," I laugh, rubbing my arm.

"It was a warning shot." He grins like he doesn't mean it. He did though. He doesn't play when it comes to Sienna which is mostly the reason I fuck with him.

And Machlan fucks with him.

And Peck fucks with him.

"So was mine," I wink.

"Don't you have somewhere to be?" Walker asks, shaking his head.

Peck fiddles with a napkin in front of him. "What about that nurse you've been messing around with? With the legs. What happened to her?"

"I haven't met her yet," I admit. "Things keep coming up. She works a swing shift thing at a hospital that's always messing up her schedule."

"Sounds like an excuse," Machlan notes with a hint of smugness.

A little unease settles in my stomach because there's a part of me that thinks so too. It has to be more than a coincidence that our schedules never match. But, when I really think about it, it's my fault sometimes. Like the time I had to go to Nana's because her insurance refused to pay for her insulin and I had to go sort it out. Or the time I had an emergency parent-teacher conference that made me cancel on her.

Focusing on that, I wait for the jitters to stop. They don't. Refusing to consider that maybe it's not the scheduling part of this little *thing* that has me off-balance and more like how much I like talking to her, I take a long, unhurried drink.

"What's that look for?" Peck asks me.

"What look?"

"That one." He points at my face.

"Probably the headache I'm trying to drink away." For good measure, I take another swig.

Walker sighs beside me. "Just tell us the story you're dying to tell."

"I don't have a story."

"You always have a story," they all say at the same time.

I down the rest of the glass as they laugh.

"Who you fucking? Where you fucking her?" Walker asks. "I went home on Sunday after dinner at Nana's and thought, 'Wow. Lance didn't tell us one story today.' You go making it two times in a row and I'm gonna have to call Blaire and see what we have to do to get you committed."

"Our sister is an attorney, not a doctor."

"Yeah, but who has rights to you?" Walker laughs. "If you lose your mind, which one of us gets to have you committed?"

"Me. Oh, God, let it be me," Machlan deadpans.

Sliding my drink down the bar, it slams into a napkin dispenser and falls over. The dribbles of Old-Fashion left in the glass slowly pool on the countertop. They go on, teasing me, speculating about everything from my sex life to offering to take an ad out for me online. Bastards.

"I hate all of you," I mutter, fighting the urge to clean up the spilled drink.

"This answers my original question," Machlan says.

"What was that?"

"Why you're in here. You're just not ready to accept the reason."

"Why is he in here?" Peck asks, side-eyeing me.

"Because he's not getting laid." Machlan says it with the biggest shit-eating grin. "Did you finally work your way through every girl on your fuck app?"

"He did it faster than even I thought he would," Walker chimes in.

Getting to my feet, I grab a few bills and place them on the bar. Fuck this. "I always get laid. That's never been a problem."

"Until now," Machlan adds.

"Jealousy is an ugly thing, boys," I call out, heading to the front door. I pause at the bulletin boards and turn back around. "The rest of that isn't a tip. Put it on Peck's tab. He's the only one of you I like."

"Hey, thanks," Peck calls out as the door slams behind me.

Climbing into my car, I get situated in the driver's seat but don't pull out. I don't move. I can hear my stomach churning, feel the prickle of something at the back of my neck, but I can't quite locate where it's coming from.

My brain is still a mess—maybe messier than before. I hadn't realized I haven't been with a woman in a while until Walker pointed it out. It feels like I have, but I haven't. It's my trademark, my hobby. What's wrong with me? Am I broken?

My cock still gets hard. I'd still fuck if an opportunity presented itself. I'm not having any unusual symptoms or urges, like monogamy, which would require a medical evaluation.

Still, something's off. I can sense it. I can feel it. Hell, I can tell. I didn't even want to talk to Jessa today at lunch. She called and it got me two things: out of a conversation with a flirty Principal Kelly and into Mariah's office.

Mariah.

"I could really go for a cupcake right about now," I say aloud with a chuckle. Turning the key, I swing down the street and head home to try to get some work done.

Chapter 6

Mariah

"Name something you only do when you're sick." The announcer sets his card down as the contestants slam the big buttons in front of them.

"Puke!" I say, shoving the spoon back in the tub of ice cream.

The female contestant looks downright smug. "Nap."

"Nap? You only nap when you're sick?" I ask, rolling my eyes. The number one answer flips across the screen—nap. "Where do you find these people?"

Scooping another helping of lemon cake ice cream into my mouth, I watch the rest of the top answers cross the board. Every now and then it crosses my mind to get up and go pick out my outfit for my date tomorrow night. I respond by taking another bite of ice cream.

Dating isn't my forte. Just thinking about it makes my stomach get all squirmy. If I were being introspective, I'd probably conclude that not having to date is one of the major reasons I prefer relationships over one-night stands or hook-ups. Talking about myself is awkward. Listening to someone else explain themselves while trying to be interesting is uncomfortable. Making it through dinner when you have nothing in common is horrific and not many men share my interests. Even if it goes well, hopes go up and, often times, dreams go down. It's a no-win situation.

Be positive. Things could always be worse.

Flipping the television off, I still. There's a ringing sound coming from down the hall. My pint of lemon cake ice cream goes to the coffee table as I race down the hallway and into my bedroom to retrieve it.

All the ice cream in my stomach starts to slosh around when I see the name: Mom.

See? Things just got worse.

Every time she calls, I tell myself this might be the day. Maybe she was at the salon and someone asked about me and she realized what a missed opportunity our mother-daughter relationship has become. Or maybe she was going through old photographs and felt guilty for not remembering when I won gold at Solo and Ensemble for my flute solo in middle school.

I let her go to voicemail a lot, but sometimes, I have more hope than brains.

One.

Two.

Three.

Inhaling a deep breath, I swipe the screen. "Hello?"

"Hello, Mariah."

"Hi, Mom. Is everything okay?"

"Everything is fine, honey. Why do you ask?"

"No reason," I say, biting a nail. "You usually just call when something is the matter."

Sighing too hard and too long, I feel the dread build across the back of my neck. I should've sent her to voicemail.

The mattress bends as I sit on the edge of the bed and listen to her go on and on about how she calls and I don't answer and how disrespectful it is to ignore your mother's calls. Every other sentence has me biting my tongue with a comeback that, while true, would incense her. As entertaining as it would be to listen to her gasp—I always get a little thrill out of it—I don't have the energy to see it through.

"Mom?" I ask, cutting her off. "Did you need something?"

The shock that someone has the audacity not to just sit and listen to her ramble has her tongue-tied. "I ... Well ... Excuse me?"

"Did you need something?" I ask it slowly. Looking around my room, a cozy nest of light greys and pinks, I wonder if I should change my sheets. I just bought a brand-new set of flannel ones that I wanted to try and the temperature at night must just be on the cusp of making it acceptable. "I'm in the middle of something, so if you could just spit it out, that'd be great."

As soon as I say it, I wince and prepare for her retort.

"Spit?" she balks. "Oh, Mariah. When are you going to start acting like a lady? I didn't raise you like this."

"Can we just ... cut around all this and get to the chase?"

I despise the pleading tone in my voice, but I hate even more the pause that stretches between us. It's filled with the unspoken disappointment she feels at being my mother. The silence is pregnant with how misfortunate she feels she is and an awkwardness that's made even worse by how our relationship dictates how we should interact with one another.

There aren't tears anymore, just a muted acceptance of the situation. I am who I am and it's not good enough for her. But it's good enough for me.

"My birthday is this weekend," she says finally. "I'd like you to come have lunch with me."

This throws me a little. "Wow, Mom. Okay. Where do you want to meet?"

"I'm having lunch brought to the house to mark the occasion. It'll be Betsy's first time here and I'd really like to make it special."

"Betsy?" I ask, trying to remember which of her friends this is. I'm sure she'll lambast me for not remembering it's her tennis friend or the one she just took a trip to San Diego with, but I truly don't remember.

"The baby, Mariah."

Blinking in super-slow motion, I realize she went there. She's usually decent enough to not openly bring up Chrissy or Eric or the pregnancy that I found out about from a mutual friend's social media post, a baby whose name I didn't even know until now.

Tears come, wetting the inside corners of my eyes, as I realize Chrissy has taken our grandmother's name. A hollowness echoes in my chest, each thought bounding around an area inside of me that should be filled with a feeling other than loneliness.

For a fleeting moment, I imagine walking into my mother's house and seeing my sister holding a baby. She never even wanted kids. I was the one who wanted a huge family and she beat me to it, just like she tried to one-up everything I ever did.

"I gotta go," I say past the lump in my throat.

"Stop it." Her tone is cold, brash, void of any empathy for me. "It's time you grow up, young lady."

"Grow up? Are you kidding me right now?"

"Eric and Chrissy are incredibly happy and they now have a beautiful little girl."

"I ... good for them," I say in disbelief.

"Yes, good for them. You should try to emulate their happiness a little instead of spending all your time in a library."

This snaps me out of it. "Well, Mother, I *was* trying to do something similar and then my sister stole my boyfriend."

"You can't steal a person," she charges back. "He was in love with her. Not you. Maybe if you had been a little more interesting, fixed yourself up a little more—"

"Nope. Not doing this today. Goodbye, Mother."

My thumb swipes the call off and holds in the power button until the screen goes black. I look at the wall. After deep breathing for a few seconds, I shove all of that garbage out of my mind.

Rummaging through my closet, I know exactly what I'm looking for. The jeans I never wear, the ones Whitney says makes my ass look great, go flying onto the bed. A soft crimson sweater that hugs my curves and I feel good in joins it. It takes more time than it should to find my nude-colored heeled boots, but they're cozied up in the back of my closet with a pair of black pumps. Both go on the bed.

"There. That should do it for tomorrow night."

The satisfaction is short-lived. So, I do what I always do when I can't settle down: head to the kitchen to bake something sweet to cancel out the bitterness.

Chapter 7

Mariah

"I should've worn the heels."

Twisting around to see the back view in the full-length mirror, I decide the jeans I laid out last night look fine. The top is cute. The shoes, though, might be too relaxed. Then again, I really have no idea.

The doorbell rings as I pick up my heels. I look at my reflection. I can't see my heart pounding out of control but I sure as hell can feel it.

"Why did you agree to this?" I whine.

The bell sounds again as if the man on the porch is reminding me I *did* agree to the craziness of a blind date and now I have to follow through.

Each step toward the front door seems to cover a mile. The knob is in my hand before I have time to come up with a plan. I freeze. Peering into the peephole, I determine he's cute, but in a television doctor kind of way. Crew cut blond hair, cobalt blue eyes that match his scrubs impeccably, and a tall, lean body that screams he ran a half a mile this morning for fun, all make him appear harmless. Although,

I remind myself as I open the door, that's what all blind dates look like at first.

"Hello," I say, smiling as naturally as I can despite the ruckus in my head. A silent prayer goes up that I don't look like one of those dogs in memes with my lips sticking to my gums in a fake smile.

His assessment is quick, yet thorough. I must pass because his broad shoulders ease. "Hi. I'm assuming you're Mariah."

"I am. You must be Jonah."

"Correct. Sorry I'm a few minutes late. I got held up in the operating room."

His words are stilted. There's some relief in knowing he's equally as unsure about this as I am.

"No worries," I tell him. "Let me grab my purse and we can go?"

"Sounds good."

Closing the door just in case he is a serial killer, I find my purse on the couch. A quick inventory confirms the small can of Mace in the hidden pocket, as well as extra cash for a cab. There's also a tube of lipstick just in case I'm wrong about this whole thing and the date goes well enough for a quick freshen up in his bathroom.

He's standing where I left him when I return. I flash him a smile while I lock up and wait for any indication there might be some sort of crackling energy between us. My keys hit the can of Mace when I drop them into my purse.

Noted, Universe. Noted.

"Whitney said you like Peaches," he says, a couple of steps in front of me. "I checked it out online. It's not fancy but, since I'm in scrubs, I thought it might work."

"It's my favorite. Have you been there before?"

He opens my door. One point, Jonah. "I haven't. I'm from Springfield originally and haven't been here long enough to see much more than the inside of Merom Memorial. The life of an intern, I guess."

"I guess. Thank you," I say, as I slip in the front seat of his sports car.

I wonder if he actually hosed the interior with antiseptic spray or it's a coincidence that the car smells like a janitor's closet. By the looks of the spotless floorboards and streak-free windows, I lean toward the spray.

He grins at me while he climbs in. "Buckle up. Seat belts are one of the easiest and most effective ways to prevent injuries in automobile accidents."

"All right. Thanks for the tip." The lock slips into the latch and I try to focus on the considerate side of him. Not the one that made me want to include, 'Yes, father,' at the end of my sentence.

The drive to Peaches takes forever despite only being a few minutes from Linton. Every topic feels like we have to move a mountain to get through the conversation. Going from discussing his job to my career back to his job is way more work than it should be.

By the time we pull in the parking lot, I want to bash my head against the window but I'm afraid if I bleed on his interior he may freak out. On the other hand, it would be more exciting than spending another hour or two like this.

We enter my favorite little place which is nestled behind a tennis court. It's cozy inside Peaches, a joint famous in these parts for their margaritas. Jonah asks me to order him a water and excuses himself for the restroom.

"Do you have a seating preference?" the hostess asks.

"Table, please," I say, looking around. There are a few that overlook the parking lot and drive-through. At least by the window I'll have something to watch. "Can we sit over there?"

"Sure. Follow me."

Setting my purse on a chair by the wall, I thank the hostess. "Can I go ahead and order drinks?"

"Sure," she says, taking a small pad out of the apron around her waist. "What can I get for you?"

"Water with lemon for him and a Coke, extra ice, for me."

"Got ya."

I get situated in my seat, shooting Whitney a text asking her what the hell she was thinking. When Jonah gets back, I drop the phone into my purse and smile at my date.

"Drinks are ordered," I chirp.

"Great." He grabs a menu off the table. "How long have you known Whitney?"

"Since elementary school. She moved to Linton in third or fourth grade," I say. "I got hit in the face with a dodgeball and she helped me to the nurse's station. We've been best friends ever since."

The waitress stops by with our drinks and takes our order. She bats her lashes at Jonah and I'm surprised to see that he flirts back, albeit ineptly. Sipping my Coke, I try to care. I don't. With a final breathy giggle, she's on her way and he directs his attention back to me.

Silently judging my choice of beverage, he lifts his glass of water with lemon to his lips. "Dodgeball should be banned from schools. There's no reason to risk a broken nose over an immature game that doesn't involve skill."

"We always lobbied to play it, so I'm going to have to disagree. It was fun."

"It's pointless."

"I loved it," I offer, holding back an awkward laugh. "Anyway, that's how I met Whit."

"She's a terrific nurse. What is it you do again?"

Blinking slowly, I wait for him to laugh. "I'm a librarian at the high school." I enunciate each syllable, wondering how on Earth this man is going to be a doctor when he can't pay attention for shit.

"I think you told me that."

"I did." *Twice already.* "I've always had a minor fascination with the medical world. I considered medical school myself, but there were too many people involved."

"There are definitely a lot of people involved," he laughs. "That's kind of the point. We're the ones who get in, elbows deep, and clean up the world. We do the work that matters."

Our plates are placed in front of us. Jonah gets a little extra smile with his. I just cannot find it in me to be bothered.

Slicing into my chicken breast, I attempt to tune them out. The waitress' giggle is abrasive and Jonah's try at conversation so painful I almost wince. If it weren't completely rude, I'd yank out my phone and ask Whitney how this guy is going to be a doctor when he has virtually no people skills. Less than even I do.

There is some weird chemistry between the two of them though, so I turn towards the window. As I chew my chicken, I'm kind of happy for him. I can't imagine that he finds this kind of thing any easier than I do and Lord knows how much I struggle with dating. Or how much I would struggle if I did it regularly.

I hear the waitress leave. I decide to direct my attention back to Jonah and make an attempt at this date, when I stop. My fork falls to my plate and clinks off the china. From the other side of the window, in the drive-thru lane, sits Lance. His window is rolled down and he's looking at me.

One eyebrow lifts as he takes me in. He ignores the guy honking behind him as he holds my glance for a few long seconds like he's not sure what he's seeing. Something must catch his eye because he turns his attention to something else.

He looks across from me.

To Jonah.

Oh God.

There's no hiding his amusement when he slides his eyes back to mine. The asshole has the audacity to laugh. The car behind him honks again as I glare at him through the glass. I can imagine the snicker that's undoubtedly toppling past his smirk as he pulls away.

Sagging back in my seat, I struggle to find room in my chest to fill it with air. It's like all the oxygen was sucked from me and replaced with curiosity about Lance. My brain races through potential situations—where is he going, who is he with, who was he getting dinner for? My stomach sours.

"You okay?" Jonah's voice drifts across the table, barely audible through my haze.

"Sorry," I say, pasting on a smile. "It's been a long day."

"You didn't hear anything I said, did you?"

My cheeks heat, like I got caught with my hand in the candy jar. "Uh, no. Can you repeat that?"

"I was saying I just got a text from the hospital," he says. "There's a new procedure scheduled in an hour I'd like to observe. It's only performed at a few hospitals nationwide and I really think it's important I stand in and see what it's all about. It would be great for my career."

Relief washes over me, but it's fleeting. When I look up again, I almost fall out of my chair.

"Well, look who I found." Lance's voice is full of amusement as he strides right up to the table, no fucks given. Dressed in dark denim and a navy blue button-down that he didn't bother to tuck in, he looks casual and delicious, despite the cocky look on his face.

I plead to the heavens that he didn't come in here just to tease me. When he winks, I know I'm screwed.

The pink in my cheeks cranks up a notch as I look from an entertained Lance to a bewildered Jonah. I should say something, introduce them, because Jonah's confusion is clear.

"What are you doing here?" I ask Lance instead. When I shoot him a look that practically begs him not to embarrass me, he just laughs.

"I was picking up dinner."

"In the drive-thru," I point out.

"And they forgot my apple pie," he says. Pride blooms on his face like he's tickled to death he came up with a lie so quickly. "I'm Lance Gibson," he says, turning to Jonah. "And you are?"

"Jonah." He looks at me briefly before turning back to Lance. "How do you know Mariah?"

"Oh, we're old friends," Lance lies. *Again.* "How do *you* know her?"

"I'm her date."

Lance takes a step back. I can't decipher the look on his handsome face, whether he's curious or irritated now. He watches Jonah far too closely for far too long.

"It's nice to meet you, but we were just leaving," Jonah says, putting his napkin on the table.

Scrambling to get myself together, to find my purse, to take a final sip of my Coke, I freeze everything when Lance speaks.

"You barely touched your chicken, Mariah."

"Jonah got a call from the hospital," I explain. "Spur of the moment thing. He's needed there so we're going to cut this a little short."

"Then perfect timing. I'll take you home," Lance says. He narrows his eyes as if to warn me, but I skirt right around that.

"Oh, no," I protest, holding up a hand. "That's unnecessary."

"I have ten minutes to get to Merom Memorial," Jonah notes. "Would it be okay if your friend took you home? I hate asking, but we're already in Merom and if I drive you back to Linton first—"

"I'll get a ride. It's fine." He may not mean to be rude, but it certainly feels that way. Who lets another man take his date home?

Still, as he gets to his feet and stands shoulder-to-shoulder with Lance, my body releases an evening full of stress. Although Lance is a giant pain in my ass, being stuck with him is better than being stuck with Jonah. At least we can argue instead of regurgitating information over and over.

"I'll pay the bill before I leave. It was nice meeting you, Mariah," Jonah says.

"It was nice meeting you too." I stand, thinking I should shake his hand or something. I don't know. Instead, Jonah leans in and kisses me on the cheek.

Glancing up at Lance, I see a fire in his eye. I hold my breath as Lance starts to take a step toward Jonah, but then he stops.

"You better get going." Lance taps his watch. "Nine minutes."

"Yeah. You're right. I'll call you." Jonah gives me a little wave before taking off through the restaurant. Lance is in his seat before Jonah is even out of sight.

"This isn't even a cheeseburger," he scoffs. Pushing the plate to the edge of the table, he makes a face. "Where'd you find this guy?"

"It's a veggie burger."

"Did you specifically look for a guy without testosterone or did it just happen?"

"He's nice," I object, trying and failing, to hide a giggle.

"You didn't think he was nice," he mocks. "And you weren't the least bit attracted to him."

I wasn't. I'm sure everyone watching us could see that. But I'm not about to admit that to Lance. Letting him think I was falling madly in love wouldn't be the worst thing I've ever done. "And how would you know that?"

He leans forward, and his cologne wraps around me. "You were sitting back in your chair, for one."

"What?" Then I look down and realize I'm mimicking his posture and leaning toward him. I shift back in my seat. "That doesn't mean anything."

He shrugs. "Maybe not. But your eyes did light up when you saw me."

"You're delusional."

Much to my surprise, he seems to consider this. "You may be right." He redirects his attention to the waitress now primed at the table.

"You aren't the man who was here before," she laughs. "Girl, where do you find these guys? I need to hang out there."

"You'd be surprised," I tell her. "The other guy said he was paying the check. Can you make sure he did?"

"Wait." Lance whips a menu off the napkin dispenser. "I want dessert."

"Lance ..." I sigh, watching him scan the menu.

"What's good here?" he asks, ignoring me.

The waitress rattles off a bunch of choices. He'd love the peanut butter pie, but I don't tell him that.

There's a touch of stubble dotting his cheeks. He works his jaw back and forth as he peruses the dessert choices. It's hard, like it's cut from granite and angled in a sharp line. My hand starts to move, to reach out on instinct and feel the roughness against my palm, but I come to my senses in the nick of time.

"I want the peanut butter pie. What about you?" He offers me the menu.

"I thought you came in to get the apple pie the drive-thru forgot?" I remind him. "Or did that slip your mind?"

"Totally slipped my mind," he chuckles. "I'm in the mood for peanut butter now anyway."

"Would you like a piece too?" The waitress asks as Lance and I exchange a knowing smile. "We have a great blackberry cobbler."

"I'm fine. Really."

"Give her a slice of the lemon pie," Lance cuts in.

"I don't want it."

"Yeah, you do. Or at least you can sit there and look at it while I eat mine."

Or I can sit here and look at you and pretend you're eating me.

Oh, God.

I can't look away from him fast enough. Lifting my purse from the seat next to me, I scavenge through it like a girl who may perish if she doesn't locate her phone.

"Did I say something?" he asks after the waitress is gone.

"Nope. Nothing at all. Just worried I left my phone in Jonah's car," I say, pulling it out like a trophy. "Whew. I wasn't sure."

"All righty then ..."

Setting it carefully next to my glass, I exhale. "I feel better now."

"Tell me about the hippie."

"He wasn't a hippie," I insist. "He's a doctor. Or going to be one. I think. I have doubts with his lack of interpersonal communication skills."

"How'd you meet him? Is this the guy you've been seeing?" He pulls his brows together. "No disrespect, but he's not exactly the type I thought you'd be having dinner with."

"Well, for the record, he's not exactly who I thought I'd be having dinner with either," I shrug. "But it's over now."

"So you won't be seeing him again?"

Considering my options, I realize I have only one. There's no way he'd believe I wanted this guy. So, I give in. "No, I'm not seeing him again. This was a blind date."

"Ah ..." Lance's voice trails off as he blows out a breath. "That makes sense."

I'm not sure how to respond to that, so I take a drink of my Coke. Just as my glass hits the table, two plates of pie slide in front of us.

"Here you go!" she chatters happily. "Does it look like rain out there? I get off in an hour and was hoping for a clear night out."

"Um, no rain," Lance responds.

She chatters on and on about her lack of plans. As I watch her make conversation easily, I wish I had that quality. There's no way I could walk up to someone I just met seconds before and chatter away about my life's hopes and dreams. But the longer I wait on her to end the conversation, the more I forget my conundrum and the more agitated I get at her for flirting with Lance.

"Excuse me," I say, butting in. "This looks great. Thank you."

"Oh," she giggles. "Yes, I'm sorry. Let me know if you need anything else." She tucks her chin and darts to the kitchen.

Lance sticks his fork in his pie, a smug look etched on his features. "Is that what jealousy looks like on you, Ms. Malarkey? I like it."

"Why would I be jealous?" I huff, lopping a big lump of pie on my fork. "She did the same thing to Jonah so don't feel special."

"Oh, I didn't feel special," he grins. "Until now."

"Why is that?" I ask before shoving a quarter of the pie into my mouth.

"Because when she did it *to Jonah*, you were looking at me. You didn't give a fuck. But when she did it *to me*, you looked like you wanted to rip her throat out."

"I did not," I protest, gulping.

"You did and it was hot as hell." An ember burns in his eyes so bright I can't even look. I'll melt. I'm sure of it.

Shoving a bite of pie into my mouth, I can't quite get it past the lump sitting at the bottom of my throat. I cough, covering my mouth with a napkin until I manage to get it down. "That's super lemon-y," I eek out.

"I bet."

"Want a bite?" I offer, trying to keep the conversation well away from the waitress and my non-jealousy.

"Nah. It's not my favorite," he says, taking another bite of his dessert.

"You're lucky I like it since you ordered it for me without knowing and you don't like it," I say, taking a sip of my drink.

"No luck involved, sweetheart." He takes another bite of his. "This isn't bad, but your peanut butter icing is unbeatable."

Charming bastard.

Sitting my fork down, I take him in. There's no pretentiousness to his words. There's nothing for me to get irritated about or dislike, just a kindness in his compliment that I know he means.

This is what bothers me so much about him. He keeps me off kilter on purpose.

"How did you know I'd like lemon pie?" I ask. Attempting to regroup and find my feet, I settle back in my chair and watch him.

"Because you always have a box of lemon candies in the middle drawer of your desk. I see them when you pull it out," he adds quickly, before I can accuse him of snooping. "Do you ever make lemon cupcakes? Can you even do that?"

"Yes, you can do that," I laugh. "I've made them but never gotten them exactly right."

"After you make the red velvet, maybe you could try them?"

"I never said I was making you red velvet anything!" Lofting my straw wrapper across the table, it hits him in the chest. "Do you think I just bake to order?"

"For me, yeah."

He hands the waitress his credit card as she walks by. "Can you ring us up?"

"Let me pay for it," I say, tugging on my purse.

"Yeah, fucking right."

"Sorry," the waitress says, standing so close to Lance her hip almost touches him. She takes his card, her fingertips brushing against his. "A man like this gets what he asks for."

"Yeah, see," he jokes as she sashays away. "I get what I ask for."

"Is that why you're a brat?"

He picks up Jonah's water glass and then sits it back down. "I almost drank from that."

"I saw."

"Were you going to let me?" he gasps.

"Hey, you get what you ask for," I laugh.

He feigns irritation. Pulling his phone from his pocket, he does a speedy review of something on the screen and then pops it away. "So," he says, leaning against the table. "What do we do now?"

"You take me home."

"We could see a movie. Do people still do that on dates or is that old-fashioned?"

"This isn't a date," I point out.

He considers this. "Yeah, I think it is. You just leveled up. From hippie to me. You're winning today."

"Do you live to annoy me?"

"No, but watching you get all hot and bothered does turn me on."

"Oh my God. Stop it," I hiss.

The table next to ours apparently caught wind of his admission and look at us over their shoulders. I can't make eye contact.

"What do you do on a date? I was serious," he says, ignoring the hushed comments beside us.

"When was the last time you were on a date?"

Tapping his chin, his eyes sparkle. "Like a real date? Or like time with a woman?"

"A date. Dinner, a movie, a walk around the lake. Even a ride around the country," I offer.

"I like the way you think." A grin tips his lips. "I haven't gone parking in years. Wanna?"

"No."

"Liar."

Laughing, we get to our feet. He sticks his credit card back in his wallet and I wonder where her number went, but don't ask. Just before we turn to leave, I catch him tossing a little wadded up ball on the table. He catches me watching.

"What?" he asks.

"Nothing," I say as innocently as possible.

"Can't go anywhere and not collect digits. It's hell being this handsome."

We walk out of Peaches side-by-side. It's a heck of a lot better than how I walked in.

Chapter 8

Lance

I'm out of my fucking mind.

Don't play with this girl, I tell myself. *She's out of your league, Gibson.*

Pausing at the back of my car, I could easily tell myself it was fate that brought us together tonight. There's leftover pizza at the house for dinner. Why I decided to drive all the way over to Peaches for takeout I'll never know.

On the flip side, it's a little like a ploy by Satan himself to test my restraint now that she's in my car. I have to keep my hands to myself. I have to get in the car and pretend like I'm in there with Blaire.

Yeah fucking right.

Glancing at her through the back glass, the moonlight rippling around her like she's some damn goddess, I want to ask the universe what I've ever done to deserve this ... this purgatory.

My cock twists in my jeans.

Yeah, buddy, I know. Don't explode on me until we get home.

"Hey," I say as I open the door. It takes every bit of self-control I didn't know I had to not just leap over the console and bite those plump, pink lips.

63

"Thank you for taking me home," she breathes. "I can call a taxi if it's an inconvenience."

"Do you ever stop talking?"

Her eyes grow wide as she laughs. "No. Actually."

Good. "You live in Linton, right?"

"Yeah. Just passed Carlson's Bakery. Little brick house. Dog-ear fence in the back yard."

"Ah, got 'cha," I say, getting into my seat. "Cross used to live there when we were growing up."

"Who is that?" she asks as I start the car.

"He owns a gym in town. He's good friends with my youngest brother, Machlan. Kind of grew up like an honorary Gibson boy."

"There are more than one of you?" she asks, her hand flying to her chest. "Your poor mother."

"Oh, no, sweetheart. There's only one of me."

Her eyes roll around in her head. "I'm sorry. I forgot who I was talking to."

"I'm going to pretend I just hit a bump to explain that little eye-roll," I tell her. "No worries."

"I wasn't worried about it," she laughs.

I pull out of the parking lot and head toward Linton. She sings along softly to a song on the radio and I almost want to turn it down to hear her voice. If I do that, I'm sure she'll stop, so I don't.

"I have two brothers and a sister," I continue. "Blaire is an attorney in Chicago." I know the first rule of history: it repeats itself. You start sharing your life's details with a woman and they think that means something. I need to stop talking. "Machlan owns Crave."

Shut. Up.

"The bar?"

"The bar," I confirm, giving up on myself. The chain of command from my brain to my mouth is clearly broken. "Walker took over Crank from our father."

She taps her fingers against the console. "I grew up in Lancaster.

When I got the job at the school, I rented the little house I'm in now."'

"Lancaster's not far. What? A twenty-minute drive?"

Her fingers stop moving. Her shoulders stiffen as she gazes out her window. I can barely hear her voice when she speaks. "You can make it in fifteen if you have to."

She worries her bottom lip between her teeth, working it back and forth. I want to reach over and pop it free. And then clamp it between my own teeth, but there's no consent and I'm not sure she'll give it to me. But that's not the problem. The problem is, I'm fairly certain it was something I said that changed her spirits.

"This is why I don't date," I note as a car passes us without switching off its brights.

"Why is that?"

"I just said something wrong and I don't even know what it was."

"You didn't say anything wrong, Lance. I just got to thinking about a phone call from my mother," she frowns.

The street lamps get few and far between as we get farther away from town. She's quiet for a long time.

"Want to talk about it?" I offer, needing her to come back around. When I'm the one who pisses her off, I'm okay with that. I don't really know what to do when she's mad at someone else.

"I don't know how to explain it," she admits. "My mom just ... let me ask you this. Does your mom have favorites? I know that sounds ridiculously juvenile, but does she prefer one of your siblings over the others?"

"Well," I say carefully. "My mom passed away a few years ago."

"I'm so sorry."

Her hand falls to my arm. Her palm is so small it barely covers half my bicep. We both look at the point of contact. I force a swallow down my parched throat, feeling the weight of her hand all the way down to my groin. My thighs ache, my balls burn, every piece of my body practically begging for more.

"I'll be sorry if you move your hand," I utter.

Naturally, she does.

"No," I continue, clearing my throat, "she didn't have a favorite. Not really. Blaire got better Christmas presents growing up because she was the only girl. Machlan had bigger birthday parties because his birthday was in December and Mom was worried it would get lost in the mix with Christmas and all that. They paid for my college and gave Crank to Walker. So, I guess I never really felt that way." Glancing at her again, I decide to press. "Does yours?"

"It's a fact my mom prefers my sister over me."

"I need to meet your sister," I mumble.

She smacks my arm. "Lance!"

Chuckling, I rub the spot she just marred. "I was kidding."

"Sure you were."

"I was," I insist, looking at her until she looks at me. "I know I'm just your friendly co-worker and ride home from bad dates, and that you get off to me every night—Ow!" I yelp as she smacks me again. "Truth hurts."

"So do lies. Wanna see?" she asks, making a fist.

"I was going to finish that by saying I can't imagine a mother being anything but proud of someone like you."

She makes a face like she might cry. It's not real, it's totally put on, but I love it.

"Think about it," I say. "You moved out on your own, got a real job, and I bet you pay your own bills."

"You're an asshole."

"And," I say, nudging her shoulder, "you're pretty as hell, smart, and sweet when you want to be. Your mother must be an idiot."

"Lance Gibson, that was nice. Thank you."

"All truth, Ms. Malarkey. All truth. Even the parts you deny." Listening to her giggle fill up my car is the best thing I've heard all day. "So your mom is a jerk. Do we like your sister?"

"No. Big. Fat. No." She shakes her head adamantly. "We don't like Chrissy."

"Got it. Do we have a dad we like? Brother? Grandma? Aunt?"

Her head rests on the seat angled a little to the side. She looks perfectly content in the seat of my car. It's hard not to pull over and, as weird as it is to acknowledge it, I don't want to *just* fuck her. I want to hear what she has to say. And then fuck her. Hard.

It's a thin, dangerous line and my toes are edging it.

"My parents are divorced and my dad has some trophy wife up in New Hampshire. I haven't seen him in years. No aunts, no brothers. Grandma Betsy was amazing, though," she whispers, more to herself than to me. Her chin drops to the side so she's looking at me. "She's who taught me to bake."

"So we definitely love Grandma Betsy."

"Definitely," she smiles. Heaving a deep breath, she blows it out slowly. "You know what, Lance? You're not a bad guy."

"I've been telling you this."

An easy little song hums through the speakers. She closes her eyes.

Her body sinks into the seat as the crinkle in her forehead disappears. I want to ask her another question, to hear her voice again, but I don't because seeing her like this is new. And I like it.

I also like the look of her breasts in that red sweater.

As we drive through the night, I imagine what life would be like without my family. Even when my brothers and Blaire make me crazy, which is often, I appreciate them. We're a tribe, along with Peck and his brother Vincent and our Nana. We'd be nothing without each other.

Imagining no Sunday dinners or church services or Friday nights at the bar with Peck getting tossed by Machlan—what would I do with my time? I take a peek at Mariah and wonder if that's why she works a lot. She has nothing else to do. No one to hang out with, reminisce with, or enjoy a meal with.

Or bake with.

The exit to Linton approaches, the turnoff lit with a bright yellow light. I look at it, at Mariah, and plow forward.

"Hey," she says, opening her eyes. "That's the exit."

"I know. I have something I need to do."

Rubbing my forehead, I know a quick exit I can take a half mile up the road and I know I should take it. I should turn this car around and head into town and get her out of my car. Stop the madness.

Squirming in her seat, she sits upright. "Can't you drop me off first? Or take me to Goodman's and I'll walk from there?"

"Relax," I instruct.

"I don't want to relax."

"Clearly." Biting my lip, gripping the steering wheel with both hands, I skip the second, and the last, exit into town. "Don't laugh."

"I promise nothing." She folds her arms over her ample chest. "Where are we going?"

"I have to go by my Nana's."

"You're kidding me?" she balks. "You have to go to your grandma's at eight o'clock on a Saturday night?"

"Yup."

"Why?"

"Reasons."

She flops back on the seat again with a huff. "You really can't take me home?"

"Sorry, sweetheart," I say with a simple shrug.

"You sure sound real sorry."

My laugh is the last sound either of us make until my car pulls into Nana's driveway a few minutes later. Parking behind her crossover vehicle, which she bought last year because it holds more casseroles for her church supper club than the sedan she had, I cut the engine.

"Two things you need to know about Nana before we go in," I say as seriously as I can. It's almost impossible not to laugh at the soberness in Mariah's face. "First, don't say anything bad about Elvis."

"Got it." She runs a hand through her long, dark locks. With every movement, the smell of her shampoo—something rich and flowery—almost kills me.

"Second," I say, pointing at her, "call her Nana."

"What's her name?"

Opening my door, I climb out. "I'm not telling you. You have to call her Nana."

She rustles around behind me then smacks the car door shut. Before I know it, she's at my side with wild eyes. "Just tell me her name. Or I can call her Mrs. Gibson, I guess."

"Don't say I didn't warn you," I say. My hands go up in defense as we climb the wooden steps Peck built a few summers ago. They creak with our weight, adding to the music from the crickets under the porch.

The house is small, built in the early nineteen-twenties. Granddad kept it in perfect condition, then Dad took over. Now my brothers and Peck and I come by and do tasks for her when she needs them done. If we don't get here quick enough, she calls a service guy and that makes us nuts.

"This place is so cute," she notes as we look across the back yard. The grass is freshly cut, probably by Walker. The remnants of Nana's garden lie dormant by the shed. "It's like a book, all quaint and lovely."

"Quaint and lovely?" I balk, turning towards the house. "Nice vocabulary you have there, Ms. Malarkey."

She doesn't bother with a comeback. Instead, she files in behind me as I head for the sliding glass door into the kitchen.

"I can stay in the car," she whispers roughly. "I don't have to go in."

"Do you want her coming out here to get you?"

She taps me on the shoulder. "She doesn't know I'm here. Why would she come out?"

"Why are you whispering?" I whisper back. We're eye-to-eye, our faces close enough that I could kiss her in a half a second. Her irises dilate as I lick my lips. "*Relax*," I say turning back to the house before I do something stupid.

Out of the corner of my eye, I see her start to reach for my hand. My heart jumps in my throat as I wait for it. She stops herself before our skin makes contact. That's probably for the best because if she touched me right now, I think I'd lose it. She'd be ass up over the deck chair in front of God and Nana. I don't even give a fuck.

Peering through the glass, I spy Nana at the farmhouse sink. She's washing a mixing bowl while doing a little hip sway to a song I'm not privy to. I consider the ramifications of this. How she'll be jumping to conclusions about me bringing a girl here. The fact that she'll tell my brothers and I'll be assaulted with endless questions tomorrow. I know she'll even invite her to dinner tomorrow because she invites everyone to Sunday dinner. But how will Mariah take that? Will it be weird if she accepts? Will she think there's more to it than there is?

"She's adorable," Mariah says beside me. "What's on her apron? Roosters?"

"Third thing to remember about Nana. Don't call them cocks. Machlan was a little hungover one Sunday at dinner and made a comment about all the cocks. That happened precisely one time."

"Got it," she giggles. "She's just so cute. Look at her dancing in there!"

"Now you know where I get my skills," I wink, shoving the door open. "Hey, Nana!"

My grandmother jumps, her hand going to her throat and wrapping around a necklace. "You scared the heavens out of me, Lance."

"Sorry," I say, picking up a cookie that's still warm from a tray on the counter. It's gooey and delicious as I stuff the whole thing in my mouth.

"You don't take a cookie without hugging me first. Oh!" She gazes over my shoulder to where Mariah is standing. Her jaw drops.

Here we go.

"Oh," she says again, her hands going to the hem of her apron. Drying the dishwater from her palms, she looks at me, to Mariah, then back to me. "You brought a girlfriend?"

"I—"

"I'm not his girlfriend," Mariah cuts in. "We're just friends."

Nana nods slowly. Removing her apron and wadding it in a ball, she sets it by the microwave. "Lance, I will love you regardless."

"Regardless of what?" I ask, popping another cookie in my mouth. "These are really good, by the way."

"Tell you what, let's just have this conversation now. There's no time like the present," Nana says, throwing her shoulders back. "The doctor on television says the best thing to do when a child or grandchild tells you they're gay is to tell them you love them anyway. That you will be their safe spot. I'm your safe spot, Lance."

"Woah," I say, taking a step back. Ignoring Mariah's hiccupping giggle behind me, I look at my lovely grandmother. "Nana, I'm not gay."

"Your parents would've loved you the same too if that's what you're worried about. And don't worry about your brothers. They'll understand."

Mariah's hand finds my shoulder. I don't even want to look at her.

"I'll still be your friend, Lance," she giggles.

"Oh, stop it," I say when my wits finally come back to me. "I'm not gay, Nana. I'm not."

"Are you sure, honey?"

"Yes, I'm fucking sure."

She gives me a warning look. "If you want to try coming in again, we can start over. But leave the language on the steps. I'll love you if you love men, but not if you continue to use that filthy language."

"Sorry." I glance at Mariah. She's eating this up. I can almost hear the jokes on the tip of her tongue. "You, I'll deal with later."

"Your secret is safe with me," she whispers, eyes dancing. She winks at me, ignoring my glower, before looking at Nana. "I'm Mariah. It's a pleasure to meet you."

"You can call me Nana. And I'm so sorry for the confusion, dear. It's just that Lance has never brought someone to my house and I just assumed that's why he was here. To show you off."

Mariah's cheeks split into a grin. "Please don't apologize. I work with him and we've all wondered about his sexual orientation for a long time. It's nice to finally know."

"Shut the fu …" I say, shaking my head.

"No wonder she's not your girlfriend with that mouth," Nana chastises me. "You expect her to kiss a mouth that filthy?"

My eyes drag to Mariah's. "It'd be nice."

She rolls her eyes, but I can't miss the rosiness to her cheeks. "I don't kiss boys with mouths that dirty."

"What if I promise to never curse again?"

"You should try that," Nana interrupts. I jump, having forgotten she was there. "I made some pudding tonight. The old-fashioned butterscotch kind. Want some?"

What I want has nothing to do with pudding or butterscotch or Nana's fridge.

"Oh!" Mariah walks by me, heading towards Nana. "I love old Pyrex dishes." She picks up the light pink bowl with pudding inside and caresses it like I wish she would my cock. "My grandma had all sorts of these. We'd bake until we ran out of things to bake and they'd all be lined up down the middle of her table in little dishes like these," she sighs. "I love them."

Nana eats this up. She's by her side faster than I've seen the woman move in years.

"My Grandma Betsy had this little light pink candy dish about like this, only smaller. She used to keep cinnamon balls in there for my grandpa."

Nana's face lights up. "I have a whole collection of these. Follow me, sweet girl."

This is not what I had in mind. "Hey, what about me?"

"Eat some cookies. There's milk in the fridge," Nana shouts as she disappears around the corner.

Sitting on a stool, I watch the doorway. Their voices trickle down the hallway and hearing them together makes me smile. There aren't girls in our family but Blaire and she's not a warm and fuzzy kind of person. Walker's girlfriend, Sienna, is around now. She comes by and chats with Nana some, but I know Nana is still lonely for the kind of attention us boys can't give her.

I consider going in the guest room with them where Nana stores her extra dishes. Popping a cookie in my mouth, I'm not really sure what to say if I go in there. It seems weird. So, I eat another cookie instead.

For just a moment, I let myself consider how this would feel on the regular. Bringing a girl by my grandma's. Doing something on a Saturday night besides being at Crave with my brothers or fucking a girl I've texted a few times on an app. In theory, it's great. If it could just be that, spending time together and hanging out with no strings attached, I could buy it. It probably wouldn't be bad.

It's also probably not possible.

I'm another cookie and glass of milk in before they're done back there.

"Yes! I roll it out with powdered sugar instead of flour," Mariah says as they come around the corner. The corners of her mouth almost touch the lashes of her eyes. Her hair is pulled back high on her head, her cheeks a gorgeous shade of pink. "You should try it. It's a neat little trick."

"I've never heard of such a thing, but I am going to try it. I'll make the boys some sugar cookies for dinner tomorrow."

"We're having cookies for dinner?" I ask, trying to be relevant. They ignore me.

"I'd love to have your carrot cake recipe too," Nana tells her. "If you share that kind of thing. Not all cooks do, you know."

They banter back and forth about recipes and I watch dumbfounded. I've never seen Mariah this animated or Nana this excited. I just eat another cookie and wonder why the world works like it does. I go out of my way to be a good person. To avoid situations that cause trouble. To not harm anyone. If karma is real, why do I get put in these positions? Where everything seems perfect on the outside when, in fact, it's not? It can't be.

"Why don't you come for dinner tomorrow, Mariah?" Nana asks.

"I'm making pot roast, potatoes, carrots, the works. If you come early, you can show me your cookie trick."

My breath catches in my throat. Mariah looks at me out of the corner of her eye, checking my reaction. I try my best not to. Having her here tonight is one thing. With my brothers tomorrow is another.

"I don't think so, Nana," she says softly.

I'm relieved. I'm also something else, something I don't want to ponder too long.

"Well, I do," Nana insists.

"I ..." Mariah clears her throat. "I have plans. I'm sorry." She watches me closely as I try to remain blank-faced. "Thank you, though, for the offer. It's sweet of you."

"That offer extends any time, honey. I'd love to have you for dinner."

Climbing off the stool, I need to get control of this situation. "I'd love to have you for dinner too."

Mariah shoots me a look as I try not to laugh at my own joke.

"Nana, we gotta go," I say. "It was nice seeing you."

Mariah takes a step towards me and stops. "Did you do whatever you came to do?"

Giving Nana a kiss on the cheek, I turn back to Mariah. "I just did."

"Did I call you and ask you to do something?" Nana asks. "Lord, I'm getting forgetful in my old age. If I did, I'm sorry."

"You're fine," I say, kissing her cheek again. "Come on, Social Butterfly," I say motioning towards the door. "Let's get you home."

Chapter 9

Mariah

Lance is quiet as he backs the car down the driveway. The moon hangs brightly overhead, but the sky is pitch black otherwise. No stars. No satellites. No glittery planets glowing from far off.

The car is cozy despite the cool evening. A song drifts smoothly from the speakers, lulling me even more into a state of contentment. It's that feeling you get when something really nice happens and you know you could just close your eyes with a smile on your face and drift off to sleep.

Peeking at Lance as he steers the car around a pothole, I wonder what it would be like to wake up beside him. Or to go to sleep at his side. Or spend the evening with him and his family.

I wonder what the rest of them are like. Are they all as wonderful as his grandmother?

Her declaration that he hasn't brought a girl to her house before rolls through my mind. Am I just that good of a friend? Was it just a timing issue? Probably. I'm grateful for it either way because I haven't felt that happy and understood since Grandma Betsy passed away.

"What?" he asks, catching me check him out. "Do I have cookie on my face?"

"No," I laugh. "I was just wondering why you took me to your grandma's."

He shrugs like he hadn't thought about it.

"Were you trying to convince her of your heterosexuality?" I tease.

"No. Clearly Nana loves me for whomever I choose to be."

"Lucky for you."

His lips part into a slow smile. "This night didn't go as planned, did it?"

"Ha." Taking a deep breath, I blow it out into the night. "It didn't go as planned, but is it weird that I'm happy about how it turned out?"

"You are, are you?"

"I don't think Jonah was for me," I wince, making him laugh. "It makes me wonder what Whitney was thinking. I mean, he ordered a veggie burger."

Lance cracks up, his hand dropping to his thigh. My eyes follow it as his fingers press lightly into his leg. The muscles in his forearm flex and I want to ask him if he lifts weights or plays basketball a lot or is just one of those people that wakes up sexy. But I don't. It's too dangerous. For me.

"So that was a blind date?" he asks. "You didn't pick him out of a line-up or something?"

"Um, no. My friend hooked us up. He was cute and I think he's probably smart if I could have gotten him to open up or something," I shrug. "But he's really not what I go for in a man."

"Now we're getting somewhere ..."

"Really?" I giggle. "Where's that?"

"What does Ms. Mariah Malarkey look for in a man?"

My mouth hangs open, but no words come out. My first reaction is to babble off hair color or nice teeth, but is that what I look for in a man?

"Cat got your tongue?" he asks.

"You know, I'm not sure what my type is."

"How can you not know that?" He takes his eyes off the road to look at me. "Don't women sit around and analyze it?"

"Not this woman. I haven't ever thought about it. It's harder to answer than you think."

He gives me a look that says I'm crazy, so I turn the tables.

"What's your type, Mr. Gibson?"

His response is instantaneous. "Big ass. Tight pussy. Nice lips."

My scoff isn't supposed to be heard. It's supposed to stay tucked inside the judgmental sector of my brain while I play it off like his response is expected. Because it is. This is verbatim what I expected him to say.

What I didn't expect is how my heart kind of tugged when he said it.

"What?" he pushes when I don't say anything. "I'm being honest."

"I'm sure you are."

"When you're fucking someone, nothing else really matters. Sure, I appreciate good breath and no gag reflex but I'm not picky."

The song switches to something a little faster temp. I turn it off. He lifts a brow, but doesn't comment.

My eyes drift closed. Fighting my brain to keep from overanalyzing every word I've said tonight, I try to just breathe in Lance's cologne and enjoy the little bubble I'm in. It's like the world isn't here. It's similar to how I feel when I read an amazing book, only this is real. At least for a little while it is.

How long I sit like that and ponder, I don't know, but Lance's hand brushing my cheek is what pulls me back to the car.

My lashes open to see him watching me with a concerned look etched on his features.

"I didn't offend you somehow, did I?" he asks quietly. He clenches the steering wheel, his forearm flexing.

"No, of course not." Shifting in my seat, wishing the warmth of his hand was back on my cheek again, I smile. "Why would I be offended?"

"I don't know. You just got all quiet on me."

"I was just relaxing," I shrug. "And thinking. I figured out my type."

"And?"

"He's loyal. That's the most important thing. And smart, someone who likes to read and wouldn't give me crap about reading in bed." The further I go into this, the easier it gets. "He'd want to be a father, have at least two kids, and not be mad if I let them pile up in bed with us. He'd love cake and baked stuff and wouldn't be adverse to stopping the car and getting out to dance because a certain song had come on."

Lance balks. "Dancing in the middle of the road?"

"Yes," I sigh happily. "It's so romantic."

"Which is precisely why I stay away from romance," he laughs. "That sounds ridiculous to me."

"You're better off focused on the ass, I guess."

"Exactly."

Twisting so I'm actually sitting sideways in my seat and facing him, I watch his jaw flex. It's an unconscious quirk. He does it when he's mulling something, when he doesn't have quite the comeback he wants.

I study him for a while. He lets me. He keeps his attention on the road and doesn't chastise me for watching.

Lance could easily be my type. He's intelligent and funny and he works hard. His heart is good, even if his mouth is filthy, and I know he likes to eat what I bake. I'd even put money on him being a good father. I'd put even more on the table that he doesn't want any part of that.

"Don't you ever want to stop chasing women and just breathe?"

"That would be a no," he cringes. "That sounds terrible."

"Why?"

"*Why?*" he repeats. "There's too much responsibility in relationships. You're suddenly on the hook for someone else's happiness."

"I wholeheartedly disagree," I shoot back. "The only person responsible for your happiness is you."

He takes the exit into Linton, shaking his head. "Not true, sweetheart. If you are in a monogamous relationship, it's your job, even if only in part, to bring happiness to the other person."

"Maybe joy," I argue. "But not happiness. Two completely different things. Think about it. Joy is something that can be spread. You can bring someone joy, just like the old saying goes. But happiness? That's an entirely personal thing. Someone else can't make me become happy if I'm not."

The lights from Goodman's Gas Station light up the car as we go by. His lips press together as he considers my stance. "Let's say we're dating," he says finally. "And you really wanted to move to Oregon, right? Maybe it's the fulfillment of your life's desire to live in Portland. The job of your dreams is there or something, I don't know. And for whatever reason I can't go and it's the only thing in the world that you really, truly want. I can't give you that. If you stay with me, you'll never really be fulfilled. You'll never be happy. Doesn't that make me a dick?"

"There are so many problems with that analogy," I laugh. "First of all, relationships are compromises."

"What if I can't compromise?"

"Then you shouldn't be in a relationship."

"Which is what I said from the start."

"But love *is* compromise," I insist. "You can't have everything you want. You have to meet in the middle."

"Love isn't *compromise*. It's *conditions*," he says, looking at me out of the corner of his eye. "You love someone *if*. They love you *if*. If you don't fulfill that condition, they leave. Ever wonder why the divorce rate is so high in this country? Because we're a bunch of hedonistic fuckers."

"So you're discussing monogamy, obviously."

Rolling my eyes, I turn to face the windshield. The car pilots onto my street. Lance turns the music back on, leaving the subject alone.

As much as I want to say he's wrong about all of that, he's not. I hate that he's not, but he's not. There are conditions to relationships and if you don't meet them, it's kaput. That's exactly what happened with Eric. I didn't meet whatever conditions he had. Probably the one about anal.

"I guess you aren't the one-night stand kind of girl?" he asks on a half-laugh.

"Hardly."

"So you're a straight relationship girl?"

"I'm not anything right now," I say, wondering if that will ever change.

"What about Jonah?"

"I hope Jonah has a nana like yours," I laugh, making Lance laugh. "I think I should date more. I haven't dated anyone seriously since Eric."

He wrinkles his nose. "Do I want to ask about Eric?"

"You don't."

The car pulls in front of my house. Whitney's car is in my driveway and a light is on in the living room. I realize I haven't checked my phone all night and I laugh when I consider how many texts are probably on there from her.

"I guess this is it," I say, grabbing my purse off the floor.

"I'm at least going to walk you to the door."

"You totally don't have to do that." I laugh as he gets out of the car and jogs around to the front. His body moves so gracefully and with such ease that I wish I would've been taping it to watch again later. "Thank you." I climb out of the car as Lance holds the door open and step into the cool evening air.

His hand finds the small of my back again as we walk up the sidewalk. I love how it nestles right in the curve. There's no fumbling like with so many men. It's almost a natural gesture and I know I'll be remembering it later.

We get to the top step and he pulls his palm away and instantly I wish it were back where it was. I wish there were a mile of sidewalk left to my doorstep.

"In a weird way," he says, "I'm glad I didn't eat the pizza in the fridge tonight."

"In a weird way, I'm glad I agreed to a date with Jonah." The softness in his features makes me blush. "Thank you for saving the day. For giving me a ride home. For taking me to Nana's. You didn't have to do any of that."

"Yeah, I didn't. But I did." His forehead creases, his eyes suddenly darkening. "I have a question."

As he takes a step towards me, his palm gently caresses my cheek, and I hiccup a breath. My chest feels like I've already run a marathon. I can't breathe, only watch his lips descend towards mine. "Yeah?"

His Adam's apple bobs as he gets closer, the scent of his cologne suddenly stronger. Muskier. *Sexier*.

My thighs clench together; my panties become pointless. As hot as every fantasy I've ever had about Lance Gibson was, it is nothing compared to this. Having him in front of me, looking at me like I'm *it* … I whimper.

"Can you change your type?" he asks, the gravel of his tone setting me on fire.

My brain screams at me to stop but my lips press together. Just as his mouth hovers over mine, the door behind us swings open.

"Oops," Whitney winces, squeezing her eyes shut. "I didn't see a thing. I'll just, um, go back inside now."

I'm going to kill her.

Lance's forehead rests on mine as he chuckles. "Probably for the best, huh?"

"Definitely," I say, breathlessly. If he can't hear my heart, he must be deaf, because it's pounding so loud it's almost all I can hear.

Whitney is a cold bucket of water but not quite cold enough to put out the flames. If he tried to kiss me again with her watching, I'd let him. I have half a notion to raise up and do it myself, but it is really probably for the best.

"I just can't believe you were going to let me," he grins.

"Um, I can," Whitney chimes in. "Damn, Mariah. I let you leave here with Jonah and you come back with that? Teach me your tricks, oh wise one."

Lance's chuckle turns into a full-bellied laugh. "I'm Lance. It's nice to meet you."

Whitney leans against the door, outright ignoring me. "It's nicer on my end, I assure you. Should I shut the door and let you kiss her?" She looks at me and then right back to Lance. "I should. I really should. A friend would. But damn it if I don't want to just look at you."

"I'm gonna go," Lance laughs. "See ya on Monday, Mariah."

"Bye."

My feet don't move until he's in the car. Then I kind of stumble in the house. Or maybe Whitney drags me. I'm not sure.

"You're meeting him on Monday?" she gushes. "Where's Jonah? What happened? Tell me everything."

"No, I'm not meeting him on Monday. I ..."

There are so many questions. The answers, though, aren't as easy to find.

"Did you not look out the window?" I ask, throwing my hands up in the air. "Isn't there some girl code that says you look out the window?"

"No," she balks. "I mean, maybe. If I thought you were actually going to be kissing a guy, I would've been a little more careful. But it's you. I just wanted to make sure you weren't boring little Jonah to death."

"Seriously? Have you ever talked to Jonah?"

She shrugs. "No. But he's cute."

"I almost unfriended you over him alone. And now you've ruined my kiss, I think we're done. It's a condition," I snort and head down the hallway.

"I said I'm sorry."

"I'm going to take a bath," I tell her.

"Then I'll sit on the floor by the tub because you *are* answering my questions!"

Chapter 10

Mariah

Sixteen. I feel like a freaking sixteen-year-old girl. Specifically, like the day when I was sixteen and the captain of the basketball team told me I was beautiful. Of course, he never said it again and continued on with his girlfriend who just happened to be Chrissy's best friend. Still, I relived that moment for years.

Lying in bed with my hair still in a weird bun from the bath, I can't wipe the goofy grin on my face. My forehead still sings with the feeling of his against mine. My cheek feels warm from the remembered heat of his palm. My heart is so full from the memories of Grandma Betsy brought out by Lance's Nana. What a wonderful and weird evening.

Lance is a lot of things. Some of them I didn't realize until tonight. It never occurred to me that he could be sweet or that he would go out of his way for ... *me*. My head scrambles, trying to process too much information too quickly. I close my eyes, but just see his face.

Just like the sixteen-year-old version of myself, I'm on the precipice of falling. Whether in love or in lust or in a slight obsession,

I'm not sure. I just know with absolute certainty I can't do this again with Lance Gibson.

He's a dead-end street. A good girl's worst nightmare.

An unnecessary problem.

There's so much potential beneath that sexy exterior. It's almost possible to be tempted to give in and play his game. But I'm not just a good girl, I'm also a smart one. Smart enough to know it's a game I'm well-versed in and one that will send me to heartbreak without passing go.

His smirk curls through my mind, like the slow, sly way the corners of his lips upturn. My back arches off the sheets, my toes digging into the mattress as I relive his touch.

My palm drags over my chest, remembering the feel of his hand on the small of my back, pulling at the towel covering my body. The air bites away at my warm skin, beading my nipples as I slip my hand between my legs. Covering the stretch of flesh connecting my thighs, a dampened heat warms my fingers.

I can't do this every night. I can't get myself off every twenty-four hours while pretending Lance is licking me. Touching me. Fucking me in positions I didn't even know I could dream up.

Dipping fingertips into my soaked flesh, I release a shuddered breath. My decision is made.

I'm going to take matters into my own hands. And then I'm going to take *other* matters in my own hands before I'm really screwed.

———

Lance

Every light in my house is on. I went room to room and flipped every switch, looking for something to entertain myself. I don't even care what it is as long as it's distracting and fully consuming.

And not Mariah.

Falling spectacularly onto the guest room bed makes the springs squeak under my weight. This doesn't help my current predicament. With every move I make, it sounds like a precursor to a good fuck and that makes my cock hurt worse.

"Damn it," I growl out loud.

Hands over my face to block out the light I just turned on, my foot bounces on the floor. It's a habit I've had since I was a kid and one I'm constantly on my students about. Sit still. Stop moving.

But I can't.

My phone buzzes in my pocket. I don't take it out. It's a reminder that I didn't check the message on my dating app. The one from Nerdy Nurse.

"You should log in and find someone to fuck, you asshole," I say to myself. "That would solve this stupid little fascination you have with Mariah."

Just saying her name makes my balls tighten.

Cringing, I unbutton my pants and try to relieve some pressure. It just gives me more room to grow.

Historically speaking, getting off cures a lot of these type of ailments. Any time I think I might actually like a girl for more than her pussy, I can just come and everything is fixed. It's almost magic. Like my jizz is some kind of anti-ship medication, proven to wash away any thoughts of words ending with those four letters.

The problem is this: I've already jacked off once since I got home. Thinking about Mariah's round ass and swollen lips only made it worse. It's like my cock is mad at me. Like it knew it wasn't the real thing and now feels cheated.

Sighing, I get off the bed and roll my eyes at the squeak. Even the bed is taunting me.

My phone is heavy in my pocket and I take it out. The notification is on the front screen from Nerdy Nurse. I almost open it. *Almost.*

I stall. I get a drink. I place my phone on the fucking counter and purposefully walk into the other room like it's a barrel of feelings I'm trying to avoid because God knows I avoid those. But it's not. It's a phone. A message from a woman I've been happily trading messages with for what feels like a long time.

Peeking around the corner, it sits right where I left it beside the coffee pot. I kind of hoped it would just vanish.

"Get your shit together," I warn myself. Like a man on a mission, I march into the grey and blue kitchen and pick it up. Then I open it and call the only person I know to call. It rings four times before she picks up.

"Hello?" she asks.

"Hey, Blaire."

"Preface this conversation by telling me if anyone is in jail."

"No," I laugh. "Why?"

"I don't know," she sighs. "It's Saturday night. You're calling late. The last time I talked to you, you were giving me a dissertation on dating apps. Machlan called a little while ago and he and Peck were going at it before the call was ended."

"I take it back. I'm not in jail. I don't know about the rest of them."

She releases a long, frustrated breath. "Sometimes you guys make me feel like I already have kids."

"When you're an excellent mother one day, you can thank us."

Her laugh, something you don't hear too much from my sister, rolls through the phone. "Not planning on having kids anytime soon. Maybe ever." As if she catches herself, her laughter mellows. "That was really inconsiderate of me."

"It's fine," I say, not wanting to go there. Not right now. "Blaire, I have a problem."

"Well, kudos to you for getting to the point without me dragging it out of you. Tell Walker to take notes." The silence between us stretches longer than Blaire's patience. "If you aren't going to tell me, let me get off of here. I have a brief due in the morning and, while you find yourself fascinating, I really don't."

"You love me."

"Clearly," she scoffs. "Now what is it?"

Taking a deep breath, I pace around the living room. "I think you need to commit me."

"What?"

"Commit me. Find a nice psychiatric hospital and just put me in it. Keep money on my commissary and I'll pay you when I get out."

"First of all, it's a commissary in jail. Unless you've committed a crime, you should be good. On that note—"

"I'm a law-abiding citizen," I interrupt.

It's her turn to blow out a breath. "Good. In that case, why do you need a psychiatric hospital?"

"Blaire. I'm feeling ... guilt," I gulp. "This is not funny."

She continues to laugh at me.

"Damn it, Blaire."

"There's a part of me that doesn't even want to know."

"Fine. I'm sorry I called you."

"Oh, stop being a baby," she huffs. The sound of paper crinkles through the line before she clears her throat. "Why do you have guilt?"

My free hand digs into my scalp as I pace the little path I've made around the living room. "Okay. There's this girl, all right? I haven't actually met her before."

"Is she an app girl?"

"Yeah. She's an app girl," I say, irritated by her unnecessary interruption. "We've texted back and forth for a while through the app and she's funny, you know? Witty as hell."

"And?"

"And nothing. That's it about her."

"I'm not following you."

"Well, there's this other girl," I say, squirming. Stopping in my tracks, my hip against the recliner, I try to discern the correct place to start explaining Mariah.

My first instinct is to start with her smile, but Blaire won't care about that. Probably not her icing either or that Nana basically bequeathed her Pyrex collection to her last night. Do I start with the fact that she's a librarian or that she thinks I'm a dick or that she tried to date a dork of epic proportions tonight?

"Lance?" Blaire asks carefully. "You still here?"

"Yeah," I groan.

"I have one question for you."

"Okay."

"Who did you meet first?"

"I've known Mariah longer," I admit. "But, like, I haven't. I mean, we work together, so I've known her like that. But not like that, if you feel me."

"I have something to tell you and you probably aren't going to like it."

"Is the only hospital you know all male? Because that won't work for me," I tell her. "I need some action even if I'm crazy."

She laughs again, but softer this time. "You like Mariah."

The snort comes before I can stop it. "Of course I like her. There's not much not to like. Except the way she razzes me. And refuses to sleep with me. And I would never tell her this, but her mint chocolate chip icing isn't my favorite."

"Lance."

"You sound like Mom when you do that," I note, a wobble in my tone. My throat goes dry as I listen to my sister.

"Is the guilt you feel because you are messing with both ladies at the same time?"

"I've never felt this way before," I say through the cotton in my throat. "I've fucked three, four women at the same time. I mean, not at the same time because I'm not sure I even have the energy for that, but I'd try if it—"

"Lance."

"Yeah?"

"Listen to yourself. I've never heard you like this. Ever."

I slip over the arm of the chair and land haphazardly across it. "That makes two of us," I say straight-faced.

"Break things off with app girl and see where they go with the other."

"Mariah?"

"Yes, Mariah. Just see what happens. What can it hurt?"

"Oh, ya know," I say, letting my head fall backwards. "Just everything."

She rambles on about taking a risk and opening myself up. Then the conversation ventures into how losing our parents made us close ourselves off from the world and how she understands that but maybe it's not the right thing to do.

"So, is the Ice Queen thawing?" I snicker.

"Go to Hell, Lance."

Sitting up, I get positioned correctly in the chair. My temple throbs with every move I make. The more I think about the rest of the conversation I want to have with her, the worse it gets.

My pulse beats in my ears. My heart pounds against my ribcage. I finally get to my feet and start the pacing again because I have to rid myself of some of this stupid, worthless energy.

"What if I know I'm not what she wants," I say, choosing my words carefully.

"Have you asked her that? Girls get upset when guys assume they know what we want. Except chocolate. It's a freebie."

"I'm being serious here."

"Me too," she sighs. "Fine. Why do you think you aren't what she wants?"

I pace. "Okay, I probably am what she wants. I didn't mean it like that."

"Oh, my God."

"But what if I can't give her what she wants? If I pursue her knowing that, does that make me a dick?"

"You are a dick," she points out. "But in this case specifically, I guess it matters why you think you can't give her whatever this is."

"What if ..." My breath is shaky as I try to pull my thoughts together and not sound like a pussy. "What if I know what kind of girl she is and what she's going to want and I can't give that to her?"

"Lance, listen to me. A relationship is like a contract, okay? Contracts are amended all the time. Let's say you two start something today. You start it based on the current situation. However, a year from now, things might change. They do change. It's life. You just amend your contract."

My nostrils flare as I exhale. "But isn't it a waste of everyone's time if I know there's a needed amendment that I won't sign?"

"Do you have a crystal ball?"

"Yeah, I do," I groan. "I know where this would lead. I purposefully stay away from women I think I might actually like outside of bed because I don't want to do this again."

"She was an asshole, Lance."

"Nah, she wasn't. Her conditions were understandable." I start to think of Britt, the only girl I've ever dated, but shove it out of my mind. "I bend over backwards not to go there and yet here I am. Feeling guilt and I haven't even fucked either one of them."

Papers rustle again. I wonder if she's listening to me and working at the same time. Wouldn't surprise me, but it's annoying too. I'm dying here and she's letting me.

"Are you listening to me?" I ask.

"Yes. I'm listening to you. You're basically talking to yourself."

"I'm just trying to explain myself. Am I not being a better man by not holding her up so that someone else can give her a fabulous life with all the trimmings. But not Jonah. Fuck Jonah."

"Who's Jonah?"

"Never mind," I sigh. "I think I've answered my own question."

Looking at my reflection, I realize how much I look like my father. Same hair, same eyebrows, same slightly crooked nose. I never wanted to be him, like Walker did. But I always admired how he ran his shit.

He was at every baseball game, mud-bog, cross-country race we entered. He'd stay up all night and help us with geometry, teaching it to himself as he taught us. More than that, he loved our mother. You could see it when you looked at him. My friends' parents got divorced or separated and I never once worried about that. My parents would be together until the day they died; and they were.

That part of my father, the man, that's who I always aspired to be. Someone to teach my kids right from wrong, to make a difference somehow by putting out these little humans into the world who were an asset to society. To someday be in Goodman's and hearing someone brag about one of my kids or grandkids without knowing I was in there. I wanted to be that guy. And that's the guy I'll probably never be.

"I think you take a chance, Lance. If she likes you, she deserves the opportunity to decide whether or not you're good enough for her."

I'm not.

"Blaire, I gotta go."

"You okay? Honestly. Don't blow smoke up my ass because I'll call Machlan."

"I'm fine. I promise. I'll call you tomorrow."

"Do that. Love you."

"You too, Sis. Bye."

Ending the call, I hold the phone in my hand. Opening the app is more because of loneliness than sex this time.

Nerdy Nurse: Fun Fact—the term boy has been used since 1154 AD to describe a male. It's believed that the word is derived from boia, which means servant.

Me: And here I thought it came from boa constrictor. Like our cocks.

Nerdy Nurse: What are you doing tonight?

Me: Just got home.

Nerdy Nurse: Hot date?

A grin tilts my lips as I think of Mariah and our non-date date. Whether it was or wasn't, she was hot. So that's a yes.

Me: Maybe the hottest ever, actually.

Nerdy Nurse: I guess I have something to live up to, huh?

My fingers race across the keys. I don't even realize what I've typed out until I hit send and the words are printed on my screen.

Me: Actually, I'm probably not going to be using this app much longer.

There's a long, probably deliberate, pause and I hope I haven't hurt her feelings.

Me: I do wish we would've gotten to meet though. I think we could've hit it off. I mean, I haven't had a conversation this good without an orgasm for, well, maybe ever.

Nerdy Nurse: I get it. I thought maybe I could figure out how to have a one-night stand on here, but I suck.

Me: You didn't tell me you sucked. On second thought …

Nerdy Nurse: Ha, ha, ha. Maybe I'll meet someone in real life who will sweep me off my feet.

Me: Don't date doctors though. I've heard bad things about them.

Nerdy Nurse: They're on my 'no go' list.

A thought crosses my mind and I toy with it for a moment. Going back and forth, I finally decide to take a chance.

Me: Now that sex is firmly off the table because although you do suck, you can't fuck, maybe some time we could meet for dinner. Just so we can put a face to a name.

There's another weird pause. Her chat bubble takes forever to start dancing to let me know she's typing. I hold my breath, still unsure as to whether or not this is a good idea.

Nerdy Nurse: I have a friend I need to check on in the morning, but I'm open after that. If you want to grab lunch somewhere?

Me: Noon-ish?

Nerdy Nurse: Perfect. Where?

. . .

Nothing too fancy, nothing too fast-food. My brain sorts through locations until I remember Peaches.

> Me: Peaches? It's in Merom.

> Nerdy Nurse: That works.

> Me: See you then.

Chapter 11

Lance

When the church bells ring on Sunday morning you can hear them all the way from the high school on the other side of Linton. You can really hear them when you have a migraine brewing and they ring out as you're walking up the sidewalk.

Last night consisted of a lot of tossing and even more turning. This guilty conscience thing is shit. No matter what I told myself to make it stop, it didn't. When I finally opened my eyes for good, I thought about hitting snooze but didn't want to deal with Nana. And it wouldn't hurt to have a bonus point with the Lord when I go to meet Nerdy Nurse.

I shouldn't meet her. There's really no point. There's something about her I want to see, to put a face with the name of the woman I've had a running conversation with all this time. A woman I've spent hours wondering about, and whose image I've been jacking off to. Maybe we'll meet and hate each other in person and I can write her off. That would be simpler.

On that note, I should be writing off Mariah too, but I can't.

Maybe I can hit the altar this morning.

"Morning," I say to the pastor, not making eye contact so he doesn't stop me. Not the most courteous thing I've ever done, but I'm sure I'll top it before the day is out.

Winding my way through the parishioners of Holy Hills, I nod and bid greetings whenever necessary. None of it registers. My mind isn't here. Turns out that having a conscience is a real thing. Having something riding on it isn't nearly as fun as having someone riding on your cock.

Nana and my brothers are sitting in their usual spot in the front right corner. Peck and our grandmother sit one row behind Machlan and Walker. Sienna sits in my old spot. I guess Walker felt like it was safer for me to sit next to Sienna than Machlan. I'm kind of perturbed by that.

"Hey," I say, slipping into my seat. I look straight ahead and hope they all have hangovers and don't feel chatty.

"Good morning," Sienna almost sings.

"It's too early, Slugger," I groan. "Let's take it down a notch, okay?"

Machlan's head pops around Walker. "Late night?"

"Yeah, for all the wrong reasons."

"But she was absolutely lovely," Nana pipes in. "Just lovely, Lance. I hope she'll come by today. Sienna will love her. Or maybe you've met her already?"

Their eyes are all on me. Even Cross knows something is up when he struts in and sinks into the pew in front of us. I refuse to look at them, not even Nana because my mouth wants to say a string of words she loathes. Also words not welcome in a house of God, but I'm not really sure who I'm more afraid of.

"No, Nana," Sienna chirps, staring at me. "I haven't met her. What's she like?"

"Nana, let's do this later," I mutter. The rip at my temple starts up again right behind my left eye.

"Nope. Let's do it now," Sienna goads.

"Is this the leggy nurse? Peck asks. "If so, I vote to hear about it now."

I glare at him over my shoulder. "Seriously. We are in a church, for crying out loud. Have some respect for the man upstairs."

"Oh, like you give a damn—" Machlan's response is thwarted by Nana's swift hand. "Like you *care*," he corrects himself. "If I remember correctly, our conversation just last week in this very pew was highly un-Christ-like."

"I don't know what I'm going to do with you boys." Nana shakes her head. "I'm going to go say hello to the pastor."

We wait until she's out of earshot before continuing the conversation. It's Sienna who speaks first.

"You know she's going to add your names to the prayer list."

"Good. I need it," I grumble. "I'm going to hell. My ticket is punched and I didn't get to do anything fun for it."

"What the hell is going on with you?" Walker asks, lacing his fingers with Sienna's. "You're acting like someone Lance'd you."

My brothers snicker. All of them except Walker. He rests his and Sienna's linked hands on his lap and watches me in a way only he can.

He has no idea why I refuse to get into a relationship, but he does know how it feels to avoid them. He fought love hard with Sienna but she broke him down. I can't let Mariah do that to me.

"Ah, did Lance get his heart broken?" Machlan chimes in.

I narrow my eyes. "No. I did not. You can't get your heart broken when you don't let it get involved."

"Then what the hell is this about?" Machlan counters. "You were up late. You apparently took a girl to Nana's. You're in here pussy-footing around."

"Sounds like you when Hadley broke your heart." Cross tosses me a wink. "What do you think, Mach?"

All heads whip to my youngest brother to see his reaction. He and Hadley, Cross's sister, had an epic ending a while back. It's not something any of us bring up. As a matter of fact, we kind of skirt around the issue of Hadley altogether.

I've postulated that Hadley is the reason why Machlan is still single. It doesn't make sense otherwise. He's good-looking, a near reflection of me, and he owns a bar. He's also not averse to love. What guy owning a bar who looks like me and wouldn't mind being in a relationship is still single? A guy who is still torn up over a girl.

"I think you can go to Hell." Machlan doesn't blink. Doesn't flinch. Doesn't even look Cross's way. Cross says something loud enough for only him to hear and they go at it animatedly.

"Need advice?" Sienna asks me softly. "I'm really good at it."

"Not really. I think I'm good."

Peck leans forward, his blond hair flopping against his forehead. "Can I say I'm disappointed this had nothing to do with the nurse?"

I contemplate not saying anything to him, but consider that if I do, there's a chance I'll feel better. I thought I'd be over it this morning. Instead, I think I feel even more guilty.

It's stupid as hell. What do I have to feel guilty for? Why did my guilt button decide to turn on? Life without one is bliss. This? This is horrible.

"Cousin," I say to Peck. "You'll be happy to know I'm meeting her later."

"For real?"

"For real."

He studies me. "For whatever reason, I expected more of a reaction."

"Well, I'm meeting her to *not* fuck her."

"Wait," Walker interjects as music begins to play. "Isn't that counterproductive? You use the app so you can get laid, right? Or have I had it wrong all this time?"

"Nope. You got it," I sigh.

Sienna's eyes are wide as she tries to make sense of the senselessness. "I'm thoroughly confused, Lance."

"Join the club."

The choir starts singing and I bow my head and hope for some guidance.

We're standing around Daisy, Walker's truck, when Nana walks up. She steadies herself on Machlan's arm.

"Who's coming for dinner? I need an idea of how many potatoes to peel."

"I thought you were making a roast?" I ask.

"I was, but I forgot to get the meat out last night. It's terrible getting old."

"You aren't old," Machlan tells her, resting his cheek on the side of her head. "You're seasoned."

She laughs, patting him on the stomach. "You coming to eat?"

"Do I ever miss a meal at your house?"

"What about you kids, Walker?" she asks.

"Sienna and I will be there."

"Peck?"

"What are you making?" He slings an arm over the side of Walker's truck. "If I bring stuff for a cheeseball, will you make it?"

"I already have one in the fridge," she tells him. "Better beat these boys over or there won't be any left." She kisses the side of Machlan's face, squeezing his cheeks in her hand, before turning to me. "Walk me to my car, Lance."

Extending my elbow, she hooks her arm through it and guides me across the gravel. We walk quietly for a bit. She waves at the pastor and again at Ruby, the little old lady who runs the town library. It's not until we're at the door to her car that she gets down to business.

"I'm sorry if I embarrassed you in front of your brothers," she sighs. "I should've thought it over before I said anything about Mariah."

"It's fine, Nana."

"I feel like a fool." She flings her purse in the back of the car. "I know better than that. I'm slipping, I tell ya."

"You aren't slipping." Opening the door, I lean on it. "What'd you think of Mariah, Nana?"

She nearly beams. "I liked her a lot. I think she's sweet and pretty and I love the way she looks at you."

"What?" I ask, standing straight. "We're not together."

"Well, you can call it what you will."

"We're not," I insist, maybe a touch too forcefully. "She's a great girl, but she's not for me." *Lies, lies, lies.*

A hand flies to her hip. "And why not?"

The exact reason is one I haven't ever discussed with her. I've only talked about it with Blaire and that's just because she knew it before I did. I'm not sure how Nana would react to what I have to say besides throwing me a pity party and I don't want that. Fuck that.

This isn't about me. I'm fine with things. I made peace with that a long time ago. It isn't about infecting others with my shit. It's about not ruining other people's lives because of my flaws.

"Look, Nana. I'm going to miss dinner, okay?"

She lifts a brow.

"I have some things to take care of." I kiss her cheek and help her get settled in the car. "I'll be there next week. Promise."

We exchange a smile and I see the concern in her eyes. I hate it. I turn to go but stop when she calls my name.

"Yeah?" I ask, looking at her over my shoulder. Her silver hair shines in the early afternoon sunlight.

"Remember what the pastor said today," she says. "Sometimes we search for happiness in the wrong places and in the wrong ways. Search simply, Lance. Don't overcomplicate it."

With a final smile, I head across the parking lot. The gravel crunches underfoot. As I climb in my car, I replay Nana's words. Whiffs of Mariah's perfume still linger in the air.

If only it were that simple, but this is anything but.

Chapter 12

Lance

This was a stupid idea.

My forehead rests on the steering wheel. It's too early in the day to second guess all of my life choices. Blowing out a breath, I look up. Peaches sits in front of me.

Inside is Nerdy Nurse, a woman I should've met at a hotel and just fucked the shit out of. Or stopped messing with as soon as it was apparent that wasn't going to happen. But, no. I've been getting ridiculous lately. I let the exchange be about more than just sex.

This is why you keep it about sex.

Air whistles between my teeth as I grab my phone and begin typing away.

Me: Is this thing still on?

Nerdy Nurse: I'm here. Are you?

Me: In parking lot. Figured you might've bailed.

Nerdy Nurse: I ordered a drink. Thought you wouldn't show up.

Me: Why wouldn't I?

Nerdy Nurse: Wishful thinking?

Laughing aloud, I exit the car and lock it behind me. Something tickles my gut and makes me wish things didn't have to end between us. I don't understand why, but I like these little exchanges.

Crossing the parking lot, I pass the spot I parked in yesterday when I came inside to check out Mariah and her date. Just like that, my need to end this with Nerdy Nurse, at least until I get my cock on straight, comes roaring back. It's not simple anymore. I might be losing my mind. I am feeling *guilt*. Until I get that shit under wraps and stop this infatuation with Mariah, I need to cool it. For all of us.

Me: I'm coming in. How do I find you?

Nerdy Nurse: I'm wearing a blue shirt. The color of your balls. 😊

Me: Nice.

Nerdy Nurse: I'm next to the drive-thru. You have about two minutes or I'm going to bail. My nerves are getting to me.

Me: Slow down, speedy. See you in a second.

The hostess is the same from yesterday and she greets me with a friendly smile. "Hey. How are you this afternoon?"

"Good. Just meeting a friend." Sticking my keys in my pocket, I rock back on my heels. "Mind if I look around for her?"

"I'll take you to her. No problem," she says, grabbing a menu out of a little basket on the podium. "Did you come for the buffet? You won't need this if you did."

I must look at her like she's insane because she backtracks. "I'm sorry. Lots of people come in on Sunday for the buffet. I just assumed."

"Oh, that's fine," I tell her. My head is so scattered I'm putting things together that don't belong together. "I'm not sure though about the buffet. Can I take a menu and think about it?"

"Sure. That's what she said too."

"I ..." The inside of my cheek starts to burn as I work it between my teeth. *Am I missing something?* "Did she say she was looking for a clueless guy? Because I'm not sure how you know who I'm looking for."

"She didn't have to tell me. This isn't my first day on the job," she snorts. "Right this way, please."

All I can figure as I follow her through the dining area is that she thinks I'm some kind of pimp. Meeting different women here—Mariah yesterday and she had just been with another guy and now Nerdy Nurse. This can't look good. I'll probably have the Feds at my door when I get home.

We round the corner toward the table from yesterday and things look even worse.

"What are you doing here?" I ask.

Mariah's head whips to the side, her eyes bulging. "Oh, my God. Are you stalking me?"

"No, I'm not stalking you. I had no idea you were here."

The hostess looks between us and backs away slowly.

"What a weird coincidence," Mariah notes, looking around the restaurant. She nibbles her bottom lip, just like she did last night. And, just like last night, I want to pop it free and suck it between my teeth.

She's beautiful with her hair up in a messy twist. The color of her silky shirt gives her a regal, sophisticated look. It's the color of ... *my balls.*

My head snaps to the drive-thru window. The very same window I sat outside last night when she sat here with Jonah. The same window Nerdy Nurse is sitting beside, waiting on me.

Oh.

My.

God.

No. It can't be. There's no way.

"What are you doing here?" I ask.

She looks around again, forcing a swallow. "Meeting someone. But, you know what, I should probably just go."

"Who?"

"No one."

"Jonah?" I ask, although that isn't the answer. She just needs to say it and confirm what I fear. Or hope. Or whatever this is that's making a mess of my senses.

"Jonah? Hardly."

Racing through every conversation we've ever had, I look for some inkling that she could be Nerdy Nurse. There's nothing. Not one fraction of a reason to even consider it was her. She's not a nurse. She doesn't work in a hospital or on swing shifts. She doesn't date men or look for quick sex—that I know of. If I'm wrong about the last one, I'm gonna be pissed.

"Let me ask you something," I say. "Why did you wear that shirt?"

I can barely breathe as her eyes meet mine. She can't be wondering if I'm History Hunk, although it's a lot more obvious than her bullshit profile. But she couldn't suspect me. Or does she?

"Why did you ask me that?" she gulps.

"Curious."

"I like the color."

"Why?"

"I just do," she says, exasperated. "Why are you asking me a million stupid questions?"

"Did it remind you of something?" I press.

She pales. Her phone clatters against the table. "Lance ..."

My heart can't decide whether to beat rapidly or to still altogether. It does some unnatural thing inside my chest reminiscent of dancing while drunk. It's all wobbly and trippy and it pukes a little to boot.

"This can't be real," I say in disbelief. "There's no damn way."

She covers her face. The redness in her cheeks blazes around the creamy skin of her fingers. To give her some room to breathe, and so I don't stand in front of her and shift back and forth like an idiot, I sit down across from her.

My brain might be confused, but my body is not. It's rioting for me to touch her, kiss her, bend her over the goddamn table and do all the filthy, questionable things Nerdy Nurse and I have talked about.

Mariah and I have talked about.

Imagining those words coming out of her pretty little mouth makes me so hard I might explode.

"I'm so embarrassed." It's said so quietly I barely hear it. "I'm so, so embarrassed."

"Why are you embarrassed?"

She refuses to answer me. Hell, she won't even look at me. It's like she's frozen in place, mute to everything outside herself. The longer I watch her fight it, the more adorable this entire thing becomes.

It's her. They're *both* her.

Who knew when I took Nerdy Nurse's words and pretended they were Mariah's I was right. *Wow.* I'd say I was a lucky bastard except neither one of them want to sleep with me.

"Things would've been different had I known it was you sending me all those dirty things," I admit. It's said with as much levity as I can muster, but I'm not kidding. Not in the least. The mere thought of Mariah Malarkey discussing my cock in her mouth and the wetness of her pussy stirs something inside me I'm not sure I can fight.

"This is mortifying," she moans.

"This is *amazing*."

"Damn it, Lance." She turns in her chair to pick up her purse. Every movement she makes is jilted, the scowl on her face cutting deep. Fuck that.

"Oh, no," I tell her, swiping her phone off the table. It's all I can think of to do to keep her from walking out. "You don't get to 'Damn it, Lance' me."

"Give me my phone."

"No."

She's never been this angry in front of me. Her eyes glow, a ring of gold settling around the blue. The flush to her cheeks hints at what she might look like after an orgasm and it's something I really, *really* want to confirm.

"Can you let me save some of the little dignity I have left?" she asks. "Just give me my phone so I can leave."

I don't. I don't even consider it. Instead, I sit as far away from her as I can with her phone nestled in my lap.

"Tell me this: why are you without dignity?"

"Are you seriously going to make me address this?" she hisses.

"Um, yeah."

"I hate you."

"I'm calling bullshit on that," I say, trying not to crack a smile. "You like me and so does the other you. As a matter of fact, one of you almost kissed me last night and this you, well, we both know what this you has been up to."

"I never would've said anything if I'd have known it was you," she growls.

I blink once. Twice. Three times. "So, let me get this straight. You'd talk dirty, filthy, actually, if I remember some of those conversations correctly—"

"Lance. Stop it."

"Fine," I say, propelling myself forward. The salt shaker rattles on the table. "You'll talk that way to some guy you don't even know but not to me? You would've let me kiss you last night, but you would've fucked some guy who didn't even give a shit about you? What the hell, Mariah?"

"It's you!" she exclaims like it's self-explanatory. "I have to see you every day. You're sleeping with God knows how many women—"

"Wait," I say, my jaw tensing. "Are you sleeping with men on that app?"

Her eyes narrow. "You know I'm not."

"I don't know shit. I'm a little mind-boggled right now to tell you the truth."

"It's nothing to you, but no, I'm not sleeping with anyone at all. App or otherwise."

"Good answer."

"Oh, go to hell with your good answer bullshit," she says. "How many women have you slept with this week?"

I don't even blink. "Zero."

She does blink.

Something in our exchange calms her a touch. She starts to talk but closes her mouth instead. We watch each other like we're having a staring contest. The longer we sit like this, the closer she gets to smiling. I hate to tell her, but I'm content with sitting here until the buffet closes because I haven't even begun to process this.

"Do you need anything?" A waitress approaches us, she's unknowingly coming upon a den of wounded badgers. "Drinks? Buffet slips?"

Without taking my eyes off Mariah, I twist slightly in my seat. "I'll tip you one way or the other, but can you give us a few minutes alone?"

"Sure thing."

Mariah breaks eye contact and checks to see if she's gone.

"I can't believe this," she says, tucking a strand of hair behind her ear. "You're History Hunk. I mean, it makes sense. I just never even imagined it."

"Are you saying I'm a hunk?"

She doesn't dignify that with a response.

"Nerdy Nurse, huh?" I grin. "That was tricky. Not that I would've expected you of all people to be hiding out under a fake name on a sex app, but I wouldn't have looked for you as a nurse."

"That was Whitney," she sighs. "My friend made the account for me and kind of threw it in my lap. I didn't want an account because of my job and working in the school and all and, besides, pretending to be someone else was fun."

Her hands cover her face again. There's no suppressing my chuckle this time. It earns me a glare, but there's no anger there. Just a beautiful girl trying to hide behind a façade.

We sit in silence for a few minutes, her playing with the salt shaker and me tapping against the screen of her phone. There are questions for days I could pepper her with, jokes for years. I could pop just by watching her flush that pretty shade of pink.

"This is mortifying," she breathes.

"What's wrong with it?" I ask. Leaning on the table, my hands clasped in front of me, I look her dead in the eye. "I wanted to fuck you when you were Mariah. I wanted to fuck you when you were the other you. Whatever," I say, confusing myself. "The point is this doesn't change anything. It just means I'm insanely attracted to you."

She bats her eyes like I misspoke and she's waiting on me to clarify what I mean. I could keep talking but decide it's better for the silence to make the point for me.

"What do we do now?" she asks. "I have to see you every day."

"Is sex on or off the table? I mean, I'll do it on or off. I have no problems with table sex," I tease. Visions of her round ass in the air, my hands gripping each globe as I slide into her warm pussy send a shot of heat straight to my balls.

"Not what I meant."

"Yeah, you're right. We both know sex is on the table. It's really a question of whether you'll allow me to participate or if you're just going to keep using your fingers and pretending they're mine."

She leans closer. "Stop it."

I think she likes the proximity, so I back away. The corners of her lips drop just enough to be noticeable and enough to tell me I'm right.

If I back away and it makes her come around, how can I be blamed for that? Answer: I can't. At least not in a way I could feel guilt over. God knows I'm avoiding that fucker.

"You know what?" I say, getting to my feet. "You're right. I don't want to make you uncomfortable and you've been very clear you want me to stop."

She's not sure whether to buy this line of bullshit or not. But as I scoot her phone across the table and it hits the side of her purse with a thud, she slumps.

This is a go-for-broke kind of thing and I don't want to be broke. I swipe my wallet from my pocket and hope I'm a good shot.

"Did you have anything? I'll pay," I say, forcing myself to ignore the look on her face. I pull a twenty that's sticking out and toss it on the table. "Want me to walk you out?"

She pulls her brows together. We both know she's waiting on the rest of it, the very Lance-like addition to every sentence I can get away with. I surprise us both with my willpower and don't give it to her.

But damn if I don't want to give it to her.

"Okay." Her possessions get compiled together as if they're the most interesting things in the world. She stands and heads to the door. This time, I make it a point not to touch her.

Chapter 13

Mariah

Each step leads me closer to the door. Each fall of my foot has me holding my breath and waiting for the moment his palm touches the small of my back. By the time I'm halfway to the door, I itch to turn around and find him. He's there. The ripple of whatever moves between us when we're near each other is roaring, almost knocking me on my ass.

On its own, that's enough. But coupled with the newfound knowledge that Lance is also History Hunk, is like going from a Category One storm to a Six in a second flat. Here I am, in a little tattered sailboat, trying to navigate this hellacious situation. The only thing that might help me stay afloat is him reaching out for me.

"Let me get the door for you," he offers. More than enough room is taken to walk around me. "Here you go."

I look at the floor all the way out, not sure what to think of all this distance. I hate it. But something about it feels almost normal in a really sad way. It reminds me of Eric and his lack of physical attention. "Thanks."

The sun is bright, making me squint, as I step outside. The door snaps closed but I plow forward. It's more than embarrassment now.

It's a fear of rejection. It's knowing who I'm dealing with and wondering how I'm going to internalize it when he's in my office on Monday making plans to bed some other woman. What do I do? Grin and bear it? Because there's no doubt that's what he's going to do. *He's unapologetically Lance.*

My pace quickens and I spy my car at the end of the row. I don't notice the custom pearly-purple paint job on the SUV on my left until it's too late.

"Good morning, honey." My mother removes her oversized sunglasses, her keys dangling in her hand. "What are you doing here?"

"Just had lunch."

I'm ten, maybe twelve steps from my car. Shuffling that way, I can cut it down to eight. Possibly six.

I can't do this today.

"I really need to go, Mom." A dull throb begins in my temple. "I'll call you later."

"You can't even make time to say hello in a parking lot?"

Her voice is too loud, too demanding, to be ignored. We've done this before. If I walk away, she will just increase the volume and half of Merom will know our business. Or, by her version of it, will think I'm a complete asshole of a daughter, in a best case scenario.

"Mom ..."

Her attention is diverted behind me. My hips pivot to turn but I stop. There's no need to look. It's Lance.

Mom's eyes go wide, the mask she uses when she's being watched falls effortlessly over her features. I'm distracted from her performance when his arm stretches around my waist and he pulls me to his side.

He's warm and solid and if it wasn't already weird, I would bury my nose in his chest and just breathe him in like a bouquet of flowers. One of my hands plants in the center of his chest to steady myself. His heartbeat pounds against my palm as roughly as mine clangs in my chest.

"I dropped my keys back there," he says, peering down at me. The greens of his eyes are filled with some nameless emotion that I could watch swim in his irises all day. "You okay?"

"Yeah."

"I'm sorry. Who are you?" My mother shifts her weight, the front of her shirt dropping. It's a patented move and many men have fallen for it. I glance up to see Lance's reaction.

He's looking at me. With a wink just for me, he turns to her. "I'm Lance. You must be Mrs. Malarkey."

"Oh, no," she says, swishing her hips. "I'm Taylor Stevens. Mariah's mother, yes, but her father was hell on wheels. We haven't been together for decades now and I took back my maiden name. Couldn't stand to be associated with that monster another day."

"I'm sorry to hear that." Lance's fingers dip into my hip, sending a proprietary impulse darting through my veins and pooling in my belly.

I almost don't want to breathe this close to him. I almost don't want to if that means pushing away and stepping back into reality. Not that I know what's real anymore. This is surely an alternate reality if Lance Gibson has his arm around me like we're lovers.

Mom studies Lance's grip on my side. The end of her sunglasses finds its way to her mouth as she tries to discern why a man like him would be with a girl like me.

Panic bubbles in my gut, overriding the foreplay from Lance, and I push away. "I need to get going," I say to him.

"Let me walk you to your car."

Mom's huff stops me. "Mariah, you are so rude."

"I'm sorry, Mom," I sigh. "I have a migraine coming on."

"Always an excuse with you," she says. "Haven't we talked about this?"

Resigned to the fight, I steady myself. "It's not an excuse."

"You always have one and then you wonder why you have nothing good in your life. It's because people don't want to coddle you, honey."

"Woah, wait a second," Lance says, chuckling to cover the anger I can hear just below the surface in his voice. "Mariah has a headache. Let's take it easy on her."

"You don't have to do this," I whisper to him.

His response is to tuck me back under his arm. This time, I rest my head against him. My body sags. He squeezes me harder.

"You obviously haven't been with her long," Mom says, eyeing him.

"That's true. But I know she has a lot of great things in her life. Me being one of them."

The smolder he emits could burn down a house. It's his special mix of cocky and confident that burrows its way into uninvited places. His rough knuckles graze the soft skin under my navel, gliding along my hip. The contact is incendiary, the friction—pure dynamite.

"Well, if that's true, why don't you accompany her next weekend to my birthday party?" Mom asks, trapping me.

"I'd love to." Lance's response is quick, too quick to allow me to intervene.

"I haven't said I'm going yet," I remind her and inform him. "I might have plans."

"With whom if it's not him?"

"I have other friends besides him."

"You do?" he asks. He bends over as I jab him in the stomach with my elbow.

"Yes. I have more friends than just you. As a matter of fact, I'm not sure I'm even your friend." The words don't come out without a laugh.

He pulls me in front of him, his hands locking behind me and dragging me against his body. Ignoring my mother, he grins. "I don't need to be your friend as long as I get the benefits."

"You mean cupcakes?" The question is breathier than I expect, huskier than I intend, but the spot in my brain that controls motor skills is host to an impressive display of fireworks going off in quick succession at the moment.

"You can call it whatever you want, sweetheart."

I laugh, pushing him away. It's potentially the hardest thing I've ever done. I'm the one who needs a cupcake for that bout of willpower.

"So you two will come?" Mom taps her lips with a manicured nail. "Your sister would love to see you."

Glancing at Lance, I snort. "Oh, I bet she would."

"Stop it, Mariah. You need to get over this. Act like the woman you are and not a child. I'm sick of your behavior."

"Act like a woman?" I fire back.

"Yes! Chrissy is beside herself. You need to suck it up and just get over it."

My chin tilts to the sky. It's a perfect, cloudless blue, like my eyes, my dad used to say, and I attempt to focus on that and not punching my mother in the face.

"I tell you what," Lance says. "If Mariah decides to come, we'll be there. And if she doesn't want to go, then we won't." He glances at me, his eyes searching mine. "But right now, we have to go. Have a good day, Ms. Stevens."

Tears dampen the corner of my eyes as he takes my hand in his. Mom storms off toward Peaches while Lance walks with me to my car. I don't try to slip my hand out of his grip because I'm not sure he'd let me.

The locks pop as I hit the button. My purse goes across the driver's side seat and onto the other.

"I'm tempted to say this day can't get any worse, but I feel like that would backfire," I sigh.

"She's a piece of work."

"No kidding."

When I turn around, he's taking me in. Not in a way that makes me think he's mentally undressing me, but with a gaze that's more intimate than that. A series of goosebumps prickles my skin.

"Thank you," I say.

"For what?"

"For coming to my defense."

He lifts his shoulders and lets them fall. "It was really just a chance to get to touch you a lot. But if you think it was for you, then good."

"Of course it was," I giggle. As my laugh dies off, so does the easiness between us. The space that was filled with nonchalance is replaced by text apps and almost-kisses and fake dates exchanged between the two of us under various names and situations. "This is weird, isn't it?"

"We're the same two people we were last Friday."

"That's a bold-faced lie."

"Fine." He gives in. "I know you don't like sucking cock with a rubber on and—"

"Lance," I hiss.

"But I knew that on Friday too. I just didn't know it was you."

I climb into my car because I need space. When the engine starts, I crank the air conditioner, despite the reasonable temperature.

He grips the top of the door and dips his head inside. His hair has fallen to the side, and his cheeks are freshly shaven.

"You know," I say, turning the fan down a bit, "if you kept your mouth shut, you could almost look sweet."

"I am sweet." A playful grin kisses his lips. The ones I almost kissed last night. "I'm settling into this role of the knight in shining armor quite nicely."

"Is that what you are now?"

"Jonah. Your mom," he razzes. "Who else will it be?"

Resting my head on the seat, I look up at him. A question lingers on my tongue. "Can I ask you something?"

"Yup."

"Why were you meeting Nerdy Nurse today?"

His eyes dart first to the building, then the opposite way to the road. He swishes his lips together like he has a mouth full of mouthwash.

The answer doesn't matter, not in the grand scheme of things. He's still him and I'm still me. But I still want an answer.

He clears his throat before answering. "You know, I'm not sure." The tables turn. "Can I ask you something?"

"I guess."

"Why did you send me a message on the app last night?"

Fair enough question. One I didn't expect to have to answer. I give the possible responses consideration, all reasonable and honest in one way or another, before settling on what seems to be the truest.

"I wanted a distraction," I admit.

"From what?"

"You."

He looks away, a lopsided grin splitting his cheeks.

"I have no business getting involved with you in any way, Lance. I got home last night and kept thinking about you and your grandmother and Whitney's inopportune timing and ..."

"And what?"

My stomach drops. "And what comes Monday?"

"Work? Cupcakes? Avoiding Principal Kelly?"

The swallow I force down my throat burns. Glancing around, I say a prayer my mother isn't watching and getting enjoyment out of this. She would too because it hurts me.

"Monday is going to be a lot easier for me as a bystander than someone who's dipped her toe in the pool," I tell him. "Whitney interrupting us was a save."

He runs a hand down his face, his long fingers stretching over his chin. "So the message last night was really to distract you from Monday. Not from me."

"No, from you," I say, wiping my palms on the sides of my seat. "I wanted History Hunk to remind me I'm desirable. That when Lance is in my office after having almost kissed me and is chatting up random girls, maybe I won't feel so boring. Or dull. Or dispensable in comparison. Because History Hunk still wanted me."

"You think that?"

"Think what?"

His voice lowers as he peers into my eyes. "You're dull?"

"I don't know. It doesn't matter. What does matter is not ending up feeling like I'm being rejected by you."

The rumble from his throat rolls by his lips. "I've never rejected you. I've practically begged you."

"To sleep with you. That's not what I want, Lance."

"Well, it is but ..."

I don't laugh at his joke. It's not funny. Whether I want to sleep with him or not isn't the point. The point is I can't. I won't.

"That's exactly what *you* want and I'm not mad about it. Why would I be? I just don't want to be one of your app girls."

"But you'd be someone else's? You'd be History Hunk's and that's okay with you?"

"It doesn't matter." I grab the handle and he steps back. I pull the door closed. Rolling down the window while I shift the car in reverse, I look at his handsome face. "I don't want things to be weird tomorrow."

"Are they ever weird between us?" he asks softly. "Hell, we can even be other people and they aren't weird. I bet we'd role play like a couple of motherfuckers."

I try to smile. I try to hold onto the Lance I hear every day. I attempt to put myself back in that box and keep things separated but I can't.

There's a nod. A little wave. There's even a fake smile as he watches me back out of my parking spot and head for the street.

There's also a feeling in the pit of my stomach that the road ahead isn't going to be easy.

Chapter 14

Mariah

All of the ingredients to make lemon bars are lined up on the counter. They've been sitting there since I got home. Two loads of laundry have been washed, dried, folded and put away. The new flannel sheets fit perfectly on my bed and the carpet in the living room smells like the lavender scented water I used in the shampoo cleaner.

It was enough to provide a semi-distraction from the day. The goal, however, was missed. While my body might be tired, my brain is not.

Extending my arms across the table, I rest my forehead on them. The water and soap from cleaning has washed away Lance's cologne. I sniff around my shirt, shoulder, forearms, and it all comes back lacking his scent.

My groan is obnoxious. It's repeated, quieter this time, as the click of Whitney's key frees the front door.

"You home?" The door clasps shut. "Mariah!" She mumbles about knowing I'm here, that my car is out front, about what a jerk I am to make her play hide-and-seek. But when she comes into the kitchen and our eyes meet, she stops. "Um, what the hell happened to you?"

I angle my face toward the table so I don't have to see her.

"Are you okay?" She drops into a seat next to me, her palm resting on my wrist. "Talk to me."

"I never should've used that app," I mutter.

"You used it? I didn't know that. I'm kinda proud."

Groaning again, not so obnoxiously since I have an audience, I drag myself into a sitting position. She performs a quick evaluation of my appearance and flinches.

"Don't be," I puff. "There's nothing to be proud of in this fiasco."

"Did you meet someone from it?" She squirms in her seat. "There are rules about meeting up with people, Mariah. You didn't meet a freak, did you?"

Lance's smile flutters through my memory. The way he showed up out of nowhere when I ran into my mother when he could've just stayed away. Remembering the way he buffered that situation makes me fill with an outrageous warmth.

"No," I ruminate before answering. "He wasn't a freak." While I'm scrubbing my hands down my face, the muscles in the back of my neck become tense. "I met someone though. Someone I already know."

"Um ..."

"Yeah."

"I'm humiliated, Whit," I cry. "I tell students every day to watch who they are online. To not do or say things they wouldn't say to someone in real life. I preach and preach and preach, setting out pamphlets about this topic. Hanging these cute little posters around the library to remind them about the dangers of social media, and what do I go and do? Exactly what I tell them not to."

I could cry real tears. Pinching the bridge of my nose, I shut my eyes and feel like a fraud. "I said things to him on that stupid app that I would never, *ever* say to him in real life. And now I'll have to see him every day knowing he knows that I said those things. I just ..."

Dropping my hand, my shoulders fall right along with it. "I just want to climb under a rock and die."

She watches me warily. "Can I ask who this guy is?"

I brace myself for her reaction. "Lance."

"The hot teacher?" she says, poker-faced.

"Yes," I grouse.

"The guy who was here the other night. Who took you to his grandma's house."

"Yes."

Her amusement knows no bounds. "Let me get this straight. Out of all the men on that app, you somehow managed to find *him*?"

It's a rhetorical question. Or it better be because I'm not holding her hand through this process.

"It is a semi-local, kind of regional app. So it's not entirely impossible, but I am leaning towards fate, Mariah." She gets to her feet and floats around the room like a cartoon princess.

"Fate? Since when is fate a form of hell?"

The spinning stops and she laughs. "Since when is screwing a hot history teacher a form of torture?"

"I didn't screw him," I mutter. *But I've fucked myself to thoughts of him a million times.*

"That's your fault."

Yes, it is.

I appreciate the few quiet seconds as she flops back in the chair again. My fantasies of Lance were just that—fantasies. Make-believe. Not real. Now my reality has been skewed, flipped upside down and it's all merging together in one ridiculously hot, yet slightly mortifying, situation.

Whitney shakes her head. "You are the only person in the universe who can find fault with an app that helped you meet a gorgeous and sexy man who already likes you to begin with!"

It's so much more complicated than that. So complicated, in fact, that I don't even know how to boil it down to make sense of it.

"How'd he take it?" she asks.

"Oh, he thought it was the greatest thing ever."

"And you should've too."

"Look," I gulp, feeling my cheeks ready to betray me. "We have one relationship, for lack of a better word, at work. What we had online wasn't really me and wasn't really him. Or maybe it was him, actually. But I *definitely* wasn't being myself."

It's easiest to leave it at that. There's no sense in bringing up the fact that he's a hook-up guy, a one-night stand—a couple nights at best. And even if I could pull off a one-night-er, I couldn't do it with Lance.

Whitney is my best friend for a few reasons. One, she's loyal. Two, she takes me as I am. Three, she can read all my nuances appropriately.

She gets comfortable, curling a leg beneath her. "So what you're saying is you are the book nerd in-person and a little vixen online?"

"No," I say too quickly.

She barely contains her laugh. "How vixen did you go?"

"I'm not a vixen."

"Clearly or you would've rode his cock like any other hot-blooded female. I saw him, Mariah. Your self-control is on a whole other level."

"Can we focus here?" I say, pulling her out of that line of questioning. "I don't know what to do."

I expect a quick chirp about how to have sex or something equally inappropriate, but she surprises me.

It's a moment you can only have with someone you're close to, a moment where you don't have to speak but thoughts are still being exchanged. Her foot starts to bounce on the floor as she grasps my panic. I, on the other hand, inflate my lungs a little more easily than I have been able to in the last handful of hours.

"I'll see him in the morning," I say, resolved. "How do I navigate this, Whit?"

"I didn't think you'd use the app, to be honest. I love that you did, but I'm surprised."

"Yeah, me too. Surprised, I mean," I clarify. "Not loving that I did it."

"Let's start there. Why did you do it?"

A sense of calm settles over me, like when you're in trouble and finally accept that everyone knows it was you who did it. You go through the motions of telling the truth because it's only going to delay the inevitable if you dance around it. You just want the conversation to be over and the fallout realized.

"I was sitting here one night right after I heard about Chrissy being pregnant." My throat is scorching as I put the thoughts I've kept to myself into the universe. "And I guess I kind of broke down, you know. Not crying and all that, but more of a pity party. Wondering if there's something wrong with me. Considering adopting a cat."

She drops her jaw in mock horror.

"Anyway," I continue, "I just needed that confirmation. I just wanted to know I could still reel a guy in. That I wasn't lame."

"You can't believe that. I won't sit here and let you say you think you're lame."

"You know what I mean."

She scoots her chair closer to mine and kicks at my foot. "I know you thought you'd be in a different place right now, but you aren't for a reason."

"I'm fine with that. Really," I insist when she looks at me like I'm lying. "I'm happy I'm not with Eric. But it wouldn't be a bad thing to have some nice, sweet, cute guy want to be with me."

The words don't make it past my lips before Lance's face pops back into my mind. It's the image of him at my car, his arms stretched overhead, a soft look in his eyes that is such a contrast to the playful one I often see.

"Like Lance?" she asks carefully.

"The end of that story would be a happy one," I laugh. "That excludes him."

"But what if it doesn't?"

"It does." Getting up, I head to the oven and get it pre-heating. "He's the most woman-hopping man I've ever known. *Ever seen.* In my office alone he talks to a different woman on the phone at least three times a week."

"But he's single, right?"

"Yes. He's single. His goal in life is to be single." The words cause a little ache to spread across my chest. "I don't fault him for that. That's not what this is about. It's about me knowing I have no desire to compete with other women for a man's attention and this guy plays that game as hard as it can be played."

Sugar and butter go into my mixer. My hand shakes a little as the vanilla is added, but I choose to think it's because I haven't eaten today and not from anything else.

"Fine." It's a simple response with no indication she's going to argue with me. This annoys me, but I try to hide it. "Guess you're going to have to figure out how to balance this then."

"That's what I said from the beginning," I grimace, busting an egg with a little more gusto than necessary.

"You said some, what, sexier things on line than you would've said in person?"

"Oh, a little." *I told him I wanted him to come on my chest.* "I want to die."

Whitney adds the lemon juice to the mixer and turns it on. "But you felt comfortable enough with him to say them."

"Because he wasn't standing in front of me, Whit. It's so much easier to tell him I want him to slap my ass or make me get off on his face when his face isn't there. When I think I'll never have to see his face."

"You said that? I'm impressed."

The dam is broken so I just roll with it. "I typed worse."

"He's probably going insane right now," she giggles. "And I doubt he'd qualify them as worse."

Putting a face, *his* face, to those words makes me almost moan in the middle of my kitchen. Typing them out was one thing when the point was to feel powerful. Knowing it was him on the other side has the opposite effect.

"I have to quit my job," I say gravely.

"You do not." She turns off the mixer. Leaning against the counter, she crosses her arms over her chest. "How does it make you feel to think he knows it was you who typed those things and he still wants you?"

Biting my lip doesn't help the smile from cracking across my lips.

"It feels good, right?" she asks.

"Yes. Fine. It feels good. But he'll tease me about it endlessly."

"Because he's a boy and boys do that."

There's nothing boy about him.

The pre-heat alert dings and Whitney glances at the oven before speaking again. "You should've considered this before you met up with him. I could've pointed that out if you would've told me your super-secret plans."

I should've considered a lot of things before I met History Hunk. Or before I used that stupid app.

"For some really, really dumb reason, it didn't seem like a bad idea. Yes, most of our conversations were sexual in nature, but it was good-hearted. It was fun. Our banter was great ..."

My finger presses into the butter as I turn away. Just thinking of Lance and the easiness of our chats fills me with a gooey sort of feeling.

"Like your banter at work?"

"Ugh. This is not helping."

At all. At work, Lance treats me like an intelligent, respectable, attractive woman. History Hunk made me feel downright sexy. Alluring. Wanted. They are two very different sides of ... the same coin? With the same guy? Processing this doesn't get any easier as the minutes tick by.

Digging around the cabinet and then the dishwasher, I find my nine-by-nine pan for the lemon bars.

"Meeting this guy didn't seem like I was meeting him for sex," I say, searching for more butter. "It felt like meeting a friend for the first time. There weren't expectations and I wasn't afraid, like I thought I'd be. It was just *easy*. Nerve-wracking, but easy."

The butter in hand, I spread it around the pan before I turn my attention back to Whitney. There's a knowing look aimed my way.

"I think everything between you two is easy, Mariah." She takes the pan and sets it next to the mixer. "Don't you see that?"

Yes, I see it. How could I not? But therein lies the problem—it's too easy.

The boiled-down truth is sitting on the tip of my tongue. There's a peacefulness that goes along with finding it in the rubble of everything else.

With one last reconsideration, I go for it. "Before this weekend, Lance was Lance. It wasn't hard to compartmentalize him in a box in my head. We'd flirt or whatever at work but there was a line and it wasn't crossed. It started at eight and ended at four. His personal life was his thing. It didn't involve me. His conquests didn't matter."

"But they do now?"

I consider her question. Neither answer, yes or no, is right. It doesn't matter because I'm still the girl from work. But it does matter because it doesn't feel like he's the guy from work anymore. All of that is muddied up now because the guy I told I wanted to feel his tongue on my pussy while his cock was halfway down my throat is the same guy who hugged me in front of my mother.

Whitney laughs when I rest my head against the cool counter. "You should've just fucked him. That would've eased some of this tension."

"Right." Standing up straight again, I go back to my lemon bars. "I'm going to have to pretend it didn't happen. Erase this entire weekend from my brain."

My friend looks at me like I've officially lost it. "You can do that?"

"I'm going to have to." With a cup of flour balanced in the air, I look at Whitney. I should just make the lemon bars and be done with it, but I don't. With a hefty sigh, I just stop pretending like it's not going to happen. "Want to make some red velvet cupcakes?"

Chapter 15

Lance

She's always early on Monday mornings. It's one of the few parts of her schedule I can predict and one the nerd in me loves. Most people struggle on Mondays. Mariah is at the school at least an hour early on the first day of the week.

While I don't always start the week on a low note, today I was late. I could say it was the extra two minutes it took for the shower to warm up or the fact that I didn't sleep last night. I could even situate the blame on Machlan's shoulders for coming over and making me some rocket fuel shit that went down way too easily, but did help the story of the afternoon come together with less prompting.

Truth is, it was intentional.

The staff meeting about homecoming festivities would've put Mariah and I across from one another in a room full of people. On the surface, that seems like the perfect way to break the ice. Assumptions are often wrong.

The third rule of history is silence is not louder than words. When things get too quiet historically, they're forgotten. The chaotic moments, the ones filled with passion and emotion—they're the ones remembered. When I see her again, it won't be in a room full of people. I won't be forced to be silent. The words I'll use aren't formulated yet, they likely won't be until the moment comes because I've tried to find the right thing to say since I left her yesterday and I keep coming up empty. But they'll come. They always do with her.

"Make sure you finish this tonight," I tell the sophomores as they gather their things. "I will take this for a grade tomorrow. You've been warned."

"Have a good day, Mr. Gibson." Two girls, who are going to cause some poor boys a lot of trouble, wave as they strut past my desk.

"Bye, ladies."

It takes everything I have not to get up and shoo them out the door. Glancing at the clock, I have four minutes until I usually trek up the stairs and slip into Mariah's room while she's getting her lunch. On most days, I'd slide my phone out of my pocket and see what my inbox looks like. Today, I slip it in my desk.

I toyed with deleting the app last night. Machlan pointed out there's a chance she could message me and if I answered that, I wouldn't be out of line. So, I didn't. But I haven't checked it since the parking lot of Peaches.

My hands undergo a quick sanitizing with some gel. I'm getting up to go upstairs when I see Ollie head away from the cafeteria. Puzzled, I go to the hallway and watch him take a long drink from the fountain. The clock ticks to 'go time,' but my feet remain in place.

"Hey, Ollie. Can you come in here a minute?"

He spins around, looking surprised. "Sure, Mr. Gibson."

Stepping by me, the same tattered shirt he wore on Friday hanging from his thinning frame, he stands next to a bust of President Kennedy.

"It's none of my business," I say. "But why aren't you in the cafeteria?"

"I, um, I eat by myself. The cafeteria is too loud."

He looks at everything in the room besides me. The clock flicks past another minute and I suck in a breath, knowing this situation likely just stole the moment I've been anticipating since yesterday.

"Okay. Fair enough. Where do you usually eat?" I ask him.

"Just wherever." His hand goes in his pocket as resignation settles over his face.

"You can always eat with me. Even if I'm not in here, you can come in and flip on the television if you want. Okay?"

"Thanks, Mr. Gibson."

The location isn't the problem and we both know it. Racking my brain for a way to fix this without making him feel bad, I tap my fingers against the desk. "I had an ulterior motive for asking you to come in here."

He gives me a lopsided grin. "What's that?"

"I need a favor."

"From me?"

Nodding, I try to bring this together as smoothly as possible. "I'm on a panel of teachers the school board put together to analyze the cafeteria food. It's not something they really want spread around because of politics and stuff like that. Anyway, I'm supposed to pick a student to get a tray every day and then report back on what they think about it."

"Okay," he draws out, smelling bullshit.

I need to fortify my story. "Ms. Malarkey is selecting a freshman and I thought you'd be a great upperclassman."

"I'm not sure, Mr. Gibson."

"Look, all you have to do is get a tray," I say, forcing a swallow. "The school will credit your account for a tray a day for the rest of the year."

He eyes me curiously. There's an element of pride sitting behind his sleepy eyes, one that makes my heart drop. It also worries me that he won't go along with my plan.

"If you don't want to eat it, you can toss it in the garbage," I add. "Just give me something in May that says how you liked it and what you hated and, just, whatever you think."

"All I have to do is get a tray and give you a paper on it in May?"

"Yes. It's not for a grade or anything. I'll even give you extra credit or something because I know it's kind of a pain for you to do this. I could ask someone else," I say, going for the guilt factor, "but I really need someone who's truthful who'll give me the report."

The relief is visible. I want to give the kid a fucking hug.

"I'll call down to the office now," I say, having to look away. "You can get your tray and start today, if you want. No pressure."

"I could do that," he says eagerly.

"Great."

He heads to the door. "I'll go now. Thanks, Mr. Gibson. If you need anything sooner from me before May, just shout."

"Yeah. Will do. Thank you."

Using my palm, I wipe at an eye that must've gotten some dust in it. I buzz down to the office and the secretary picks up.

"Hey, this is Lance," I tell her. "Does Ollie's lunch account have anything on it?"

"I'm not supposed to tell you that," she says. "But ..." There's typing on the other end. "No. It doesn't."

"Can you stick twenty bucks on there and I'll come down this afternoon and talk to you about it?"

"Sure can."

"Thanks."

My head goes into my hands. On some level, this is why I got into teaching in the first place. But it's also the part no one explained to me beforehand. Mouthy kids, errant students, even ones who don't give a damn—I can handle that. Hungry kids? Neglected ones? Kids who don't have a pot to piss in? Those I can't.

A knock raps at the door. When I raise my head, I can't look anywhere else.

Mariah is standing there in a yellow dress that's belted around her waist. Her hair is down today and in her hand is the little bag she carries her lunch in.

She's prettier than ever and I realize that's probably some sex-deprived colored glasses kind of thing. But as she tries to decipher whether or not to say something, I want to storm across the room and plant my lips on hers.

"Hey," she says, switching the bag between her hands. "What's going on?"

"What do you mean?"

"I was getting my lunch and sort of overheard a part of your conversation with Ollie." She smiles sheepishly. "Don't even start with the eavesdropping stuff."

"I was in *my* room this time," I say, getting to my feet. The sun didn't change positions out the window, but it sure feels a lot brighter in here now. "I do find it interesting you'd go out of your way to listen in on my conversation, even when I don't come to you to have them. More adorable than strange, if you're wondering."

She grins. "I think it was my name that stopped me in my tracks."

"Still eavesdropping," I tease. "Would you like to come in?"

The grin falters. Reality settles in, creasing the lines on her forehead. "Should I?"

"The door is open. Pun intended."

Her eyes roll, but it's enough of a joke to get her to move. She comes inside and does a full three-sixty of my room. "This looks nice."

"I get that a lot."

"*Your room* looks nice."

"So nothing about the shirt?" I ask, tugging on the neckline of my button-down. "I wore it thinking it was the color of my balls."

"Lance ..." She gulps. "I don't know what to say."

"I do."

Pacing around my desk, I lean against the front. She fidgets with her bag. Her nails are a shade of pink which is weird because she usually doesn't paint them. But I don't ask. Now isn't the time.

At around four this morning, as I was watching a cooking show on television, I came up with a half-assed plan. I don't want to make her so uncomfortable that she doesn't want to see me. While I'm trying hard not to touch her, I have no intention of ceasing to see her. I haven't lost my mind.

"I won't mention the app if it makes you uncomfortable," I promise. "I will say I loved seeing that part of you—now that I know it was you—and I find it hysterical that we were messaging all this time and didn't know it. But I'll let it go."

"You will?"

"I will. But if I get a paper cut, I'm coming to you for those nursing skills you promised to show me."

She swings her lunch bag and it hits me in the arm, but there's a happiness on her face that's priceless. Keeping a side-eye on her, I head to the door and swing it shut.

"What day do we go to your mom's?" I ask. "And do we get to meet the sister? Because if she's anything like your mom, I'm gonna get a drink before we go."

"We aren't." She opens her bag and takes out a baggie. "I'm not going."

"Can I ask two things?"

"Yeah."

"First, and most importantly, what's in that baggie?" Raising a brow, I hold out my palm. "It looks like dessert."

She takes a nibble and shrugs. "Lemon bars. You don't like lemon."

"I'm assuming you made me something?"

"Nope."

My jaw drops. "Fine then. Second question is why are we not going to your mother's party?"

"I am not going to my mother's because she's impossible. And my sister is going to be there with her husband and their child and I have no interest in seeing them."

Reaching out, I make a point of taking a lemon bar from her bag. She watches me with a heated gaze. That part I ignore. For now.

"May I ask why?" Bringing the bar to my lips, I take a bite. It's sweeter than I thought it would be, brighter in flavor. Not really lemon-y, but fruitier. "This is really good."

"Thanks."

"Back to the sister?"

"You're so pushy," she notes, putting the baggie back in her bag.

"And your point?"

She rummages in the bag again, but more aimlessly than before. There can't be that much crap in there to take her this long. Still, I refrain from pestering her even if it's harder than hell to do.

"My sister," she begins, forcing a swallow, "married my ex-boyfriend. Like, six months after we broke up they got married."

"You're shitting me."

"I'm not."

Smacking my tongue off the roof of my mouth, things start to make more sense. "You're thinking if she married him that fast ..."

"That they were screwing around while we were together? Correct."

I wonder vaguely what my reaction looks like from her viewpoint. Utter confusion as to how a guy who wanted to be tied down with a woman would walk away from Mariah? Pure venom spikes in my blood toward a man I don't even know for putting that look on her face—like she's not worthy of someone's first choice.

Fuck that guy.

"You're right," I say, polishing off the lemon bar. "We hate her."

"You have no idea," she grumbles.

Shoving off my desk, I take a few steps toward her. Her perfume is different today. It's still soft and feminine, but sexier instead of floral. Or maybe that's her pheromones I'm picking up on. Either way, I feel my stomach knotting like it's threatening to send instructions to my groin. Like I should show her just how desirable she is.

"If you change your mind and want to go, I'm happy to go with you. Just as friends," I say, hands up in the air when she snaps her gaze to me. Because I want this to feel normal, I add a little at the end. "But if there are benefits involved, I'm game."

She laughs. "I'm not going, but thanks. Now, back to Ollie. What's up with that?"

"If he asks you, we're in charge of a student panel to study the cafeteria food. You picked a kid, I picked a kid. Got it?"

"Oh, Lance," she says, reading between the lines. "You're kidding me."

"I put money in his account today. I don't know what's going on with him, but fuck, Mariah. How does a kid go hungry in this country in this day and age?"

"Believe it or not, that's one reason I bake a lot and bring it in."

"I thought that was just for me?" I pout.

Her giggle winds the knot even tighter. "Sorry." She heads toward the door, the clock threatening to tip as the bell rings. "If I can help, let me know. I'd love to."

There's no reply from me because nothing I could say would be well-received. I've managed not to blow it so far today. Keeping my mouth shut now would probably be wise.

Except, I'm not wise.

"I have things you can help with ..."

She laughs, steps into the hall and disappears as the bell rings. My class begins to fill as students file in. They murmur their hellos and I ask them about their weekend on auto-pilot, all the while replaying mine in my head.

The tardy bell is set to ring when Stacy comes waltzing in. "Hey, Mr. Gibson," she sing-songs.

"Better get to your seat before that bell rings."

"I have something for you."

Dropping my pen, I look up to see a red cupcake in a yellow liner sitting in the palm of her hand. "Ms. Malarkey sent this down for you."

"Thank you," I say, taking it from her.

"Mr. Gibson?"

"Yeah?"

Looking up at my student, I see a look of pure glee. She leans towards me and whispers, "You two would have gorgeous babies."

"And you're tardy," I say, motioning toward her seat as the bell buzzes overhead.

The cupcake goes on the corner of my desk and Stacy's comment gets filed away to a part of my brain I don't want to revisit.

Chapter 16

Mariah

"How's it going this week?" Whitney asks. She joins me at the trunk of my car and takes in all the desserts lined up. "It kills me you make all this and give it away." Swiping up a banana cupcake with peanut butter icing, she shrugs. "I'm keeping one."

"Fine," I laugh. "That can be your payment for helping me deliver them."

"You could at least buy me dinner."

"You could do this out of the kindness of your heart too," I note, handing her a tray.

"All my kindness got soaked up by a screaming three-year-old at around two this morning in the emergency room," she says, wincing. "I think I'll abstain from sex."

I give her a look, lifting a tray of lemon bars from the trunk and closing it.

"For like two days," she adds with a laugh. "So, how did it go with Lance?"

We meander through the garden at the back of the nursing home. A few residents are outside, some in wheelchairs, enjoying the pretty day. The door to the game room opens into the expansive outdoor area.

I love coming here to bring baked goodies and books and sometimes slippers or lip balms. It makes me feel connected to humanity in a very peaceful way.

"It's not going badly," I admit. "It's not so different from before, really. He still drives me crazy, makes lewd comments, only now he works in a lot of vague references to conversations we've had."

"I love your love," she sighs happily.

"You're insane."

"I'm not nearly as crazy as you are. You just don't see it."

I see it, but I'm not about to admit that to her. I am crazy. Ridiculously so. I haven't been able to get off in days because the easiness of fantasizing about Lance is now too messy. Every day, every smirk, every lick of icing off his lips makes me want to freaking scream. All four afternoons this week when he didn't make a call in my presence, when I didn't even see his phone, made me giddy.

Tempering myself, writing notes on my desk like 'truth' and 'wisdom' don't even help keep my spirits at a sane level. It's going to come crashing down on me one of these days because leopards don't change their spots and neither do guys like Lance.

I haven't deleted the app off my phone in case he messages me at night. I want him to, even if I don't necessarily want to see the string of those messages. Every evening when I climb in bed and scroll through social media, I have a little pep talk with myself. Tomorrow could be the day when everything goes back to normal. When the fun with me is over, and he moves on to someone new. I should prepare for that. I try. It's occurred to me that this will be like a death—you can't ever really prepare for it until the other person is gone.

"Ah, it's Mariah," Gretchen says from her wheelchair by the aloe vera plant. "What did you bring us today, honey?"

"I have banana cupcakes and lemon bars," I tell her as the chatter increases in the room. "I have some other goodies in the car."

"Can I have a lemon bar?"

"Let me check with the nurse and then I'll bring you one, okay?"

After getting the okay from the staff, we start dispensing the goods. I drop off the one red velvet to Mr. Henry before working my way back to Gretchen. "Here ya go, sugar."

"These little visits just make my week," she beams. She takes the lemon bar and holds it in her hand. "How was your day?"

"Good. How was yours?"

"Good, good. Same old stuff in here day after day. That's why we love seeing you." She takes a bite of the dessert. "Tastes just like the ones I used to make."

"I bet they're not as good."

She pats my hand. "Where'd you learn to bake, anyway? Your mama?"

"My grandma, actually," I say, kneeling beside her wheelchair. "She was a lot like you. Sweet and beautiful."

"Ah, now you're just being polite."

"Not true. I saw Mr. Henry checking you out when I walked in."

She laughs, but touches her cheek as it flushes. "He asked me to play chess with him later tonight. Do you think I should?"

"Heavens yes you should! He's handsome, Miss Gretchen."

"He is, isn't he?" she giggles. "What about you? Do you have a handsome man you spend your evenings with?"

"Sadly, no," I say, thinking immediately of Lance. Wondering what it would be like to spend an evening with him, what we would do, what his habits are, I'm jostled by an elbow to the rib by Gretchen. "I dazed off."

She sinks her dentures into the lemon bar and throws her head back. "This is delicious. Make these for whoever he is you're thinking of and you'll win him over."

I study my friend. She's one of the sweetest women I know and I look forward to seeing her every time I come here. Deciding to take a gamble, I go for it. "I made them for him," I say.

"So there is someone."

"Not really," I sigh. "We're more like friends."

"So not the good kind?" She raises a brow. "I'm old but I'm not dead, honey."

Laughing, I grab a chair and pull it over to her.

"Tell me about him," she instructs, the lemon bar now gone.

"It's long and complicated."

"As are all the good stories."

Looking around the room full of people on their last years of life, I wonder what choices they made they now regret. Which risks were worth it, which ones hurt badly but they'd turn around and do them again if they could.

"Were you married, Gretchen?"

"I was. For forty years. He was a good man," she says, her eyes sparkling. "Kind of a menace when I first met him, but he panned out all right."

"A menace? You have to explain that."

"He was always in trouble, forever giving me grief about things. He was what my mother called a neighborhood kid, meaning the neighborhood took care of him. His mother was a wretched woman. Just awful."

"How did you meet?" I ask, trying to imagine her when she was my age.

Rearranging the pillow behind her back, she gets situated before going on. "He was friends with my older brother. He'd tag along for meals a lot of days or Mama would leave a bottle of milk on the stoop for him to take if he didn't stop by. One day he kissed me by the chicken coop and told me if I kissed another boy, he'd beat the tar out of them," she laughs. "I never kissed another boy for my whole life."

"I love that."

"My daddy didn't," she laughs, thinking back. "My mother just loved him though. She kind of took him in and treated him like one of her own."

She pauses her story to talk to the nurse. Her evening meds are delivered and it's a process I've watched happen a few times. It's so regimented and carefully executed that it amazes me they can do it correctly so fast.

When she turns back to me, she picks up where she left off. "He passed away back in ninety-four. Said his only regret was not making peace with his mother."

A heaviness sits on my shoulders as I relate to a man I never knew.

"What is it, honey?" she asks.

"Nothing. I just have an iffy relationship with my mom too. I kind of understand where your husband was coming from."

"Do the two of you speak?"

"Kind of."

She takes a moment to let that sink in. "Want some unsolicited advice?"

"I'd love some," I say, letting her take my hand in hers. "What do you have for me?"

"Don't be a grudge holder, Mariah. I was one for years. My good friend passed away when we were in our thirties, she just had a baby, and her car went over an embankment and into a river. We had some stupid fight that I don't even remember at this point. I was devastated for years. I still regret it. I never thought I wouldn't get the chance to talk to her again."

"I try," I tell her, thinking of all the times I try to be peaceful with my family. "I answer most of her calls. I listen to her tell me what a lousy person I am."

"Well that's not true." She squeezes my hand. "Maybe I should have a talk with her."

I give her an appreciative smile as I wonder what it would be like to have someone like her in my corner for real. I can't imagine her being disappointed in or taking sides against her loved ones.

"She has a party coming up this weekend for her birthday," I tell her.

"Are you going?"

I make a face.

"You should go. Be the bigger person."

"But she invited my sister and the two of them together are just poison to me."

"Take Whitney," she says, pointing at my friend who's feeding a cupcake to Mr. Henry. "Take her before she ruins my chess game tonight."

Laughing, I watch my friend tease him with a dab of icing. It's clear Mr. Henry is having the time of his life. Still, I turn to my other friend and wink. "Whitney has nothing on you, Gretchen."

"Damn right." A somber look crosses her face. "I want you to remember something for me, okay?"

"Okay."

"You can't choose how people treat you or the actions they take. They get up in the morning and have to see the ugly things they do reflected in their face." She rolls her wheelchair back and then centers it in front of me so we're face-to-face. "You, dear girl, only have to live with how you let them affect you. When you look in the mirror, you get to see all the pretty that you are inside and which you radiate."

"Sometimes they make me feel really ugly," I admit.

"Because you let them." It's the simplest answer she could give and the one that hits the hardest. "When you get to be my age, you start thinking a lot about death. You look back on your life and think of all the people you already lost and know the people you see around this room will start dropping like gnats."

"Gretchen!"

"It's true," she shrugs. "But listen to me—life isn't that complicated. It's meant to be lived with those we can't live without."

"That sounds pretty complicated."

"It's not."

It's such a simplistic way of looking at things and couldn't possibly hold true. There's no room in that philosophy to account for the unknown: other people, or emotions, or the bad things that can happen to us.

"You live your life and you fill it with all those people who make you feel like getting up in the morning. The ones who give *you* life. And the rest of them?" She blows a breath. "The rest of them you just let go."

"Even if it's my mother?"

"Maybe," she shrugs. "Maybe not. Here's a rule of thumb for you: treat people how you'd treat them if you knew they'd be dead tomorrow. Because they might be. Sometimes that means forgiving and moving on and sometimes it's just forgiving. The key to it is finding your joy and what you need to do for you—not them."

The events coordinator taps me on the shoulder. "We have a man who just came in from outside and didn't get a cupcake. He's very upset. You don't have any more, do you?"

"You know I do," I laugh. "I'll go grab them." Before I get up, I look back at Gretchen. "I appreciate you, you know that?"

"You bring me joy. Great joy, Mariah."

I make my way outside. The sun is a bold orange with its promise to dip behind the horizon. Thinking about what Gretchen said and then about baby Betsy and my grandmother, I know what I want to do.

Unlocking the car, I get into the back seat first. My purse is on the floorboard and I pull it up next to me.

Grabbing my phone, I flip through the screen until I see the app. Just the green logo with blue letters make me feel like a different person. Stronger. More confident. And it's not until I swipe my finger over the image and see Lance's icon, that I realize why.

This is why it was so easy for me to open up to him. He doesn't *just* make me feel good in general. He makes me feel good about *me*.

With each tap of my fingers on the screen, some of my confidence gets wiped out by nerves. I hit 'send' in a flurry before I can talk myself out of it.

> **Me:** Any chance you'd reconsider that date?

The little bubbles appear almost instantly and I hold my breath until the words he typed appear on the screen.

> **History Hunk:** Oh, probably. My schedule is pretty open at the moment.

What does he mean by that? Am I bothering him by asking? Maybe he's over this. Maybe he has a date.

Chewing my bottom, lip, I type out the fastest answer in the history of texting.

> **Me:** Well, if you're busy …

> **History Hunk:** STOP. I'm free. Tell me when and where.

My fingers are swift over the keys, falling right back into the groove.

> **Me:** My mom's house. Saturday afternoon? *bites nails*

> **History Hunk:** I'll bring Mace.

> **Me:** You're the best.

History Hunk: You haven't seen the start of it. 🌚

Me: Gotta go.

History Hunk: Chocolate cupcakes tomorrow? Peanut butter icing?

Me: Bye.

Chapter 17

Mariah

"My, you look beautiful today." Lance starts the engine and pulls out onto the street. "Did you do something new to your hair?"

"Why are you being weird?" I laugh, fastening my seatbelt. I have no idea how we can fall into such an easy rhythm, like this is what we do and nothing awkward ever happened, but we do and I'm more grateful for it today than ever.

He looks at me over his shoulder. "I read a book on manners. It said I should compliment you when I see you."

"I believe the first thing you said to me was, 'I knew you'd cave," I say, yawning.

"I tried." He wrinkles his forehead. "Sleepy?"

"A little. It hit me around two this morning what I was up against today. Makes it hard to sleep."

The car pulls onto the highway toward Lancaster and the address I gave Lance earlier. The traffic is light, the sun bright. Now that we're in the car and on the way, a sharp, almost bitter sensation has its claws in my gut.

Instead of focusing on that, I focus on Lance.

He's wearing a collared shirt the color of jade with a pair of dark jeans. He's chosen to don the pair of black glasses I love which he wears on occasion. It's the confidence, I think, that his glasses portray that makes me swoon when I see them on his face. There's a fraction of stubble along his jaw that lends a casual vibe to his ensemble It's glorious.

Tucking my hands under my thighs just so I don't touch him, I try to refocus my attention on the road ahead.

"What's the game plan today?" he asks.

"What do you mean?"

"Well, are we going eye-for-an-eye or playing nice? I can do either, but I'd like to have some operational direction before we go in."

Pulling my bottom lip between my teeth, I worry it back and forth.

There's no telling how this is going to go. I haven't seen Chrissy in forever except for an accidental run-in at the pharmacy during Easter. Every interaction between us is heated, the result of a lifetime of competition that I didn't sign up for.

It hurts. When I was a little girl and Mom and Chrissy would take off to do a pageant or go for a girl's day at the spa and I was left home alone, I would get angry. Not that I wanted to do those things; I just wanted to be included. Then, in my early twenties, I switched. Numbing myself from it was easier. I didn't need them. When I met Eric I was sure I'd met the man I was going to start my own family with—and then he leaves me for them. It was like he conspired with the enemy and they all laughed in my face. The pain, the anger, wasn't just from losing Eric. It was from losing him to *them,* losing him to the same people he was supposed to protect me from.

"I don't know what the plan is," I admit. "Maybe we should just go back home?"

Expecting a witty retort, I hold my breath and wait. Lance surprises me instead.

"I think we should go," he states.

"Why?"

He mulls over my question, tapping out the song on the radio against his thigh. We speed around a car and he takes a drink of coffee from a to-go cup before turning to me.

"I think we should go because I'd give anything to celebrate a birthday with my Mom," he says.

My heart pulls at his expression. He looks so lonely, even though I'm right here, so I pull his hand off his thigh and hold it gently in mine. The contact isn't the bolt of lightning it usually is. It's a soft, gentle buzz that I feel in every cell of my body. In return, he gives me the slightest upturn of his lips, but that's all.

"I'm sorry your parents passed away," I say. His hand is warm and firm, sturdy just like he is, as I roll it over in my palm. His fingers move against mine in a lazy dance that feels entirely too good.

He squeezes my fingers, holding them tight for a long second, before pulling his hand away. He uses the now-freed palm to turn the steering wheel leading us off the highway and into downtown Lancaster.

"My family isn't like yours though," I say. A bubble of anxiety hits me as we stop at the first light in town. "It's almost like they aren't my family. I'm just an attachment. I got thrown in at the last second like those apple pies at fast-food joints that you add for ninety-nine cents and then never eat. That's me."

"Come on," he jokes. "You're at least the chocolate pie."

"I don't know ..." I say, the end of my words tinged with a laugh.

"You want to leave? We leave. You want to be the last person there? We stay. I'm here *for you*." He looks me dead in the eye and I fight hard not to let him see me melt into a puddle. "If things get rough, just climb on my back and I'll haul your ass out." His head goes side-to-side like he's thinking. "I might grab your ass on the way out though. Just warning you."

"You'd hate that, wouldn't you?"

"Hell no," he grins. "I might do it just to show your ex what he's missing."

My face twists up as I come to terms with seeing Eric. There's a question dangling in the air but Lance doesn't ask it. I wait until we hit the next stoplight and then just ask him what's on his mind.

"This Eric, that's his name right?" He asks as I nod. "How serious were you?"

I think back on the day he broke things off with me. How he called me at work and asked me to come right to his apartment because he wanted to talk. How that day I thought maybe, just maybe, this was the talk I was waiting for—the one that came dotted with a simple ring and a promise of a lifetime.

This is not something I want to discuss with Lance. It's somewhat embarrassing, even though I know it's not necessarily a reflection of me. It took me a long, long time to even semi-believe that and I'm not to the point where I can rock that attitude like it's my job. Yet.

"I thought I'd marry him," I admit. "I knew he'd been looking at rings because he left a browser open on the computer. I was really just waiting on him to pop the question," I say, refusing to look at Lance. "Then he breaks up with me out of nowhere, so I figure he's getting cold feet. It happens. But then six weeks or something later, I'm asked to come to lunch at Mom's and there he sits with Chrissy."

"Your mom just let this happen?" he asks in disbelief.

"Oh, yeah," I nod enthusiastically. "It was my fault I was boring and didn't fix myself up or stay exciting. What's a man to do?"

Lance's knuckles turn white as they grip the steering wheel. The tires bark a little as we take the final turn. I watch him in awe as he physically reacts to this story. That he cares enough, in any respect, to even react at all is both a little shocking and mind-blowing at once.

As the house comes into view, my breathing becomes ragged. I blow out a measured breath as the car climbs the hill up to the driveway.

"Here we are," he says, parking behind a giant white SUV. "If I need bail, call Walker. You'd think Machlan because he owns a bar and this is more his speed, but he'd just find Eric and go at him for round two."

Swatting his shoulder, I giggle. "You won't need bail. They aren't fighting people. Just assholes."

"Yeah," he says as he pops open his door. "But I am fighting people and I have a thing against assholes."

He shakes his head, warning me not to open my door as he rounds the corner of the car. I sit like a princess, waiting for my door to be opened. It's amusing and endearing at the same time because, although he's done this a few times, something is slightly different about it now. And I'm okay with that.

"Listen," I say as we start up the long sidewalk lined with rose bushes. "They are different from me."

"I met your mother, remember?" he groans.

"Yes, but today will be different. Today she has Chrissy and the baby." My throat is tight as I force a swallow. "They're her pride and joy. I'm used to it. I know what it's going to be like. But—"

He whirls me around to face him. Startled, I gasp but the breath falls slowly away as my eyes catch up with his.

He peers down at me, his green eyes sparkling. "You're here because you're the bigger person. I'm here because I'm with you. If they try to make you feel any less than you are—less smart or beautiful or talented—it's because *they're* insecure."

There are hundreds of responses to that, but I can't seem to utter a single one. His compassionate words have incapacitated mine.

My heart pounds as his hands cup my cheeks. "If I even think you're starting to let them get to you, we're gone." He presses a sweet, simple kiss to the center of my cheek. It's the most unloaded kiss I've ever received from him, but maybe my favorite one too.

Like a fool, I just nod, unable to come up with a coherent reply.

Lacing our fingers together, ignoring my sweaty palms, he leads me to the door. He presses the doorbell, still holding onto my hand.

Each second that passes feels like a lifetime and I want to turn around and go. I have no idea what to expect other than knowing I'll be leaving with the understanding of how much I fail to make the cut in my mom's eyes. That's a given.

As we wait on her, the good ol' script that always runs through my head starts playing. It reminds me that *her* mother died when she was ten and her grandmother passed away before that. It's not totally her fault she doesn't know how to behave in this role; she's never been shown. It's an excuse, I know, but one that does make her inadequacy a little easier to swallow.

The door opens. Mom is standing on the other side, a baby nestled in a soft pink blanket in her arms. "Good morning, Mariah," she says. "I'm so happy you could make it."

The sight of her with the baby startles me. I knew Chrissy's daughter would be here and it's really the main reason I agreed to this idiotic idea. But seeing the little button nose sticking out of the top of the blankets is enough to sock the wind right out of me.

Lance swoops in for the save. "Happy birthday, Taylor," he says, squeezing my hand. "It was nice of you to invite us."

"What a wonderful surprise," she coos. "I was sure you wouldn't come."

"Why wouldn't I?" he asks.

She looks at me out of the corner of her eye. "I'm sure you have more interesting things you could be doing today than accompany my daughter."

My initial reaction is to turn away and head to the car. Her jab coupled with the sight of the baby is a bit much for the first twenty seconds, but Lance's hand grips down on mine. "There's nowhere else I'd rather be."

"How sweet," she purrs. "Come in. Your sister and her husband are already in the living room. I was going to invite some friends to brunch with us, but thought we could have a family get together instead."

It crosses my mind that she might intentionally be trying to drive me crazy as we head through the foyer. The house is nothing like I remember it. It's nearly all-white now with lots of gold mirrors. Oversized vases sit here and there with sprays of fake flowers jutting out the top. There's nothing comfortable or home-like about any of it, not that it felt like a home when I lived here.

We go through a newly-rounded doorway where the crystals from a chandelier send sparkles of light throughout the room. We turn a corner and I stop in my tracks.

Chrissy and Eric are standing along a wall of windows. They're clearly awaiting our arrival. Lance takes a step closer to me as I try to maintain my composure.

My brain is muddled trying to decide what I should say or need to say or whether or not I should say anything at all.

Chrissy looks older than the last time I saw her. Her hair is now a reddish brown and her cheeks fuller than before. She reminds me of our father, in a way, and I wonder if she's seen him lately.

Eric sports a beer belly that sticks out over the buckle of his belt. His hairline is receding slightly, even earlier than I predicted. There's no twinkle in his eye, no joke on the tip of his tongue, and I wonder what I ever saw in him to begin with.

"Hello," Lance says, breaking the ice. "How's everyone doing?"

Eric darts across the room. "Hi. I'm Eric." He offers Lance a hand, pointedly ignoring me. Lance bites back a smile as he shakes Eric's hand.

"I'm Lance. Nice to meet you."

"You too." He looks at me and then right back to Lance. "That's my wife, Chrissy, and our daughter, Betsy."

Lance forces a swallow. "This is my girlfriend Mariah, but I think you already know that."

My elbow finds his side and I can feel his body shifting with a silent chuckle.

"Nice to see you, Mariah." Eric nods in my direction before rejoining my sister a few feet away.

I don't want to look at any of them. It's safe tucked against Lance's side, depending on his predictable way of taking the reins when I need him to. I just wish we were some place else together.

"How are you, Mariah?" It's Chrissy's voice, soft and careful, that breaks the awkward silence.

"I'm good." I pull my gaze away from Lance and settle it on my sister. "How are you, Chrissy?"

"I'm good." She tries to give me a smile, but seems to be unsure whether it's the right thing to do.

"Mariah," Mom calls out. "There are appetizers in the dining room. I know how hungry you get and it'll be a few minutes before brunch is ready."

It's a dig. It's a dig as deep as the Mariana Trench. My teeth grind together knowing it'll likely be the first of many.

Lance crooks his head so he can look me in the eye. It's like he pulls me in, reminding me of who I am and who I'm not. "You okay?"

"Yeah." Giving him a quick smile, I turn to my family. Mom is still snuggling the baby on the sofa. Since she's the real reason I agreed to this, I make a play. "Can I hold Betsy?"

Mom seems thrown by my question. My sister looks at me, slightly less thrown than our mother.

I don't say anything and neither does she, but we quietly agree. Heading to the sofa, I wait as my mom lays the baby still swaddled in pink in my arms.

"Oh," I say softly, pressing the blankets down so I can see her face. My eyes fill with tears as I take her in. Chrissy's long, dark eyelashes and Eric's full lips are present. I gasp when I see her tiny birthmark just above her upper lip like mine. "Hey, you," I whisper, my voice shaky. "I'm your Aunt Mariah."

I feel a connection to this beautiful little angel that supersedes the emotions I have about her parents. She's tiny and innocent and deserving of so much love that I hope I can be a part of her life in some meaningful way.

Raising her to my lips, I press a kiss to her sweet-smelling skin. My heart clenches as I hold her close, rocking her gently back and forth. When I open my eyes, I'm looking at Lance.

His brows are furrowed, his jaw working back and forth. He

doesn't look angry as Chrissy approaches me. He doesn't look worried either. He looks like he's thinking about something that is taking every bit of his mental power to process.

"Isn't she perfect?" Chrissy whispers, coming up beside me. There's a hesitation in her tone, like she's feeling me out.

"She's beautiful," I say softly. "She has my birthmark." I pull her away from my chest and look at her again. "You are so pretty, Miss Betsy. Your great grandma would've loved you so, so much."

"Let me see her," Lance says, reaching for the baby.

I'm not sure I heard him right. But, sure enough, he takes the few steps toward me with his arms outstretched. He holds my gaze as I lay the baby in his strong arms.

Our skin brushes against one another's as we make the transfer. It sends a rush of warmth down my spine that I can't explain, but know I want to experience again.

I watch Lance take in Betsy from a few steps back. He looks so big holding the tiny little baby. She doesn't even take up the distance from his hand to his elbow. He holds her like he's done it a million times, like holding a baby is a routine thing he does every weekend. There's no clumsiness, no protest from Betsy to give her back to someone who knows what they're doing. She sleeps just as soundly in his arms as she did mine.

"You're a cutie," he tells her. "You look a lot like your Aunt Mariah and that's totally a good thing." He lifts his eyes to mine and then drags them to my sister. "She's gorgeous. Congratulations."

"Thanks. Um, she has so much hair," Chrissy says, a nervous edge in her voice masked with an abundance of cheerfulness. "I hope it stays kind of curly like this."

I'm not sure who she's taking to so I don't bother responding.

With a final look at the baby, Lance offers her back to me. "You want her?"

"Yes," I say, feeling her nuzzle up to me. It's the most wonderful feeling in the world. Her little eyes open slowly as she gets comfortable. "Hey, there," I say, as she tries to focus on me. "How are you, sweet baby?"

Her lips twist in a cry that's not really a cry.

"I think she's hungry," I say, turning to my sister. I hand her over, still unsure how to navigate this with Chrissy. I can tell she wants to talk, to pretend like we're long lost friends, but we aren't. We were never friends and I haven't forgotten.

Once the baby is settled in Eric's lap with a bottle, I exhale. "Congratulations," I tell both of them. Or neither of them. I don't know.

"Thank you," Chrissy says. "I'm glad she got to meet you."

"Me too," I say, rocking back on my heels.

"I'd like to add to this little tribe," Mom declares out of nowhere. "Do you think you and Mariah will be discussing children soon, Lance? I'd love her to finally settle down."

"Really, Mom?" I ask, disdain thick in my voice. "Are you really going to do this today?"

"Do what, honey? I'm just asking about your plans. That's all."

Lance lays a hand on my arm. He looks at my mother. "Whoever Mariah chooses to be the father of her children will be a lucky man."

"Are you saying you're not up for the job?" She doesn't even try to pretend she's not putting him on the spot. "Is that what I'm hearing?"

"Mother," I growl, glad I'm no longer holding Betsy. My fists are clenched at my sides as I watch her play one of her maddening games.

"I think you should let your daughter decide who she wants to procreate with and you should worry more about whatever is burning in the kitchen," Lance shrugs.

As soon as he says it, I smell the odor of burnt toast. Mom must too because she gets to her feet and heads towards the kitchen.

"Babies come when the time is right, but I'm starting to wonder if she will ever find a man to settle down with," Mom says dryly like she just commented on the color of the sky.

"That's none of your business," I sputter.

Lance smiles at my mom. "Maybe Mariah is pickier than most women. Maybe when she does settle down, it won't end in divorce."

With her eyes narrowed in our direction, Mom heads through a doorway to the right. The room heaves a collective sigh as soon as she's out of sight.

"You have to cut her some slack," Chrissy says. "She's under a lot of stress right now."

I must not have heard her correctly. "She's under stress?"

"Yes. You know she doesn't handle it well."

"And how does that make up for the other years I've been alive?" I ask.

"It's not you, Mariah," she contends. "She just can't deal normally like you or I can."

"It is me and that's fine. It can always be me," I shrug. "I don't care anymore. That's where you both lose."

There's something freeing about putting that into the world. A weight is lifted off my shoulders as I watch Chrissy's reaction to my words.

"Mariah ..."

"No, Chrissy," I say, shaking my head. "No."

"I ..." Chrissy looks at Betsy on Eric's lap before looking back at me. "I'd like to talk to you alone one of these days. Do you think that's possible?"

There's no easy answer to this. I have so much to say to her and yet nothing at all. So many years' worth of questions but none of the answers even matter anymore.

I look up at Lance and he smiles down at me.

"Maybe," I say to Chrissy. "Let's talk about it later."

Chrissy agrees, forcing a smile. "Come on, Eric. Let's check on Mom."

Lance's chin dips as soon as they disappear. "I'd like to talk to you alone one of these days. Do you think that's possible?"

"You're talking to me alone right now."

"Talking was a euphemism."

I giggle, twisting in his arms so I'm facing him. If there is one easy part of today, it's being with him.

He looks at me with an incredulous, almost reverent glimmer in his eye and the entirety of it—that look, his gorgeous face, the way he stood up for me today and let me lean on him—is too much.

I'm sure I could've faced this on my own, but it was so much easier with him by my side.

Every brick I've stacked between us is starting to fall down. It's getting harder and harder to remember why I shouldn't want anything to do with Lance. It's becoming impossible to tell myself to stay away from someone I've been attracted to for so long, especially now that he's showing me so many sides of himself.

He rests his chin on the top of my head, lacing his fingers together at the small of my back. It feels good to be able to rest on him for a moment, feel the strength of his arms around me.

"What the fuck is wrong with your mom?" he asks.

"I warned you," I giggle.

"You couldn't have prepared me for that. Wow."

"I'm never prepared, even though I know what's coming."

He kisses me just behind the ear. I'm running on adrenaline and his touches; his sweet little gestures are enough to make my head nearly explode.

"You're driving me crazy," I breathe, feeling my body go limp in his arms. "Seriously, Lance. I can't take it."

"What do you want me to do?"

"Be a dick," I laugh. "Stop being sweet and kind and touching me …"

He rolls his hips ever-so-slightly against me. "Do you feel how hard I am for you?"

"I think you're always hard."

"This isn't for some app girl or another version of you. I'm so fucking hard for *you*, Mariah Malarkey, that I can't stand it. But I will stand it because you hold all the cards. Why I'm okay with that, I have no fucking clue and it might be my undoing," he chuckles.

Feeling more confident, more brazen than I've ever felt in my life, I turn and stand on my tiptoes. It's my mouth on his ear, my breath hot against his skin. In a voice so low I can barely hear it myself, I whisper, "I'm so wet for you, Lance Gibson, I'm going to have to take my panties off."

His jaw falls to the floor. I get a quick glance at it before I have to look away so he doesn't see the pink in my cheeks.

"Come on. Let's get lunch," I call out, walking away as quickly as I can.

Chapter 18
Lance

"He's a monster," I add, not sure what more to say. Eric has been attempting to make small talk the entire meal. Two things are clear: one, he's no Einstein and two, his sense of humor is nil.

He continues on about the new fighter out of Crew Gentry's gym in Boston like he knows something about fighting. His terminology is all wrong, explanations of fighting styles downright backward, and he fumbles through it with the confidence that only an idiot can have. It's kind of impressive in a strange, uncomfortable way.

Keeping an eye on Mariah, I take off my glasses and clean them with a napkin. She's said just enough during the meal to remain polite and sophisticated. Her back, though, is rigid. Her shoulders are as stiff as a board.

While I listen to Eric babble on, I rest my arm over the back of her chair. She leans toward it. I only notice because I'm paying attention.

My hand goes to the back of her neck, working the tense muscles back and forth. My touch alone causes her to relax some, but as I press back and forth, her entire body slackens.

She molds to my hand. She bends as I press on her delicate skin and she shifts in her seat. My fingertips stroke up her spine and draw back down. Listening to Eric's stumbling story takes more effort than I care to spare.

"I hear what you're saying," I say in an attempt at getting him to shut up, "but Pike isn't as strong on the ground. I know he's with Gentry now and that was his specialty, but he doesn't have the skills Crew had. Not yet, anyway. Watch his footwork while he's standing and then watch him scramble when his back hits the mat. He wants to be upright."

"I guess you're right."

No shit.

Betsy's cries can be heard softly from the living room. Chrissy shoves away from the table, but Taylor gets to her feet first. "Let me go, Chris. I can't enough of those precious snuggles."

Chrissy settles down across from Mariah once again. While she chitchats with Eric about Betsy's feeding schedule, Mariah focuses her attention on me.

"You okay?" I ask.

"I'm fine. You?" she asks sweetly, like she already knows the answer. She rests her palm on my thigh. Her fingers flex against the denim, taunting me with how close she is to my cock.

I haven't been able to erase her tease from earlier. I've sat the last forty-five minutes wondering just how wet she really is.

It still surprises me when she says things like that, things that remind me of Nerdy Nurse. It was sexy before, but paired with the proper librarian I know from my nine-to-five makes it perfection. This is the thing songs are written about.

Dirty, raunchy, hip-hop songs.

Maybe sweet country ones too.

This is my problem.

We trade a secret smile. My hand clasps around the corner of her shoulder, pulling her closer to me. Eric's gaze sits square on the side of my face. I want to look at him and tell him exactly what he's missing, everything he tossed away. The problem is he's been inside her and I haven't and that little detail gnaws away at me until I'm almost raw inside.

It's not a competition. She doesn't want him. It's my thigh her hand is on. But there's a carnal need swirling around my gut, begging me to mark her. To leave an imprint on her that she won't be able to forget as easily as she's forgotten him. To bind her like she has bound me.

Drawing a line down her arm, I lean towards her, angling my head away from the others, I whisper, "Still wet?"

"Are you still touching me?" she breathes. "Pretty self-explanatory."

"Your hand is killing me," I warn. "If you move it any closer ..."

She leans her head just enough to block anyone from seeing my reaction as she glides her palm down my swollen shaft. Hissing, I move in my seat, trying not to make a spectacle but almost coming undone.

"You're evil," I tell her.

Mariah's eyes dance with a lightness I'm not sure I've seen before. It makes the entire dinner, including the forced conversation with Eric, and even the weird looks from Taylor worth it to see her this way. Her laughter pulls Chrissy's attention our way.

"So," Chrissy says, hands clasped together, "how long have you two been together?"

"Oh," Mariah says in surprise. "Um, well, we ..." She grips my thigh as if jostling me to help.

"We've known each other a while," I explain. "A couple of years, actually."

"That's great. You look very happy," Chrissy coos.

"We are," I reply, trying to smoothen my features. "I feel like I'm constantly finding new layers to her I didn't know existed."

Mariah's nails bite into my thigh as she scoots herself closer to me. "How sweet," she says. Her arched eyebrow is nothing less than a coded *go fuck yourself*. It's all I can do to not laugh.

"You're sweet," I wink, watching the arched brow go higher. "Then you're ..." The words fall as her hand rests on the crotch of my pants. It's like she's hit the mute button and I suddenly can't speak. Every bit of focus is now directed to the spot where her palm sits heavily on my dick. "You're full of surprises."

Pressing my palm on top of hers, I wait for her to pull back. She doesn't. Suppressing a growl, my insides rioting with all they have, I work her hand harder against me. My cock is so swollen there's no way I could stand up right now.

Mariah, on the other hand, just looks at her sister with the most subdued look on her face. "We are. Just having fun." She turns to me sweetly, as she inches her fingers even closer to my shaft. "Are you having fun today, Lance?"

Chuckling to cover the burn in my throat, I swallow. "Absolutely." Lifting my hand from hers, I scoot it onto her lap. I work her dress into a ball. "I think you're a barrel of fun."

As soon as my skin touches the silkiness of her bare thigh, the hand that was touching me goes to her throat. A small laugh escapes as she responds to something her sister says, but she doesn't look at me.

I turn in my seat, angled towards her, and toss a few words back at Eric to keep him talking. Moving my fingers towards her inner thigh, I let the weight of each fingertip rest against her before moving the next. Each touch dries my mouth, tangles my gut, and sends my heartbeat soaring in my ears.

She's soft and smooth. The muscles in her legs tighten as she spreads them, moving one in my direction, opening herself up for me, making my blood turn to fire.

"Yeah, not much of a hockey fan," I tell Eric when I realize he's waiting for a response. He's satisfied with this and goes back to whatever he's watching on his phone.

Chrissy is telling us about Betsy's last doctor's appointment, lost in the flow of a story that is sure to take a while. Mariah watches her with what would seem to anyone to be rapt attention—anyone but me. I know her better than that.

The heat from her pussy reaches my hand as I move my fingers forward. I cup the inside of her thigh just inches from her panties. She steadies her features but doesn't flinch.

Studying the side of her face, my skin suddenly not big enough to contain everything trying to spill out of me, I lift one finger. With my palm pressed into the top of her leg, I creep one digit towards the apex of her thighs.

Her breathing shakes as she pulls in lungful after lungful of air. My chest matches hers move for move.

Her skin is damp from the heated desire nestled between her legs. The edge of her panties form a distinct line around the curve of her hip to a sweet spot beneath her. I fix my gaze on the pout of her lips and try to remember that there are other people here.

"Eric," she says, "how is your mother?"

My laugh is covered by a cough as I drag the edge of my finger beneath the lace covering her slit. It's wet even there, the dampness creating an all-too-easy path along the side of her pussy.

She laughs again, this time with a tremble. Her body flexes forward as if she's craving the contact as badly as I am. There's no way that's true. I've wanted this woman for as many days as I've known her.

Betsy's cries from the other room pulling her parents' attention elsewhere. Mariah sags back in her chair, a move that just gives me more access. As our lunch partners murmur amongst themselves, I slip my finger to the edge of her opening.

Her cheeks burn red. She reaches for a glass of water as I shift in my seat, the tightening in my balls so fierce I cringe. She's so wet that her juices trickle down my finger, so hot the moisture from her body dampens my hand.

Just as the glass reaches her lips, I sink the tip of my finger into her opening. Her eyes fly wide as her shoulders drop in relief.

Eric's voice is on the periphery of my senses. It'll have to wait.

With every push of my finger into her body, her muscles tense around my pointer. My stomach twists into a knot I'm sure I'm not going to be able to unthread.

"I'm going to check on Betsy." Chrissy's voice is barely audible over the rush of blood pounding in my ears. I follow Mariah's eyes which are trained on the couple leaving the room.

"God," she moans as I slip in a second finger. "I want to hit you for doing this right here."

I still. "Want me to stop?"

She gulps a breath before turning to me. "Yes."

My fingers withdraw immediately, the knot in my stomach straining.

She looks around in desperation, her eyes darting in a circle around her. Shoving away from the table, she yanks the hem of her dress back down. Her eyes hood as she looms over me.

Mariah has turned me on so many times. But not a single one of them, neither as Mariah or when she was promising me filthy things under the alias of Nerdy Nurse, has made me harder than I am right now.

"I'm losing my mind," she breathes, a roughness to her tone that is the final fray of my self-restraint. "Follow me."

She takes my hand, guiding me to my feet. Our footsteps tap across the tile. We go through an arched doorway and take a right.

Rounding a set of stairs, there's a room tucked in the back. She twists the knob and we enter a butler's pantry. It's painted light grey with a set of cabinets lining the smallish, rectangular space. Shelves hang on the top starting a few inches off the cabinets and extending to the ceiling.

The door shuts behind me, a lock clicking into place. I look over my shoulder.

She's standing in the middle of the room. Her eyes are almost feral as her chest bounces with each hefty breath.

A series of thoughts sweep through my mind as I look at her. I have no problem with one-night stands. I prefer them. I own them.

But a rustle of uncertainty surges through me when I take her in and she doesn't look like a one-night stand and I don't know what that means.

"Are you sure?" I ask her.

"Shut up, Lance."

My hands are on her face, my lips crashing against hers before either of us see it coming. Her back slams against the door. A box of cereal rattles off a shelf and falls to the floor.

Her mouth works effortlessly against mine, her hand tangles in my hair. She tastes of cherries as her mouth opens for me. My tongue parts her lips, lapping against hers. She moans, but my kiss swallows it.

Each second together feels like it took a second too long to arrive. Each moment bleeds into the next creating a dizzying high that rivals any I've ever had. I break contact with her mouth only to dot kisses across her chin and down the gentle slope of her neck.

Her body bends to mine, continuously moving to scratch the itch that is only going to be soothed with an orgasm.

"This," she gasps, as I pull her dress over her head and toss it onto a nearby shelf, "is so inappropriate." She leans forward, dragging our mouths together again.

"Like you care," I say between kisses, fumbling with the latch on her bra.

She opens her eyes. Narrowing them as she bites down on my bottom lip, she shimmies her shoulders out of her straps. Her breasts are held up only by the cups of the soft pink bra that barely contains the gorgeous mounds.

"Fuck," I hiss, kissing down her neck, yanking down the satin cups. Her breasts spring free. With one in each hand, I pull her taught nipple into my mouth. Mariah's hips roll into me as she moans, her fingernails scraping against my scalp.

Hooking my fingers through the delicate bands of her panties, I give them a pull. They break free as easily as my willpower.

I take her in like a teenager seeing a woman naked for the first time. She's so fucking beautiful with curves around her hips, her breasts, and a softness to her legs and stomach. I wish I had more time to appreciate this, to revel in how lucky I am to be the one with her right now, but I don't. That'll have to come later.

"Why do you still have clothes on?" she pants.

"Because you're naked," I say, kissing a line across her from hip-to-hip. "It's kind of hard to stop licking you."

"If it's only kind of hard, then we better stop."

I stop. It's actually painful to break contact, get to my feet, and face her without touching her again. But I manage. Somehow.

Slipping off my shoes, then my socks, I kick them to the side. I refuse to let her look anywhere else as I unbutton my shirt and send it flying. My pants and navy boxer briefs drop to the floor and go skidding to the side with the rest of my shit.

A smile tickles her lips as I palm my cock.

"Is this hard enough for you?" I ask.

The air between us sizzles, our gazes heating the space until it's too much to take. We meet somewhere in the middle, our lips crashing against one another. Her hands wrap around my neck, her legs around my waist. I press her back to the door again, the shelf on the wall rattling at the force.

My shaft is buried between the ridges of my abs and the softness of her belly. She reaches down, touching the pre-cum glistening on the head.

"I have no condom," I say, pressing my lips against the top of her shoulder.

"Now's not the time to tell me that." Her head hits the door, the sound thudding through the room.

"I'm clean," I promise. "Had a check-up last month."

She cups my cheeks, pulling my face to hers. "Why should I trust you?" she asks, nibbling my bottom lip.

Squeezing the cheeks of her ass, I groan. "Because I'm not an asshole. Good enough for you?"

"Fine. I'm on the pill."

"Fabulous. But are you clean?" I tease, sliding my tongue into her mouth.

She laughs, pulling away. "Fuck you."

"I want to, but I have to be safe too."

"Yes, of course I'm—"

I'm inside her with one thrust, parting her flesh with a single, solid stroke. She yelps as her muscles pull at mine, cinching my cock like a sheath.

"I'm inclined to believe you haven't done this in a while," I chuckle. The head of my dick is pulled back so hard by the tightness of her pussy that it almost hurts.

"Just shut up and fuck me, Lance."

"Yes, madam."

I bury myself in her. She's soaked, her pussy burning inside for me. I shove myself inside her again, feeling her pulse around my throbbing cock.

She softly moans, her eyes fluttering open like she's in a haze she's can't get out of as I pound into her. If I had my way, I'd keep her here permanently.

She feels too good wrapped around me. Too good in my arms. Too fucking gorgeous, and she's glowing from what I'm doing to her. *Me*. A man who has no business touching a woman like her.

I'm an animal, a guy that intentionally keeps emotion out of the equation when sleeping with a woman. So why in the fucking hell does this not feel like a normal, run-of-the-mill fuck?

"Hey," she breathes.

"Yeah?"

"Don't stop."

———

Mariah

• • •

A slow, sexy smile stretches across his face as he presses himself all the way until he hits the back of my pussy. I'm held between him and the door, his body sweaty against mine.

The butler's pantry smells of sex and sugar mixed with Lance's cologne.

I can barely breathe from the adrenaline, barely process the fact that he's inside me. I'm dying for him to move, dying over the fact that he's looking at me in a way I can't deal with.

His chin lifts, his throat on full display. It leads to a set of muscled shoulders, a symmetrically perfect chest, and abs that make me whimper.

Tilting my hips forward, he doesn't miss a beat. He rolls into me again, filling me with his rock-hard length.

He works himself against me, swirling across my clit. With each movement the door rattles, the cookbooks lining the door above us rustle against the shelf.

"Hold on," he says.

Wrapping my arms around his neck and legs around his waist, he cups my ass in his hands and walks me to a counter. Pushing aside a cookie jar and a canister of flour, he sets my ass down on the cool marble.

My legs dangle off of the edge. My breasts sit on the top of my bra, my hair hangs in my face which is assuredly smeared with make-up, but I hold my breath as he takes me in.

"You're fucking gorgeous," he growls.

I'm sure I've looked prettier, but I've never felt it more than I do right now with this man eyeing me like he wants to devour me.

"Show me," I whisper.

His hands grip my hips almost too hard, dragging me towards the end of the counter. I reach for his cock, but he squats down instead.

He parts my legs and crouches between them, giving me a mischievous grin. His face inches closer to my opening until his tongue slides between my legs and laps at my wetness.

"Oh, my God," I groan, my hands propping me up behind me.

All I can see is the green of his eyes dancing with mirth as he watches me absorb the pleasure he's doling out.

"Sit. Still," he says, pressing on my stomach to hold me down.

"You're so good at this," I say as he inserts a finger into my hole. His tongue licks up to my clit before he sucks it into his mouth. "Fuck you for being so good at this."

He chuckles against me, the humming of his throat making everything worse. Better. I don't freaking know. My head spins, the relief I need is so close I can taste it.

"I'm going to come," I groan.

Then he stops.

"What are you doing?" I ask through gritted teeth. I feel like a baby when I almost whine as he stands. "Lance!"

"Yes, you are." He scoops me back up. I link my ankles at the small of his back. "You're going to come on my cock."

He's inside me, splitting me in two, pounding me with no fucks given about the noise we're making or the sensitivity of the situation. My back slams into a wall next to a rack of spices as my body screams around him.

His eyes are trained on me, his jaw tense. I want to return the favor, watch him watch me, but I can't keep my eyes open as the pressure inside me soars.

"I'm so close," I beg as he slides inside me again.

"Mariah?" A voice comes from down the hall.

I snap my attention to Lance through a blur. It's just clear enough to see him grin.

"Bite my shoulder," he instructs, "because I'm not stopping."

"Mariah?" My mom calls out again.

He twirls his hips as he's balls-deep inside me. It's enough to tip me over the edge. My legs shake, my body goes slack. I bite down on his shoulder.

His skin is hot and hard in my mouth as he pounds into me. Growling under his breath, he presses me harder against the wall.

His cock swells as he empties himself into me. It only makes me shudder even more.

Every muscle in my body aches. The light in the pantry is too bright. The bolt of delicious orgasm melts me from the inside out as it rolls through my veins with every movement from Lance.

His thrusts weaken while my bite turns into a slack-jawed kiss. I pop a final, lingering press against the center of his shoulder before pulling away.

He quiets, still inside me, as I take in the definite circle marring his tanned skin. He looks at it too and laughs.

"Sorry," I say, half-heartedly.

"I'm not." He slips out of me and drops me easily to my feet. Kissing the top of my head, he lets his lips linger a moment longer than necessary. "I've fantasized about the things you'd say while you come."

As I smack his chest, the buzz of the orgasm starts to dissolve and a tinge of reality works its way back in. I slip my bra back up and find my dress as the truth of his words hits me. Pausing, I look at him. I almost don't want to ask in case I heard him wrong, but I do want to know. "You've fantasized about me, huh?"

He scoops up his clothes and starts covering up the body I could look at forever.

"Yup," he says, buttoning his shirt. "But not one of them was as good as that."

My cheeks ache from the smile stretched across them as I search for my panties. I never thought he fantasized about me. Not really. Maybe wanted me for a quickie here or there, but never an all-out fantasy.

"Mariah?" A knock comes against the door. "Are you in there?"

Grabbing my panties from behind an oversized can of soup, I whip my head to Lance. He looks no worse for the wear.

"What are we going to do now?" I say, half in shock. "Oh my God, Lance."

He snakes his arm around my waist and puts his lips to my ears.

"I think you need to go to the restroom and clean yourself up. I just came so fucking hard."

I swat his shoulder. "I'm serious!"

"We walk out like two consenting adults. Ready?" he winks.

"Not that I care, but what is she going to think?"

"That you're one lucky lady," he laughs.

Before I can overthink it anymore, he tugs open the door. My mother is standing on the other side. She looks at me, then at him, in surprise.

"Oh," she says, swallowing roughly.

"Mrs. Stevens, you need to have someone look at this lock. It's sticking," he says blandly.

"Really?" She looks at him, then at me. "I haven't had any trouble with it."

Lance grabs my hand, lacing our fingers together. He looks at me. "Trouble seems to creep up in the strangest places."

My brows pull together, a question on the tip of my tongue, but my mother speaks before I can.

"Did you like what I've done with the pantry, Mariah?"

Starting down the hall, Lance right behind me, I call out, "Your pantry is memorable, to say the least."

Lance laughs, the sound wrapping around my heart. I just hope this isn't one of those strange places where trouble creeps up.

Chapter 19

Mariah

"Thank you for lunch."

I take a step away from my mother. Physical interactions are something I haven't mastered with her. They always seem contrived or like they're only done in a room full of people because that's what's expected of her. They're never warm, never safe like I imagine a mother's hug should be. This time is no exception.

"I'm so glad you came, Mariah. And I'm even happier to see you with a man." She turns to Lance, pulling him into the same generic embrace. "I know Mariah is a little difficult to deal with, but I hope you'll stick around. Maybe encourage her to spend some time with her family, get out and do something besides sit in that library all day. She has so much potential."

"I can't even with this," I mutter. "Are you serious right now, Mother?"

"Mrs. Stevens," Lance says, pulling away. He casts me a warning glance over his shoulder. "With all due respect, maybe if you were a little nicer to Mariah, she'd come by more often."

"I see," she nods. "She's played the victim card with you just like she does with every man."

"The victim?" I ask. "Me? That's a new one."

"She just means you—"

"You probably should stay out of this," I say, cutting off my sister. "Nothing good will come from you chiming in at this point."

She gets a disapproving look, one she's practiced for years. It used to scare me as a child. I'd immediately back down for fear she'd charge forward and call me names or hurt my feelings. As we stand just a few feet away from each other, she tries it again. Maybe even unknowingly. I can't find a fuck in me to give.

Lance laughs, reaching for my hand. "Thanks for lunch. You ladies have a wonderful afternoon."

He guides me out the door. My mom's sharp goodbye as we leave, Chrissy's request to call me sometime—none of that matters enough to even turn around and acknowledge it. The only thing I want to do in this moment is suck up every minute with Lance.

Unlike the times before when he's touched me, this feels different. More intimate. Maybe it's just because I know what it feels like to have him inside me, I don't know. But it sends a whirl of emotions through me that I don't have time to sort.

The late afternoon sun isn't as warm as it was earlier and I shiver. He pulls me into his side, running his hand up and down my arm as we descend the stairs to the sidewalk.

"That wasn't as bad as I thought it was going to be," I note, looking up at him. My hand shakes as I place it on my chest, the excitement from the day starting to wear off.

"You were so tight ..."

"Not what I meant," I laugh. Each echo of my chest feels like I'm sloughing off some of the stress from the day. Like I'm casting all of that off and leaving it here, in Mom's yard, behind me.

"That's totally what you meant and, if it's not, I didn't do you right."

"Oh, you did me right," I say, blushing. "We just had sex in my mom's house. What is wrong with me?"

"Hopefully just a very sore pus—"

"Stop it," I giggle as he opens the car door.

He spins me around to face him. "You were brilliant in there today and I'm not just talking about the pantry. Although, your performance in there ..."

I smack his chest. He tosses me a wink as I climb in the passenger's side.

His shoulders seem broader, his chest fuller, as he crosses in front of the car. I can smell him on my clothes, taste his kisses. Feel the remnants of his onslaught between my legs.

Clenching my thighs together as he climbs in, I watch him get settled. Much to my surprise, he doesn't look at me or say a word. He flips on the engine and pulls around the circular driveway and onto the road.

I wait for him to crack a joke or to reach out and touch my leg. He does neither. When he does move, I hold my breath until I realize he's switching on the radio and not coming near me.

It's odd that he's not brushing my shoulder or touching my leg. I can't help but notice it. I tell myself it's just because I want the contact and maybe I'm reading too much into it. Maybe it's just everything from the day taking its toll, but there's still a tangled up ball of nerves that's starting to fray in the pit of my stomach.

Watching the scenery pass, I want to say something to break the silence. I hate it. It's not what we do. I hate it more that I don't know *why* we're doing this now.

Summoning all my courage, I twist in my seat to say something when he speaks first.

"In all seriousness, you handled yourself so well today."

"Thanks."

"Your sister seemed to put her claws away."

"Yeah. I haven't processed that yet."

"Your mother, on the other hand ..." He makes a face.

I settle back in my seat and try to find our normal rhythm. "My mom is a piece of work who will never change."

"What about Chrissy?" he asks carefully. "Do you think she

could've changed? Or is this just an 'I know when to put it on' kind of thing?"

My shoulders rise and fall. That's been in the back of my mind too all day, but I haven't sorted it. "She's always been able to turn it on and off, but today she was almost ... nice."

"I agree. Definitely worth a thought," he notes. "And can we discuss Eric?" He presses his lips together. "He has the personality of a sloth. But sloths are kinda cute in their own way, so I feel bad even equating them to him."

"Hey," I giggle. "I saw you two chatting it up. I thought you were besties now. Which, by the way, was a super strange feeling."

Lance gapes at me, stopping at a red light. "Am I that good at acting? They pay them a hell of a lot more than teachers."

"But you didn't hate going today, right?"

"Nope. Didn't hate it." He looks me up and down for a moment too long. The car behind us blares their horn. "Might've liked it too much."

We speed forward, quiet again, as we mull over his words. There was a sincerity to them, a lack of playfulness I've come to expect from him, that has me a little worried. That *too much* might be a bad thing.

Closing my eyes, I remember the look on his face as I had him follow me from the table. The look in his eye as the pantry door snapped shut. The glimmer in those jade orbs as I asked him why he was still dressed.

That was me. How, I don't know. I've never done anything like that and to think I just did it, to Lance, no less, has me not wanting to ever look him in the eye again.

But I process the afternoon as we make it back onto the highway on the other side of town and hit the exit towards Linton, and I can't find an ounce of regret.

Today I was powerful. I made choices and decided what I let impact me. I was in control. I was a version of myself I really like.

"Thanks for coming with me today," I say quietly. "I appreciate it but, um, don't want what happened between us to make things weird."

I think he's going to ignore me or at least come back with something I don't want to hear. When his palm rests on my thigh, I instantly melt into the seat.

"I think I could've fucked you in the middle of the table and things might've been weird for your mom, or Eric, but not for me," he grins. "Come to think of it, I wish I could've shown that bastard what he was missing."

"Trust me, that's not what he was missing," I scoff.

"What's that mean?"

"Nothing."

"Come on," he chides, bumping my arm with his. "Spill it."

"Let's just say there was no pantry sex with Eric."

"So, you didn't bite his shoulder?" he teases. "Or coat his balls with your come?"

"Oh my God," I say, burying my face in my hands.

"That was hot as hell."

"I can't talk about this."

"Why? You should own that, Mariah. You're sexy as fuck."

I start to respond but give up and just look out the window instead. Without the hormones flooding me, it feels a lot different to say these things.

"You're back to the librarian, huh?" he chuckles. "Imagine if I could get you that worked up in the library."

"Will you stop?" I laugh.

He squeezes my thigh before removing his hand. "I loved seeing you like that back there."

"Oh, I bet you did."

"Not just naked, but let's just put it out there right now that I'll never, ever forget that sight."

I look at the floorboard, concentrating on a stray piece of napkin.

"But more than that," he continues. "You were confident. Classy. In control."

"I don't know what happened to me," I say. "I usually let my annoyance at my mom win and kind of blow up or don't show up to start with. Today felt ... good."

He's grinning when I look at him.

We ride along in silence until we hit the exit for Bluebird. I can't help but think of how different things are as we pass Goodman's than they were when we passed it a few hours ago.

I think I won a little in the power balance with my mom. Maybe my relationship can be repaired with Chrissy. And Lance ...

He handles the car with ease, singing the words to a song on the radio to himself. There's no doubt he's mulling over a thought, one I'm not sure I want to know. One I'm not sure I know how to process.

I'll never look at him the same. It has nothing to do with knowing how he feels inside me or what his lips taste like after they've been all over my body. It has everything to do with him going with me today, providing a shield when I needed it.

I'll never look at him the same, but yet nothing's changed between us. We're still two people with an insane chemistry that we can never let combust.

As the wheels hit the ramp, Lance speaks. "Want to take a drive? I know a little place we could go."

While the thought of curling up next to Lance and watching the sun start to dip behind the trees is, by definition, an excellent thought, so is the idea of not getting my heart broken by him.

"I better get home," I tell him instead. "I have some cupcakes to make for tomorrow."

"Lemon?"

I let the sunlight warm my face. "Is that what you want?" When we pass Carlson's Bakery and he still hasn't answered, I look at him. There's a look in his eye I can't place. "Lance?"

"I was debating between lemon and red velvet." He pulls his car against the curb in front of my house. "I can never quite make up my mind."

"Maybe I'll surprise you."

He squeezes my leg a final time before getting out. Before he closes the door behind him, he pokes his head back inside. "You always surprise me, Mariah."

By the time I get my purse, he's opening my door. The walk to my stoop is slow and I wonder if he wishes the day didn't have to end just like I'm wishing too. Tomorrow brings another day filled with unknowns. There's a fear replacing all of the excitement inside me, a fear that I'll second-guess my decisions today, all night, and tomorrow I'll realize I somehow didn't see the whole picture.

But when I look at him and he touches the side of my face as I stand in front of the door, I know that's partially not true. I won't regret today for as long as I live. And if this is the whole picture, if only for today, then I'll have to deal with the rest of it as it comes.

"Thank you for letting me accompany you today," he says.

My heart melts. "Thank you for accompanying me."

I hold my breath as he draws his face lower, pressing a kiss to the apple of my cheek. "Goodnight."

"Goodnight," I sigh.

I wish I could ask him in or tell him I changed my mind, to take me on that drive after all. But I just had sex in my mother's pantry. I have to balance that out with logic at some point.

Turning to unlock the door, I yelp as Lance's hand swats my behind. He's jogging down the sidewalk when I turn around.

"What was that for?" I ask.

He stops at the car and grins. "I just wanted to touch your ass."

"You're impossible."

He climbs in the car and starts the engine, honking as he speeds away.

Chapter 20

Lance

I'm about to throw back a shot of tequila when the doorbell rings. Setting it down with more force than necessary, a little splashes onto the dark kitchen countertop.

Unbuttoning the second button of my shirt, I yank open the door. Peck is standing on the stoop, a plate covered in tinfoil in his hand.

"Nana sent leftovers." He says this like I couldn't have guessed.

My stomach growls. "Guess it's good timing." Popping open the door, I step aside so my cousin can walk in. "You just leave Nana's? It's late."

"Nah, I've had that in my car a while. Ran by Crank to work on a motor I took apart yesterday and got caught up in it. Didn't realize I was there so long."

"I do that grading essays," I say, taking the plate from him.

"You could've said anything and I would've agreed. Television, a book, porn. But essays? Fuck that," Peck laughs. As we enter the kitchen, he motions towards the shot of liquor. "That good of a day, huh?"

Hunger forgotten, I slide the plate down the bar. It hits the coffee maker with a thud.

I've paced these floors all damn evening trying to work out this kink in my brain, this fucking blip that seems to be overriding all sense and sensibility.

Lifting the shot glass, I swallow the tequila in one gulp. It burns like hell, making me cringe. "That shit is horrible," I say, smacking my lips together. "Reminds me why I stick to Old Fashioneds."

"So, why are you shooting tequila?"

"Peck. I have a problem."

He eyes me warily as he pours himself a shot and downs it.

"How do you do that without flinching?" I ask.

"Practice. Lots and lots of practice," he says, wiping his mouth with the sleeve of his flannel shirt. "Wanna talk about that or your problem?"

Pulling out a chair, I sit at the table. Peck follows suit.

"Fine," I say, wishing I would've brought the tequila to the table with me. "I have this ... what word do I want to use? This ... discomfort," I say, not happy with the word selection but going with it to hurry this along.

"Um, I think this is a discussion to have with Nana. Or your doctor."

"Shut the fuck up," I laugh. "It's not like that, asshole."

"Good because I love you and all but I don't love you enough to hear about excretions and shit."

I reach as far as I can to the side and grab the bottle of tequila. One more time and I have the shot glass too.

As I'm pouring another swallow of fire, I ignore Peck's curiosity. I pretend like he's not there until the shot has settled in my stomach and I feel the tinge of numbness only a good tequila can bring.

"Okay," I say, licking the bitterness of the drink from my lips. "I think I'm experiencing feelings, Peck."

His laughter is unexpected. It bounces off the walls of my kitchen, the sound amplifying as it rattles around me.

"If I hadn't drunken this shit, I'd be knocking you off that chair." I laugh, not able to keep a straight face.

"You'd be trying, lover boy."

"Have I ever told you I hate you?"

"Not in a while," he grins. "Good to know you haven't lost all of your damn mind."

The tequila sloshes in the bottle as I spin it around and around. "I might've. Or I might be. Fuck this shit."

"All right. Slow down. What's happening? Or who is happening?" His eyes light up. "The nurse. It's the nurse, isn't it?"

"She's not a nurse."

Peck leans back in his chair. "Okay."

"It was the nurse, only she wasn't a nurse. I actually know her in my real life. Not that the app isn't real life, but you know what I mean."

His smarmy smile from the other side of the table makes me pour another shot.

"I do know what you mean," he says. "Continue on."

"I told myself I'd just fuck her. But that was before I knew who she was. When she was just the librarian—"

"Wait." Peck shoots up, leaning forward on the table. "The nurse is the librarian? The one you're always talking about who bakes cupcakes and stuff?"

"That," I say, pointing a wobbly finger his way, "is true."

He motions in a circle and laughs. "Keep going."

"So now I'm in this Catch-22, right? I mean, as the librarian, I like her as a person, but I totally want to fuck her. And as the nurse, I totally want to fuck her, but I kind of like her too. Now they're the same person and I like her and want to fuck her and I did fuck her at her mom's house today and now I have all these weird thoughts in my head that I can't get rid of and I think ..." I down the shot.

Peck takes the tequila bottle and places it in front of him. "I think you got more than a little pussy today, cousin. I think you went and got yourself fucked."

My forehead hits the table. The room spins but I'm ninety-nine percent sure that it's just my imagination, just like I hope the rest of this fuckery is my imagination too.

I was *this close* to not taking her home. It would've been so easy to just drive to my house or to Bluebird and spend a few more hours together.

Why do I want to spend actual time out of bed with a woman?

I don't want to want this. I don't want any fucking part of this but it doesn't seem like I have a voice in the matter.

I love touching her, feeling her light up as our bodies connect. It doesn't even have to include my cock, which is a new thing for me. I can control my dick. Plenty of practice there. But the rest of this? Wanting to hold her hand? Touch her face? Fucking talk to her about cupcakes and books and family stuff? What the hell do I do with that? Who am I?

And since when does thinking about a woman screwing another man bother me? It's a given. People aren't monogamous. Having to interface with Eric today and knowing he had her before me, that somewhere in her beautiful little mind she remembers what his cock felt like, made me want to knock him out. I want to erase that from her brain and fill it only with memories of me.

Fuck. This.

"I'm going to go out on a limb here. I'm not saying this for your ego," Peck says, "because we all know that isn't an issue."

"Go to Hell," I groan, my stomach twisting with the drink.

"No, I don't think I'll join you tonight in Tequila Town. I like my insides just the way they are."

"I hate you."

"You've said that." He chuckles at his own stupid comeback. "Anyway, I'm going to assume she likes you."

This is enough to get me to lift my head. "Of course she does. Everyone likes me."

"How could they not? Feel that charm?"

"She was feeling something and it wasn't just my charm."

"Good God," he scoffs.

"She said something similar, yeah."

He gets to his feet, taking the tequila with him. "If she likes you and you're all crybaby over her, what's the problem?"

My head throbs as I raise it solely for the purpose of glaring at him. Instead of narrowing, my eyes close. All I know is that Peck's hand on my shoulder keeps me from falling out of my chair.

"Get me some water." I place both hands on the table. "Who let me drink that shit?"

"You're a grown up. You did it yourself." The faucet turns on and off, then a glass sits in front of me. "Here. See if this helps. Did you eat today?"

I grin up at him and he shakes his head.

"Food, Lance. Did you eat food?"

"Yes, Peck. I ate food." I sip the water, but the extra fluid in my stomach doesn't help anything. Scrubbing my hands down my face, I try to wake up and pay attention. "Okay. What did you ask me?"

"I asked you what the problem was."

I could tell him the truth. Mariah is *way* too good for me. I could tell him the other truth—that I would never be able to meet her conditions. I could go further and tell him the rest of the truth but I don't really want to say any of that out loud. Just thinking of it has the alcohol sitting at the base of my throat.

"I'm going to tell you a little something about relationships, Peck."

"Gee. I can't wait."

My glare is better this time. He at least sits down.

"They all come with a condition," I tell him. "Like, we can be together but you must not have sex with other women. Or I must be able to go through your phone at any time to ensure you're behaving. Or you must make a certain amount of money." I force a swallow, the saliva hitting the pool of acid in my gut. "Or you must be willing to father x-number of children and have a house by the lake. That kind of thing."

"Sounds about right."

"I could never meet Mariah's conditions."

My stomach rolls and I have to close my eyes to keep it from spilling over. I blame it on the tequila, which I don't consume much, but I'm fairly sure I'd feel just as sick saying that out loud even if I weren't half-inebriated.

"Do you know that?"

"Yup."

"You've had this conversation then?" he asks, the lines on his forehead creasing. "You've asked her to have a relationship?"

"Fuck no," I wobble. "But I know her well enough to know what her conditions would be."

Or what they should be. She should want everything the world has to offer her. She probably does. Nah, she does. I know she does. Why wouldn't she?

He rolls his eyes and sighs. "I love how you think you know what she wants."

"I don't think. I know."

"And those are completely unacceptable to you? You'd rather not be with the only woman I've seen fuck you all the way up than compromise?"

I nod slowly to keep from puking all over the table.

"What do you want from me?" he asks. "Sympathy?"

"I don't want your sympathy. I didn't even ask you to come here with your dumbass questions."

Peck leans back in his chair, tapping a boot-clad foot against the hardwood floors. He crosses his arms over his shirt and watches me for a long time.

I sip the rest of the water, trying to clear my head. If Peck hadn't shown up, I could've been in bed by now. Asleep. Not thinking about Mariah.

"What's her condition?" he asks.

My lungs constrict as I consider telling Peck the one thing no one knows but Blaire. My head feels heavy, threatening to fall off my shoulders and roll around on the floor. I may as well let it because as soon as I say this, my nuts will be gone.

"Remember just after I graduated high school?" I ask. "And I was in that car wreck down by the lake? It was right before the Water Festival."

"Yeah. You missed the entire festival that year. Were in the hospital for a couple weeks, right?"

I nod. Focusing on the knives stuck to the magnetic wall behind the stove and not on Peck, I decide I can't talk to Blaire about this. Even though she knows, she's too clinical about things. I couldn't tell Walker or Machlan. All that leaves is Peck.

He sits across from me like he has all the time in the world. There's no judgment in his eyes and I know even after I tell him there won't be. It's not who he is.

I clear my throat. "My lung was punctured. A broken rib. What-ever." I cough once more, like somehow it's going to help my lungs fill with air. "Um, I also found out then that I most likely cannot have kids."

Peck's leg stops tapping. His arms fall slowly to his sides, dangling towards the floor.

My brain replays those words in a sick-mashup with the doctor's face as he told me the results from my scan. The way Blaire's hand felt as she held mine. The feeling of having fatherhood stolen from my body.

I get to my feet and shuffle to the counter and pour myself another shot. Peck doesn't stop me.

"So, there you go," I say, looking at the overfilled glass.

The room is quiet except for the hum of the ice maker. I don't know what I want Peck to say, just that I want him to say something.

"Guess you see my point now." I stare at the pool of liquor. "I might be an asshole, Peck, but I'm not cruel."

"The only cruel part of that is the universe's cruelty to you."

"Don't I know it."

Leaning against the counter, I look at Peck. He's younger than me by five or six years. A good guy, hard worker, heart of gold. Someday he'll make a woman a good husband and a kid or two a great father. Something he'll never know how much I envy.

My heart shreds in my chest as I allow myself to think about the future. How I felt when my parents died and realized one day my siblings would all have families of their own and I wouldn't. No one would want someone as broken as me—not for the long haul. Not to build a life together. I could adopt, want to adopt, actually, but a woman isn't going to willfully give up her ability to look at a child and see her own face, those of her mother and grandmother first. I couldn't even ask that of someone.

"I went into teaching because I love kids," I say, hearing a crack in my voice I hate.

"Do they know that for sure?" Peck asks. "I mean, maybe things have changed."

"They haven't changed. I'm infertile. My balls don't work."

I eye the tequila again. This time, I shove it away.

The words coming out of my mouth are mine, but damn it if they don't sound like they're a million miles away. Maybe it's my wishful thinking that I weren't here right now having this goddamned conversation.

"I don't know what to say, Lance. I'm sorry."

"Yeah. Me too."

He stands, pushing in his chair. Then he leans on the top, his arms dangling over the top rung. "This explains a lot though."

"Like what?"

"The dating app. Why you never bring girls around. You were shoving everyone away, huh?"

Making a face, I shrug. "Not really. Just not letting them get close enough to have this conversation, you know?"

"Does this mean you love me?"

"Shut the fuck up," I laugh.

He joins in, his chuckle a lot freer than mine. "Look, I admire your consideration for this ... what's her name?"

"Mariah."

"Mariah," he repeats. "I appreciate how considerate you're being. But shouldn't you see if it even gets to a point where this conversation would take place?"

"Are you fucking serious? I'm not so drunk I just misheard that, am I?"

"You don't know what will happen."

I swipe up the glass and down it. It's not as bad this time. "I know exactly what will happen with her, Peck. Ex-fucking-actly."

"The fact you can say that when you're drunk as hell is impressive."

I let my stomach settle. My language skills while drunk aren't what's impressive, but I don't tell Peck that. I don't explain it's the fact I can still think logically and reasonably that's surprising.

That I want to call her but I don't.

That I want to drive to her house and feel her skin on mine but I don't.

That I got the woman I've wanted for a long time for a few hours to myself today and it wasn't nearly enough, yet I back away.

That I have no fucking clue how tomorrow at work is going to go knowing I was buried inside her this afternoon.

All of that? That's impressive.

"This girl isn't one I can forget. She's not another pussy, another screen name, another color hair in a hotel bed that I'm reminded of when looking at a box of crayons."

"So you love her."

"Hell no."

"Sounds like it to me."

"And you also think you love Molly McCarter. I think your reasoning skills are inept."

He laughs. "And you're batting a thousand tonight, buddy." He heads to the bottle and pours himself a shot. "You can drive a man to drink." The liquor goes down a lot smoother than it did for me. "What's your plan?"

"My immediate plan is to go to bed, jack off, and then sleep."

"I'm thrilled to know that."

"You asked," I point out.

"I meant with Mariah."

Of course, he meant with Mariah. I just don't want to answer that.

How do I tell him on the heels of telling him I can't have kids that watching her with Betsy today made me wonder what she would look like holding our baby? I wanted to know what if felt like to be Eric and standing at lunch with my wife and child?

That I never wanted to know what that would feel like until I met Mariah.

There's an emptiness in my soul, a hollowness I haven't felt since Britt left me shortly after the accident. When she told me she loved me but couldn't imagine not being a mother and packed her bags and left for LA.

That hurt. That felt like an ice pick straight in the gut and I didn't even necessarily want to have kids with her. It was a talking point only. A possibility after two years together. But imaging those words coming out of Mariah's mouth seems to hold a whole hell of a lot more potential to inflict a pain I couldn't absorb.

I also couldn't live knowing she'd never know the sound of a baby's heartbeat from inside her womb. Or what it was like to buy maternity clothes. Or the feeling of being sick in the mornings from incubating a life inside her because of me.

Sure, there are sperm donors and all kinds of other ways to be a parent and that's all fine. But I couldn't give that to her and *that* kills me. It feels like I'd be lacing my problems onto her and I wouldn't do that to anyone.

"I need to go to bed," I mutter, squeezing my temple. "Can you let yourself out?"

"Yeah."

Shuffling to the doorway, I partially lambaste myself for drinking so much and partially rip my own ass for not going back in the kitchen and finishing off the bottle.

"Lance?" Peck calls out behind me.

"Yeah."

"I'm really sorry."

I head off down the hall. "Me too, Peck. Me too."

Chapter 21

Mariah

"What did you make today?" Tish breezes in the doorway, catching me before I head to the lounge for my lunch. She peers over the tin of desserts. "Lemon and red velvet?"

"It was a long weekend." I type away at the keyboard to avoid her gaze. "Help yourself."

I almost called in sick today. The anxiety of seeing Lance almost got to me. I was up all night, until a quarter to four, thinking about this mess.

If I only think about the good parts, a smile graces my lips that I can't wipe off. If I think about reality, it fades pretty quickly.

"What's that all about?" Tish asks, pointing my way.

"What's what?"

"That snarl."

"It's not a snarl," I laugh, giving up the typing ruse and turning to face her. "You're a pain in my butt."

"Mhmm," she says, biting into a lemon bar. "These are good."

"Thanks."

She finishes off the piece before dusting her hands over the trash. "Now spill it, sister."

"I have nothing to spill."

Her hand settles on her popped-out hip. She gives me her no-nonsense look.

Looking out the door, I don't see Lance. I'm typically downstairs and back up in about 4 minutes from now and he's waiting for me. Whether he will come up today or not, I don't know. But I don't see him.

"Tish, let me ask you something."

"Sure."

"When you were dating around, would you ever have messed around with a man who you knew wasn't what you wanted?"

"I'm going to need more to go on."

Sighing, I look out the door again. "Let's say you wanted to settle down, have a quiet little life somewhere. Raise a family. That kind of thing. And then you met a guy who just ... makes you laugh and smile, makes you feel confident in yourself. I don't know how to explain it. But what if you knew that guy was never going to be the guy in the little house with the little kids."

"I'd say he was a waste of time then."

My heart drops. "Exactly."

"Unless," she says, pulling her shirt snug over her chest, "he looked like him."

"Who?"

"Hey, ladies," Lance calls, stepping inside my office. "Do I not get my two, three minutes of privacy in here before you come in?"

"Yeah, Mariah. Step outside so Lance and I can have our private time," she coos, ending it with a laugh. "Looking sharp today, Mr. Gibson." She steps around him, mouthing something I can't even begin to make out as she leaves the library.

My palms sweat as I take him in. Dark pants and a crisp white shirt with a green tie the same color as his eyes hanging down the center. The tie is loose, like he's been working it all day.

"Good afternoon," he says, shutting the door behind him.

"Hello."

"You look beautiful today. I love that color on you."

"Stop with the book manners stuff," I laugh.

He shrugs, heading for the cupcakes. "Ah, you made both."

"Only because I was bored."

I watch him select the one he wants, noticing the dark circles under his eyes. His cheeks lack the color they usually have and the greens of his eyes are a little duller than normal.

"Up all night?" He asks, peeling away at a red velvet cupcake. "Thinking of me?"

"Hardly," I scoff. "I made those and was in bed by eight-thirty." *Lies, lies, all lies.*

"Better than me. My cousin came by and I may have had a little too much tequila."

"I can't drink that," I say, frowning. I wonder if what happened yesterday afternoon had anything to do with him drinking so much. I don't recall seeing him with a hangover ever before. The idea leaves me feeling uneven.

"Does it make your clothes fall off? If so, I have a flask in my car I can go get." He bites into the cupcake. "Big fan of the cream cheese icing. Not quite as good as the peanut butter, but close."

I go back to my computer screen, needing a distraction from the way his mouth works back and forth. Things are too normal, too we-didn't-fuck-like-monkeys-yesterday.

The room becomes too small for the two of us as I remember the heat of the pantry yesterday as we slipped off our clothes. His cologne reminds me of the taste of his skin when I bit into his shoulder and I wonder if my teeth marks are still there.

All night I wondered how he would react once the orgasm wore off and reality set in. How he couldn't just not message me back because he would see me every day unless one of us changed jobs. I'm not egotistical enough to think I'm any different than anyone else he sleeps with. Not really. Maybe we know more about each other. Maybe things between us have taken some obtuse turn. But none of that changes the fact that Lance is Lance and I'm me.

"I wasn't going to come up here today," he admits. "I was going to stay in my classroom like a responsible professional and work through lunch." He chomps down on another cupcake. "Yet, here I am."

"Why?"

"Why what? Why wasn't I coming up here or why did I decide to?"

"Either," I offer, chewing on the inside of my cheek.

My hands drop from the keyboard, my attempt at distraction pointless. There's no way I'm going to be thinking of anything other than him. I haven't in the last however many hours. I'm certainly not going to pull it off with him standing in front of me.

He takes another bite and considers this. "I thought maybe you wanted space or that I should give it to you. Or, quite possibly, it's just what I do historically after sex."

"Fair enough."

"But," he adds, almost taking a lemon bar but picking up a third cupcake instead, "I then realized that was ridiculous. We were friends before you came all over me. So why in the hell can't we have both? We're very, very good at both."

"Because your language is horrible, you eat all my cupcakes," I say, "and your come was still leaking out of my vagina this morning."

I didn't mean to say that. But as the cupcake falls out of his hand and lands icing-first on top of book order forms, I'm glad I did. It takes him a full five seconds to regroup.

"See?" he says, his white teeth shining. "I come in here to be friendly and you make it dirty."

"Yeah, *I* made it dirty because *I'm* the one who brought up our interaction yesterday. Try again."

"No, I brought it up but it's still your fault."

"Oh, really," I laugh, crossing one leg over the other. "And how do you figure that?"

He leans forward, his grin as mischievous as I've ever seen it. "You make it impossible not to want to lay you on the top of this desk and see if I can't fill you up again."

My thighs burn I'm squeezing them so hard, my mouth watering at the thought of his body on mine. He knows exactly what I'm thinking and, by the look he's giving me, he's thinking the same thing.

"Are you wet for me?" he goads, thinking he's getting the best of me. *Game on.*

Holding his gaze, I make a point of slipping my hand under my desk. His pupils widen, his Adam's apple bobbing as he watches me. My finger glides through my slickness. I hold it in the air, inches from his face. "I'd say so."

His eyes burn, his temple pulsing, as he watches my finger move in the light.

"The question is, Mr. Gibson, are you hard?" I drag my gaze from his face to his swollen crotch and nod. "Looks like a yes."

"Why do you do this to me?" he asks, sticking out his bottom lip.

"You asked. You didn't have to know. I could've sat here all day with my thighs stuck together and nobody would know that but me."

A low rumble escapes his lips. "What are you doing after work?"

"I have plans. You have icing on your lip."

He ignores the second part of that. "Cancel them."

"And why would I do that?"

"Because I want to take you somewhere."

"The last time I went out with a boy as friends we went to the arcade," I sigh.

"Were you twelve?"

"Eleven. That's not the point."

"What is the point, Mariah?"

The atmosphere shifts in the room, the question that's been on my mind all weekend now spoken aloud. *What is the point of all this? A good time assuredly, but can I make it just a good time?*

How am I going to feel next week when he's making plans with another girl or stops coming in for cupcakes? Pretty freaking shitty and that's after sleeping with him one time.

Sex is great. Really, really great. But I can't break my own heart—

because it would be me doing it at this point—just to get off a few times.

"Lance," I say, "this isn't a good idea."

"Why not?"

Turning the tables, I look at him. "You want to know why? Fine. This is why: there's nothing good that can come out of this."

"I thought you came just fine."

I roll my eyes. "We can play word games all day but it doesn't change reality. We are co-workers."

"We're both incredibly good-looking."

Although I smile, I keep going. "We have a friendship of some sort that doesn't seem to be impeded by our activities this weekend. Let's keep it that way."

"But why? Clearly we can play both sides of the coin and not impact the other. You're just as argumentative and hard-headed today as you were on Friday."

"And you're just as infuriating and difficult, but that's not what I'm talking about. We want different things, Lance."

"You don't want to come?" he grins.

"No. I mean, yes. Ugh." I lock my jaw and stare at him. "I hate when you do this."

He plants his hands on my desk. "If you say no, then no. I'll not ask again." His eyes darken with resolve. "I've struggled with this all night. As long as we're clear that we're just having fun, like what you were looking for on that app, then why not? We're adults. We enjoy being together. Why can't it just be that simple?"

Because it never is.

I breathe in his cologne, knowing exactly what the scruff of his face feels like against my belly, and consider telling him no. It can't be that simple. It's not that simple. In a month's time I'll look back and be so head-over-heels for him that I won't be able see straight. Back-to-back broken hearts isn't on my agenda.

The thing is, even though I know it's best for my heart, I can't do it. Being around him makes me feel alive. Strong. Smart. Sexy. I like who I am when I'm with him.

Before I can make a decision, there's a knock at the door. Lance gives me a quick look, one that says this isn't over, and opens the door. Ollie walks in, his hands stuffed in the pockets of his oversized jeans.

"How are you?" I ask, getting situated behind my desk

"I didn't mean to interrupt," Ollie says.

Lance puts a hand on his shoulder. "Ms. Malarkey and I were just having a quick planning session."

"About the lunch program?" he asks.

"Yup." Lance looks at me and grins. "What can we do for you, Ollie?"

"I need some help and, um, I didn't know who else to ask."

The frivolity of the last few minutes is erased from Lance's face. In its place is somberness and a compassion for this kid that reduces me to a puddle of goo.

"Sure, buddy," Lance says. "What do you need?"

Ollie looks at the floor, shuffling his feet back and forth. "Well, I need to pass Family and Consumer Sciences. I missed a midterm test and Ms. Holden said I could do it if I could find someone to supervise me by Friday. She has a Beta thing and can't do it and I didn't know if maybe you could stay after school one day to help me out?"

The look on his face is downright pitiful. His hair, in desperate need of a cut, is flopped on his forehead. Eyes that could be full of joy are filled with an anxiety no high school student should know. My heart breaks for this kid.

"What's the test?" Lance asks.

"I have to make a cake." Ollie shrugs. "It's that or a casserole but a cake seems easier."

"Cakes are my thing," I say, shoving my chair back. "Can I help?"

He looks at me like he's just seeing me. "You want to help?"

"I mean, I could," I offer, looking at Lance for relief.

Lance takes a cupcake and hands it to Ollie. "Here. Taste this. Homegirl here can outbake anyone."

There's no way not to beam at his compliment.

"Mrs. Holden said it had to be a teacher though," he notes. "Are you a teacher, Ms. Malarkey?"

"Oh. No," I reply. "I'm not."

"Well, this guy is," Lance says, wrapping an arm around Ollie's shoulders. "And I'd love to watch you bake a cake. I have to monitor detention tomorrow, so I'll move those rascals into the Family and Consumer Sciences room and we'll whip up something to rival these cupcakes."

The relief is evident. Ollie's shoulders fall as he peels the paper away from the cupcake. "Mr. Gibson, that would be great."

"No worries." Lance is cut off by the bell sounding. "Now get to class and I'll be down there in a second."

"Bye, Ms. Malarkey. These are great, by the way," Ollie says, motioning towards his half-eaten cupcake.

"Thank you, Ollie. Have a good day."

He's out the door as the library begins to fill with the sixth period study hall. Lance turns his back on the doorway but before he can speak, a freshman sticks his head in the door about a book rental.

By the time I get the student taken care of, Lance is gone.

I recover the cupcakes and get situated back at my desk. Fingers flexed, ready to type, I mentally remind myself: falling in love is the objective, but not with Lance Gibson.

Long game over short game. Marathon over sprint. Love over lust. *I think.*

Chapter 22

Mariah

The door to Carlson's swings shut behind me as I step into the late afternoon sunshine. A take-out bag in my hand, I hit the sidewalk for the short walk home.

Lance was gone before I left work. It's not altogether unusual, but I expected him to hang around to finish our conversation. When his car wasn't in the spot next to mine and he didn't jog up behind me, my spirits sank a little.

"How'd your day go?" Whitney asks.

"Fine," I say, juggling the phone between my hands.

"I'll try again. How'd your day go, Mariah?"

Laughing, I shake my head. "It was fine."

"Did you see Lance?"

"Yes."

"Stop it with the short sentences." The line gets crackly as she sighs into it.

"Okay. Yes, I saw Lance. Yes, he was gorgeous today. Yes, he brought up the weekend and asked me to cancel my plans tonight and I told him I couldn't."

She snorts. "You don't have plans tonight."

"So?"

Stopping on the curb to let a car go by, Whitney reads me the riot act. She blabbers on about not knowing a good thing when I see it and how I can't win at anything without taking some risks. She clamors on and on until I'm on the other side of the street.

"Will you quit it?" I ask, exasperated. "Taking risks means there's a potential positive outcome to a situation. There's not with this."

"How do you know that? Have you asked him?"

"I know that because I know him, Whit."

"Sounds like a load of bullshit to me."

Switching hands with the phone and my take-out, I attempt to fortify myself for this conversation. "It's not bullshit. I'm not judging him. I knew who he was well before I ever let my feelings get involved. I just need to keep a foot in reality over here."

"Have you asked him what his reality is? He should get a say, don't you think?"

"Of course he has a say and he's made it very clear." My heart drops at the thought. "I need to be just as clear about what I want and what's real."

"This is about Eric, isn't it?"

I wish I could say it's not. I wish I could say none of what I feel, none of what I worry about, comes from that place. When you've been hurt as badly as I have, the pain might go away but it leaves a scar behind to remind you not to repeat it.

"I'm not like you," I remind her. "I get swept up in my feelings and fall in love way too easily. Hell, I was thinking Eric was going to ask me to marry him and he was screwing my sister." I kick at a pebble on the sidewalk. "It's too easy to forget what I know in general. But with Lance, he could wipe out my entire brain if I let him."

"I still think you should see what happens. People have a way of changing what they want, Mariah."

"Yeah, well, we'll see." A horn blasts me from behind. I grit my teeth. "I gotta go, Whit. Call me later."

"Ok. See ya."

Spinning on my heel, ready to give someone the finger, I almost stumble over my own two feet. A car pulls up beside me, the driver's side window down, and the most handsome face I've ever seen smiles at me from inside. "Hey, you," Lance says.

"What are you doing here?" I ask, not quite believing my eyes.

"I told you to cancel your plans." He stops the car next to me, shutting off the radio. "Considering you had no plans, I figured I was safe to pop by anytime."

My heart leaps in my chest. I didn't plan on seeing him tonight but now that he's here, I love that he is. I can't let him know that though. At least not readily.

"I did have plans," I tell him.

"Fine." He rolls his eyes. "You had plans. But you cancelled them, right?"

"No."

He doesn't flinch. "All right. Well, cancel them now so we can get on with it."

I start walking down the sidewalk. His car rolls alongside me.

"You look beautiful," he offers.

"Will you stop the manners thing?" I laugh.

"I didn't use it that time. You're supposed to follow a compliment with another line. This time, I spoke from the heart which is in the manners book, but not a method I've tried until now. Like it?"

"You're impossible."

Stopping at the base of the path leading to my front door, I feel my confidence wobble. I'm not sure what to do now that he's here. Surely him being here means something. But when you're trying not to read too much into it, you lose perspective.

Before I can think about it too much, Lance directs the conversation for me.

"Go grab a book and come on. That's all you'll need," he says. The car goes in park. "Maybe a jacket if you get cold easily."

"I haven't even eaten yet." It's a weak argument, but at least it's not me giving in right away.

"Bring it with you then."

"Fine," I say, heading up the walkway. "I'll be out in a minute."

"Don't forget to cancel those plans!"

I flip him the bird as I unlock the door. It takes a couple of minutes to spritz myself with some perfume, grab my sunglasses and a jacket, and to swipe the book I've been reading off my nightstand. It might only be two or three minutes, but it's long enough for logic to kick in.

This is not going to help anything. There's no way we can keep our hands off each other and each touch frays my judgment.

Pulling open the curtains just enough to see him in the driveway, I notice he's out of the car playing with the neighbor's puppy. He throws a stick and the little black ball of fur goes after it, topples head-over-paws, and then races back for a scratch behind the ears.

Damn it.

I think back to what Whitney said. That maybe people change. *Could Lance change? Could he want to be the type of guy who settles down to raise a family? Could I change? Could I just go with the flow and see what happens?*

He tosses the stick again for the puppy now ripping across the lawn. If I don't go, if I play it safe, I won't spend time with him again. I'll stay inside and maybe bake something or open a book or clean the bathroom. But if I take a chance, I get to feel this little zip of excitement. Feel like a person who has something to wake up for tomorrow. I get to smile again.

I'm sliding into his car before I even realize I've left my dinner in the foyer. He wastes no time jumping in, switching on the engine, and backing out of the driveway.

The windows are down, the fresh air whipping through the car. I pull my hair up into a quick up-do to keep it from tangling. Lance watches me with rapt attention.

"Road," I say with an elastic between my teeth. "Watch it."

He laughs, nodding. "What did you get at Carlson's?"

"A bacon, avocado, and tomato sandwich but I forgot it at home."

"Excited much?" he grins.

Jabbing him with my elbow, I get my hair twisted and secured. "What do you get from there?"

"Roast beef, usually. They have a really good pesto wrap thing that I only order when no one is around."

"Why?" I giggle.

"Because what man orders a fucking wrap?"

"You, apparently."

"And if you ever tell anyone, that'll be it for you."

"Gonna kill me?" I tease.

"No. Withhold the dick."

"Oh, gee. Please. Not that," I fake cry. He glares, making me laugh.

The car takes a quick left and into the parking lot of Goodman's.

"What are we doing here?" I ask.

"We need drinks and they have the best ice."

"Truth. I found the pebble ice here my first day in town," I say, getting out of the car and closing the door. "Their Coke is good too."

"It's a fountain machine. They're all the same."

"They are *not* all the same. Some machines are better than others."

"I don't think so."

"I know so," I tell him as the automatic doors slide open.

Goodman's is a typical Mid-West gas station filled with pre-packaged donuts and the scent of too-strong coffee. Old men in bib overalls stand around the corner talking about crops and combines and farm animals.

There's something I love about this place. It might be because whenever I walk in, everyone stops and waves or that the time I had a flat tire, every old man in here tried to help me fix it. It's an old-fashioned sense of camaraderie in the small town that I appreciate.

"Hey, Lance!" A man three times his age with duct tape around the top of his shoe calls out, coffee cup in hand. "How are you, bud?"

"I'm good, Dave. How are things with you?"

"Not bad. I told Walker last week I hadn't seen you in a while."

Lance waits for me to join him at his side. "Been busy," he says. "You been hanging around Crank?"

"Ah, a little. With my wife gone now, I've been trying not to sit at home all the time."

Lance frowns. "Her funeral was really nice though. I'm sure she would've loved all the carnations. I think every carnation in town was at her service."

Dave beams. "It was. Made me proud." He pulls his attention away from Lance. "I'm Dave," he says, extending the coffee-free hand my way.

I take it and give it a soft shake. "I'm Mariah. Nice to meet you."

"You Lance's lady?"

"Ah, well ..."

"Yeah. She's my lady all right," Lance grins, wrapping his arm around my neck and pulling me towards him as I blush. "You know how it goes. You have to keep reminding them until they believe it."

"This one here is a good one," Dave says, shaking a finger my way. "Comes from good people. All of those boys are good."

"But I'm the best," Lance whispers into my ear. "Dave, we gotta go. I'm taking her up to Bluebird before it gets too dark."

The old man tosses a wink, like he and Lance share some secret. "You kids have fun."

"Give Walker a hard time for me," Lance tells Dave as he moseys out the door.

We make our drinks and Lance pays. We're almost back to his car when a cute guy with blond hair comes our way. A hat is pulled snugly over his forehead, a Metallica t-shirt that's been washed a time too many is stretched over his broad shoulders. On his face is a shit-eating grin.

"What's going on?" he asks, coming around my side of the car. "Is this Miss Mariah?"

"How do you know my name?"

Lance drops his head and sighs. "Mariah, this is my cousin Peck. Peck, yes, this is Mariah."

"Nice to meet you," he says. He smells like engine grease and Old Spice as he pulls me into a hug. I look at Lance but he just throws up his hands and unlocks the doors. "I've heard a lot about you."

"No, you haven't," Lance corrects him. "Now get out of here."

Peck's eyes are a pure blue, the color of the ocean in pictures of exotic places. There's nothing but kindness reflecting back as he looks at me.

"You have, have you?" I ask. "What's he been saying?"

"Oh, just that—"

"Peck, I'm warning you," Lance growls.

"Just put your glasses on and get in the car and read a National Geographic for a while," Peck teases him before looking at me. "How do you deal with him?"

"It's hard," I say, looking at Lance over my shoulder. "He gets so grouchy. And bossy. Is he this way with you?"

"Nah," Peck laughs. "He's just showin' off for you. Around the rest of us, he knows his place."

"That's with my foot in your ass in a minute," Lance tosses over the roof of the car. "Can we go now?"

Laughing, I turn back to Peck. "It was really nice to meet you."

"Same." He salutes Lance. "Have fun." With a final grin, he jogs into the building, the purple bandana in his back pocket flopping in the breeze.

I get settled in the seat next to Lance. "I have a question."

"Shoot."

"I don't want to make this weird between us at all ..."

Just saying that makes it weird. I look at the floorboard where a piece of gravel sits all bright against the black carpeting.

"Mariah? Ask me," he says.

"Fine." I take a deep breath. "I guess it's not so much a question as a statement."

He lifts a brow. "Fine. Say it."

"Fine." I take another deep breath. "I really do like spending time with you. People always make assumptions and that has to put you on the spot a little because I know what you think about those type of things, but—"

"Hey." He waits for me to stop talking before he continues. "I like spending time with you too. If I didn't, I wouldn't keep doing it."

"Okay," I say, looking straight ahead. "I just wanted to get that out of the way."

He laughs as he pulls out of the gas station. "I'm glad we got that settled."

Chapter 23

Mariah

"Wow," I say, stepping into the soft grass. "This is amazing."

Lance leans on the hood of his car, an arm extended towards me. Like on auto-pilot, I step next to him and take in the view.

The entire city of Linton can be seen from up here. There are pine trees and tulip poplars dotting the hills that flow on all sides of this peak. On the left there are fields with muddy ruts and to the right the trees have been knocked down on the gentler slope.

"This is Bluebird," Lance says, resting his cheek on the top of my head. "We used to come up here drinking when we were young and dumb. And in the winter, my brothers and I still get together at least once and slide down that side just to prove we aren't too old to do it."

"Looks painful."

"It can be," he chuckles. "Peck always devises some crazy sled and tests it out. One year it was an inner tube sprayed with cooking spray. Last year he used a piece of Plexiglas that almost killed him."

"He seems really nice," I note.

"He is. We all give him hell, but he's a good guy."

We stand still for a few moments, taking in the scenery. Lance's heart thumps steadily, his chest rising and falling in a way that could put me to sleep if I let it. Every time I'm with him, I just want to be with him more. Every time I want to be with him more, I know I better watch myself because if the rug gets pulled out from under me, it's going to hurt like hell.

"What do you do up here?" I ask, pulling away.

"Lots of things," he says, strolling to the back of the car. "But today, I have about a hundred essays to grade."

"Sounds awful," I kid, joining him at the trunk. He pulls out a blanket and a worn leather briefcase before latching the lid.

I follow him to the front of the car where he spreads the multicolored blanket out on the grass. "Nana made this," he tells me. "She made each of her grandkids a blanket when we graduated high school."

"And you're putting it on the ground?"

"Trust me. She'd be happier to hear I'm using it than have it rotting in a closet somewhere."

We grab our drinks and my book and settle on the blanket. The sun hovers over the tops of the trees, a large, orange circle that seems to shine just for us.

The only sound is the crinkle of Lance's papers and the occasional swirl of the pen against them. The air is tinged with the scent of pine and the spice of Lance's cologne.

My book rests on my lap, a love story with a heroine loved by two drastically different men. I've wondered what it would feel like to be loved by two heroes, but now that I sit on top of this hill with Lance at my side, I wonder what it would feel like to be loved by one, everyday kind-of-guy.

A guy like him.

"What?" Lance's voice startles me, bringing me out of a daze I didn't know I was in. He removes his glasses and wipes them on the end of his shirt. He watches me with a careful curiosity. "Something wrong?"

"No. Nothing is wrong."

"Um, yeah. Something is going on. I can tell by the way you're looking at me."

I'm not about to tell him what I was thinking, so I glance down at the stack of papers next to his side. "What made you want to be a history teacher?" I say off the cuff.

"Honestly?" He places his glasses on his lap. "I couldn't imagine working for an asshole eight, ten hours a day. I saw what my dad went through owning his own business and I didn't really want that either. I didn't want to spend my entire life at work like everyone else."

"But why teaching?" I ask.

"Well, I dislike most adults," he laughs. "Kids have always been more my speed. They're pretty innocent most of the time and you can still mold them into becoming something good for the world. So, it was either that or becoming a veterinarian and I don't like getting bitten. Most of the time."

We exchange a grin as he clamps the shoulder I marred a couple of days ago. My body hums with the memory. Instead of going there, I keep us focused.

"Was there a moment though when you knew teaching was it for you?" I ask.

"What's with all the teaching questions?"

"I'm curious."

"When did you know you wanted to be a librarian?" he asks, turning the tables.

"When I was eight and we took a field trip to the library," I say easily. "I walked in that building with its dusty shelves and tattered covers and knew it was where I wanted to spend every day for the rest of my life. Now you. When did you know?"

He stretches back, his hands on the line where the blanket meets the grass. His watch sparkles in the sunlight, his forearm flexed beneath it.

"When I was in high school, there was a girl in my grade who was going through some shit at home. We all knew it. It was a different time then though, people didn't get in other people's business like they do now. Know what I mean?"

"Yeah. It was a different world then."

He nods, gazing off into the distance. "Her dad killed himself accidentally in a hunting accident the year before and she never really got over that, I don't think. I remember her sort of not being in the gymnasium, not being in the cafeteria, not really participating in classes we had together."

His tone gets soft on the last few words. He works his jaw back and forth as he relives a memory I'm not privy to.

"What happened?" I ask.

"She killed herself."

The sentence is harsh. Black-and-white. So final. The reality of the end of a little girl's life, a child I didn't know, spirals over my skin, chilling it to the core.

"Oh, Lance. I'm sorry," I say.

"We all went to the funeral," he continues, not moving his eyes from the tree line below. "I remember sitting there and wondering why no one helped her. How all of these people sort of let her down, you know? I think I knew that day I'd be a teacher or somehow working with kids. I'd be the guy who maybe sees those things and helps somebody out."

"That's why you're so great with Ollie, huh?"

He shrugs. "It's hard to explain."

"You explained it just fine," I promise, resting my palm on his calf.

"My mom was always beating us on the head to be decent people," he says, dragging himself into a sitting position. He takes my hand when I start to pull it away and places it on his knee, his hand pressing on top of it. "She had four kids. All of us were healthy. All of us were bright, capable kids. Almost every night at dinner, piled around a round table in her kitchen, we'd say our prayers. When we'd open our eyes, she'd be sitting there, one hand holding Dad's, just watching us almost in awe."

The picture he's describing comes to life in my imagination, a woman with dark hair like Lance's and brighter eyes, smiling back at him. I can see them all sitting at a table, passing around bowls of homemade dishes, the room full of a love I've never known.

My heart aches at the vision. It squeezes, craving to have something fill it in a way Mrs. Gibson's heart must've been full.

"She would tell us," he continues, "that we couldn't rest on our laurels. That we were given more blessings than other people for a reason and that was to help those who needed a hand or an extra set of eyes or ears."

"She sounds amazing. I can't imagine being raised by a woman like that."

He chuckles. "She was tough as nails though. There were expectations and we had to meet them."

"Like grades and stuff?" I ask as he squeezes the top of my hand.

"Kind of. I guess we had to work to our potential. But she better not catch you back talking or driving by a broken down car or not holding a door open at the grocery. That happened to Machlan once. Poor guy," he says, smiling at the memory.

"She sounds lovely."

"She was lovely." He sighs, seemingly content with the conversation. So, I press my luck.

"What was your dad like?"

He wiggles on the blanket, taking a moment to get comfortable again. "Dad got up every morning at four forty-five. He was out the door by five-thirty and rolled in a few minutes before six every evening. We had supper at six sharp and then he'd take out the garbage while two of us kids did the dishes and Mom relaxed. Then he'd take one of us outside to do something. Throw a ball, work on a car, head to the bait shop. Whatever it was that needed done or we wanted to do."

"I love that he made you do the dishes," I giggle.

"Oh, trust me. These hands have met their fair share of dishwater," he laughs. "If it needed done, he didn't care if you were a boy or a girl. Blaire took out the trash, she took her turn mowing the lawn. Us boys would clean toilets and mop floors. You were never too good to get your hands dirty," he smiles.

"I think I would've loved him."

"I did," he admits. "I always envied my dad in a way. He was a man's man, you know, without the chauvinism. He was proud of his family. Proud of us. But if someone said something cross to him, he'd kick the fuck out of them."

I burst out laughing, my hand slipping out from under his. "I didn't see that curveball."

"Let's just say Machlan got it honest," he laughs. "I guess Dad was a ruffian back in the day too. I hear stories now sometimes about him in the eighties in the pool hall downtown."

"Days of the pool halls," I sigh. "I had this little fantasy for a while growing up that I would walk into a pool hall and some bad boy would whisk me away."

"Sounds like you watched too many Patrick Swayze movies."

"There's no such thing," I giggle. "My first crush. I wanted to have all his babies."

Lance's smile falters. He scoots around again, a wrinkle dotting his forehead. "What about now?"

"What about now what?"

"Do you still want to have babies?"

I'm not sure if it's because he doesn't look at me when he says it or if it's the tone he uses to pose his question, but it feels like it's a set-up of some sort. I give him a second to turn to me, but he doesn't. He keeps his gaze across the hills towards the setting sun.

"Yes. I want to have babies," I say, my voice soft. "I've always wanted to be a mother. What you had growing up, I didn't and I always wanted it. I wanted to create my own little family who had dinners together and took vacations together and built forts together with blankets in the living room on rainy days."

He nods his head, working his jaw back and forth. "You'll be a great mother."

"Thanks," I whisper. "I hope so."

There's really no reaction from him.

"What about you?" I ask. "Do you want to be a father?"

He starts to laugh, but the little lines around his eyes that come out when he's amused aren't there. There's a crease instead, one that is foreign to me.

Sitting up, he licks his lips before turning to me. His eyes shine with something that causes my heart to ache.

"I always wanted three boys and a girl, just like my dad. I wanted the girl to spoil like he did Blaire and the boys to tell about my glory days." He almost smiles, but not quite. "I think I grew up in such a comfortable, happy home that I just wanted to replicate it."

"Can I ask you something?"

He shrugs.

"Why are you so anti-relationship now? It seems counter-productive if having a family is what you want."

"Maybe ..." He forces a swallow. "Maybe I'm not sure how much like my dad I really am after all." He swipes up his glasses and puts them back on his face. "What about your dad? What was he like?"

It's a definite, intentional change in topic. There's so much more to his story, one I want to know. I can't press it; it's not my place. And as that little piece of reality splashes me in the face, I feel like I've been hit with a bucket of cold water.

"My dad was meh," I say, trying to move my thoughts to the new conversation. "He calls sometimes, but I think he really just said 'screw it' and wrote us off."

"I can see him writing off your mom, maybe even your sister. But not you."

"Yeah, well, I'm inclined to think I should've been more unforgettable too," I laugh.

"Have you heard from Chrissy?"

"Nope. Maybe I will, maybe I won't. I'm not hedging my bets either way."

"Do you want her to?" he asks, wrapping his hand around my ankle.

I shrug. "I don't know. Can people like that change, Lance? Can she go from being a total, outrageous asshole and then become this sisterly person?"

Could you go from being a man whore to a monogamous man?

Biting down on my tongue is the only way to keep that thought from slipping out of my mouth.

He squeezes my leg and thinks. "I used to say no. Tigers, stripes, all that. But lately I've been considering maybe people can change. I don't know."

"Okay, let's say they can. But do they always revert back to what they were?"

"Maybe people are less like tigers and more like ... onions."

"People do stink," I giggle.

"True," he says, shaking my leg. "But maybe they're also *layered*."

"So what you're saying is that as you go through life, you shed layers?"

"Maybe," he shrugs. "Or, as you go through life, it sheds them for you. I think of Cross, right? He dated this girl named Kallie for years. Cross was a pure hell raiser and Kallie had enough and left. Maybe if she would've stayed, he would've still been high on her sofa," he laughs. "It's possible her leaving made him shed a layer. Now he's an all right guy."

"Maybe," I sigh. "Maybe having Betsy made Chrissy shed a layer."

"And maybe it didn't," he adds. "Whether we want to think people can change or not, we have to remember that history says things are not only cyclical but also fairly predictable. Remember that."

That's what I'm afraid of.

"What's that look about?" he asks.

"What look?"

"That one." He points at my face. "The one that looks like you were ready to cry."

"I was just thinking about cycles and predictability and how I hope I don't try blue eye shadow again."

His laugh is free and loud. He leans back again, the stress melted away from his shoulders. "I bet you look just as pretty with blue eye shadow on as you do now."

"That's a bet you'd lose, Mr. Gibson."

"I can't imagine you wearing anything and looking bad."

I bask in his words, feeling the wash of power settling over my skin. "Thanks."

"You're welcome." He bites his bottom lip as he takes me in. "Want to shed something for me?"

"What do you have in mind?" I ask, fluttering my lashes.

Resisting the urge to reach up and kiss him takes everything I have. I want to climb on top of him, inside him, surround myself with him in every way. My skin craves his hands on my body, my lips die for his mouth on mine. When he's in control, all I can do is relax and feel a way I can feel with no one else.

Biting my lip, I wait impatiently so I don't appear too needy.

He laughs. "Just come here, will ya?"

"I'll think about it."

He lunges towards me, knocking me on my back as I yelp into the evening air. My laughter fills the top of Bluebird Hill as Lance hovers over me.

Looking down intently, his chest matches the rise and fall of mine. He brushes a strand of hair out of my face as he studies me.

"Some people have to peel away their layers to get to the good stuff," he says. "You're already there."

"Stop being so sweet," I whisper. "It makes you irresistible."

"I'm irresistible way before I kick in the sweet factor," he teases.

I pretend to mull that over as he lowers his face to mine. Our mouths move together in an effortless, easy dance that distracts me until I can't think of anything else.

Chapter 24

Mariah

The lavender scented bath water laps against the sides of the tub caressing me. The candle I lit on the vanity flickers in a delicate sway. Shadows are cast against the white tile walls of my bathroom and I close my eyes and just breathe in the peacefulness.

Lance dropped me off a few hours ago. He walked me to the doorway and kissed me like it was the end of a date. Like there was a promise of more. Like tomorrow might have him pulling up beside the curb to see me again.

Even though I love his angular jawline and fiery eyes and funny sense of humor, what makes me feel the giddiest is the way he looks at me.

I run a hand from the base of my throat, between my breasts, and into the water. It skims over my rounded stomach. It's a part of me I've always hated—the pooch, I call it. No number of crunches, sit-ups, or planks would rid me of the excess belly fat surrounding my belly button. Tonight, though, with my hand clasped over that area, the grimace I usually wear while touching that part of my body is gone.

In its place is a small smile as I think of Lance placing kiss after kiss on my navel as if it were the sexiest stomach he'd ever seen. I remember how he touches me in every possible place and does so almost reverently. How when he looks at me, it seems like he's only seeing a beautiful woman and not all the flaws I see when I look in the mirror or put on a pair of jeans.

Now that I know Lance, he's not what I expected. He's somehow more than all his parts combined. He's more than the sexy, intellectual from school and more than the alpha, quick-tongued womanizer from the dating app.

I don't think I was quick to judge Lance Gibson. I just think, maybe even hope, I might've pegged him wrong.

———

Lance

The water is hot as it flows over my body with the shower head on its strongest setting. The spray pelts my skin on a selection that works well in the morning to wake me up but right now is just another uncomfortable annoyance for me to have to deal with.

The look in her eyes tonight was my own doing. She wouldn't look at me like that if I would just leave her alone. I know the way it is when we're together, there's this intoxicating chemistry that I've never experienced with someone else. A connection I'm not sure I've ever even seen another two people have—it's that good.

This isn't lust. I could write a book on that. It's not an obsession, either, or one of those situations where you want someone you know you can't have. Been there, done that—on both the giving and receiving end. What exists between Mariah and me is altogether different.

Am I in love with her? I hate to think so. Am I that hedonistic? Do I have that little self-control?

The fact that it even crosses my mind is enough to make me

shudder despite the temperature of the water dousing me from above. I thought I had the love and commitment issue covered. Thought I had a shield up to prevent me from having serious feelings towards anyone ever again. But even with Britt, I didn't feel this gone. I just know that when I think about the future, I associate it with Mariah and it's cast in gold.

It makes me sound like a pussy I know. But it's the truth. And whether I'm a pussy or not doesn't make it any less true.

In a perfect world, she would be the one for me. Hell, even in this imperfect world, she's the one for me. But the one we live in is colored by an accident from years ago that made me less of a man than so many of my contemporaries. And while the thought of her with someone else makes me want to rip them apart limb by limb, I also want to smack myself when I consider what it will do to her if I keep up this charade.

She'll have to decide at some point whether she wants me or wants the future she's always imagined. Sure, I could let her decide as Blaire and Peck suggested. But that's the biggest dickhead move—to force *her* to choose. To make her be the bad guy. Fuck that.

There's no way I can put her in a position where she can't win.

I'm not stupid. I know the shaded signals, what the meaning is behind her touch, the look in her eyes, the smile that she only gives me. She's falling in love as fast as I am. And, if I truly love her, and I'm inclined to think I do, I can't ask her to make that choice.

Chapter 25

Lance

My bag hits the chair with a thud.

"Brandon, you sit over there," I say, pointing to a little table in the corner of the Family and Consumer Sciences Room. "I don't want to hear a peep out of you unless it starts with, 'Excuse me, Mr. Gibson' and is followed by a question pertinent to the subject matter you should be studying as defined by the State of Illinois. Got it?"

"This is gonna blow," he groans.

"It's detention. It's supposed to blow. That's the point."

He tosses his books on the desk and collapses in the seat like he's been sentenced to the electric chair. I toy with the idea of pointing out he's being a baby and cause and effect and all that jazz, but choose to pick my battles with this kid instead. This isn't the one to fight.

I left the door to the room open on purpose. With each squeak or tap of soles down the hall, my eyes flicker to the opening to see if it's Mariah.

It's funny how routines become your norm. Then when change comes to your habits, even simple little differences, you feel thrown off in every aspect of your life. Tugging at my tie, I keep my gaze on the empty the hall and hope she walks by. She does not.

I haven't had a drink since the night with the tequila and Peck, yet I feel drunk. Or hungover. Just a cloudy-headed haze that I can't clear out. Decision making skills are one of my finer assets. I pick a direction and go. But I'm so unsure about what I should do with Mariah right now that I question my sanity.

As my tires hit the asphalt parking lot this morning, I was adamant I was backing off. Not being a dick, just giving this thing between us some time to cool down. Then as my ears picked up the lunch bell this afternoon, I found myself standing outside of the library warring about whether I should go in or not.

I did, but by the time I made that decision, half of the lunch period was over. It was just enough time to wet my whistle. I left her office needing to see her again but knowing more than ever I really, really shouldn't.

"Ollie," I say, spinning around. "You ready?"

"Yeah."

"Don't sound so excited." Patting his shoulder as I walk by, I enter one of the little kitchenettes lining the back wall. Each kitchen station is separated by a counter top. "Did Ms. Holden give you a recipe or something to go off of?"

"It's right here." He points at an index card on the counter.

"You mean the instructions to bake a cake fit on that thing? She did give you instructions, right?"

Ollie grins. "That's all I'm allowed to use. No online resources, no video tutorials."

"She's hardcore," I say. I slip my phone, that I'd pulled out to look up a cake baking how-to, back in my pocket.

"My ma cooks," Brandon calls out from the corner. "You have to get out all your ingredients first."

"That did not start with 'Mr. Gibson,' Brandon."

"I'm trying to be helpful," he contends.

"Doing the history assignment I gave you today would be helpful."

He rolls his eyes, but goes back to the paper in front of him.

Ollie fumbles his way around the little island, checking the index card and pulling various items from the drawers and mini-fridge. Next, he goes to the cabinets and pulls out measuring cups and spoons.

I hop up on the counter, pretty certain this sort of thing is against the health department codes, and watch him try to figure out what to do.

"First step," he says, running a finger down the card, "is creaming."

"That's what she said!" Brandon shouts from across the room.

I look at Brandon with a sigh. "Really?"

"Mr. Gibson, that was funny as hell," Brandon laughs. "He walked right into that one."

"Just do your work," I tell him. "Focus."

Ollie goes back to work, digging around under the sink until he finds the stand-up mixer. He lugs it to the counter. He then searches in the drawers for the paddles.

Silverware clamor together as he makes the simple task sound like a bull in a china shop. Brandon starts to comment on it, but wisely refrains and goes back to what is most likely drawing inappropriate images on his notepad.

Ollie pounds around for a while longer until the paddles are snapped into the mixer. He drops the butter into the bowl and plugs it in. Nothing happens. "Mr. Gibson? Do you know how to turn this thing on?"

Hopping off the counter, I head his way. "I'm not supposed to help you, but that thing should've come with an owner's manual."

"It probably did," he shrugs. "And we were probably taught how to use it in class."

This straddles my teacher conscience. Thinking it over quickly, I turn to him. "Ollie, do you have any plans to go into baking?"

"No."

"Cooking? Chef school—culinary school?"

"Um, no."

That's enough for me. I search the thing all over and can't find the switch. Next thing I know, Brandon is at my side looking too.

"How can it be this complicated?" I mutter. "Didn't either of you pay attention in class?"

"No," they say in unison.

"This is ridiculous," I sigh. "Look, people made cakes long before they had mixers. Read the instructions. Does it explicitly say you have to use the mixer? Or can we get out of this on a technicality?"

"Beat in the mixer on medium-to-medium high for three to four minutes," Ollie reads.

"Naturally," I groan.

Brandon lifts the cord and the red light on the front of the machine turns on. "It was right here," he says proudly.

"I wondered how many of you it would take to get that thing on." Mariah's voice rings from the doorway.

My head snaps in that direction to see her leaning against the door jamb, a coy little smile on her lips. Her bag is hanging at her side, her hair falling around her shoulders. I wonder if this is how she looks coming home after working all day. That thought gets shoved right out of my mind for all of our sake.

"This is unnecessary," I say, knocking the top of the machine with the back of my hand. "Just another overpriced gadget."

"Like the stereo system in your car?" She shoves away from the door and struts into the room.

"No, not like my stereo system," I say, looking at the boys like she's crazy. They laugh. "What are you doing here anyway?"

"It looks like Ollie needs help." She drops her bag at the station next to us. "What are you working on?"

"Hey. He's supposed to do that on his own." I shake my head at her.

"I'm not doing it for him, but I think I'll supervise. You know, since it took three of you to turn on the mixer."

She tosses me a wink before turning back to the students. "Chocolate cake?"

"I haven't had chocolate cake in forever," Ollie sighs. "This is a butter cake recipe. Can we make it chocolate?"

They all look at me.

"Talk to the supervisor." I throw my hands up before hopping back up on the counter.

Mariah moves effortlessly around the kitchen, giving Ollie tips and chatting with the boys while she takes inventory on what's already out and what's yet to be done. They laugh at her jokes and lend her a hand when she tries to reach the vanilla from the top of the cabinet above the sink.

There is a bundle of papers I need to sort in my briefcase—a stack I planned on going through while Ollie made his cake. If it were just him making the cake, maybe I would. But there's no way I can take my eyes off her.

"Add your sugar and get it creaming," Mariah says, pushing her sleeves up.

I watch them for a minute, Brandon specifically. He's paying less attention to the baking than he is the curve of Mariah's hips.

"Brandon," I call out. "Head back to your desk."

"But I really want to help," he grins. It melts off his face quickly as he sees my reaction. It takes just a few steps for him to make it to his seat and slink back in.

I remind myself he's a teenager. Mariah's not interested in him. Still, he has testosterone and my natural reaction is to get him away from her.

I'm so fucked.

Mariah helps Ollie measure the sugar. I'm pretty sure he could've done it himself, but he seems more than delighted in a very innocent way at having her help him.

"Does your mom bake with you?" she asks, handing him a spatula.

"I'm a foster kid, Ms. Malarkey."

"Oh." There's a squeal in her voice before she composes herself. "Does your foster mother bake with you?"

"I've been in six foster homes in the last ten years. I can only remember one doing that kind of thing with me," he shrugs.

There's a sense of defeat in his tone, a finality that shows he accepts this is the way things are. This is the way they're meant to be. I glance over at Brandon and he's watching too.

"That must be rough," Mariah says. "I'm sorry you've had to go through that."

"Better than staying with my sister. The last time I remember seeing her she had a needle sticking out of her arm."

I have to turn my head so they don't see me cringe. Rubbing at my forehead like I have a headache, I try to wrap my head around his situation.

"Well, I can kill two birds with one stone." The baritone voice rumbles through the room. The football coach stands a few feet into the room, a collared shirt with the team logo on the chest. "How long is detention, Brandon?"

"Another hour," he replies.

"Okay. Get to the War Room as soon as you're done. You're getting behind with these detentions."

"I know, Sir. I'll be there." Brandon lifts his pencil and does a great job at pretending he's working on his paper.

Coach Collins' gaze then roams across the room and settles on Mariah. "Mariah, can I talk to you for a minute?"

"Sure."

She's all too chipper as she prances to the doorway to talk to the new coach who's fresh out of college. I've seen him around outside of school and, much to my chagrin, he comes across as a pretty decent guy.

I want to snatch her up, wrap my arm around her waist and pull her back to me. Whatever he's saying to her isn't library-related. There's nothing about the library that would make her head fall back in laughter like that.

Mother fucker.

My blood threatens to pop the confinements of my veins. My temples throb as I try to appear impassive despite being on the edge of exploding.

Ollie flips on the mixer. The roar of the machine grates through the room, flipping butter and sugar together in a bowl that squeaks every time the paddles turn inside. Gone is the sound of Mariah's laugh. I can no longer hear broken pieces of their conversation and it's all I can do not to march over there and insert myself in the middle of whatever they're talking about.

My phone buzzes beside me. A message bar is positioned across the screen, reminding me to update my dating app.

Pursing my lips together, I look back at Mariah. I wonder if this is how she felt when I was in her office talking to other women? She couldn't have, not really. I wasn't seeing her. Not like we have been now. Still, I would've felt a variation of this even before I knew she was Nerdy Nurse.

What the hell does that mean?

Coach leans towards her his hand pressing on the wall just above her head. She doesn't seem to mind as she looks up at him and laughs. It's too close, too intimate. My hand shakes at my side, twisting into a tight ball, as I watch this asshole think he's making a move on her right in front of me.

He touches her hand as he talks and I think I'm going to come out of my skin.

"Ollie!" I call out over the roar of the mixer. "That's good."

He flips the switch. "But it needs another two minutes."

"Call it two minutes. Move along."

The coach reaches out and places his hand gently on her shoulder. I slide off the counter and head to the window before I do something stupid.

The courtyard outside is bright and peaceful. A few birds play in the grass. A heaviness sits in my chest as I realize this isn't going to get any easier. My reaction to her isn't going to ease up and other men aren't going to stay away from her because I've somehow invisibly marked her as mine.

"Mr. Gibson?" Ollie says from behind me. I hold up a finger without turning around.

Sucking in a deep, ragged breath, I turn around. Brandon is standing next to Ollie, holding a spoon.

"What are you doing Brandon?" I ask, annoyed.

"He needed help and you ignored him."

Taking off my glasses, I head across the room just as Mariah finishes with the coach. She's all smiles as she joins us.

"What are you doing?" she laughs.

"Sifting dry ingredients," Ollie shrugs.

"You're wearing more of them than anything." She pulls him to the side and dusts him off, white flour puffing off his shirt. "Why are we doing this today again?"

"I missed it the first time and it's a requirement," Ollie explains.

"Why'd you miss it?" I ask.

He shrugs. "Overslept."

"Get one of those new alarm clocks that flash color," Brandon says. "That thing scares the shit out of me every morning."

"I could sleep through a war. By the time I finish at the farm after school and then put in a couple of hours cleaning carpets with Red Henry, I'm beat."

Mariah takes a step back. "You work two jobs?"

"Yeah."

"Isn't there a law about that?"

"Probably," he says simply. "I'll be eighteen in six months. I don't have a choice, really."

"I'll be eighteen next month and I'm not working two jobs," Brandon chips in.

A ripple flows through my stomach as I take in what Ollie's saying. Mariah chews on her bottom lip, her eyes meeting mine.

"You won't be homeless on your birthday either." Ollie's statement is harsh, but said with enough kindness that it doesn't feel as sharp as it is. "As a foster kid, I get some basic government services for a certain time. But I can leave if I want and, well, my foster family is pretty shitty." He lowers his head. "That makes me sound ungrateful, doesn't it? I'm not. I swear. I just don't want things held over my head anymore."

I think Mariah is going to hug him. She leans forward like she does before she reaches for me, but her arms don't extend. It's like she's not sure what to do. I can't blame her because I don't know what to do either.

My mind starts racing, trying to figure out how to fix this.

"So you just … what?" Brandon asks, walking back to the kitchenette. "You live in a box?"

"I won't because I have some money saved." Ollie sprays a pan. "But if I didn't, maybe."

"That's a bunch of shit." Brandon looks at me. "How's this true, Mr. Gibson?"

I can't find the words for a minute, nor can I find the gumption to get on him for his language. "I don't know," I admit. "Ollie, if you need a place to stay, tell me."

"I'll figure it out."

Mariah walks to the counter where I was sitting, her back to us. I want to go to her and hug her. Make her laugh like she did with Coach Collins. Instead, I take in the two boys from very different backgrounds looking at me for answers.

"This isn't fair," Brandon insists. "This is so far from fair it's fucked up and I know you're going to tell me to watch my mouth but that's the only way to describe this." He looks at me, at Mariah, at Ollie, and back to me.

I think back to my life growing up, a semi-charmed one in comparison. How we took vacations and had pets and didn't have all the things we wanted, maybe, but we always had enough. I think of the accident and the way it tore our lives apart. How Britt left and then my parents died and how I worked for years to protect myself from any sort of pain or from causing pain to someone else. And how now I'm in love with the woman I'm more or less sure was created with me in mind. It must've been a version of me who didn't go on that gravel road back in the summer over a decade ago though. Because now the life we could've had, the one I know we would've had, should've had, is impossible.

"Life isn't fair, guys." I hold the bowl while Ollie scrapes the rest of the batter into the pan. "You're born with a hand of cards."

"Like in poker?" Brandon asks.

"Kind of. And each year you go through life, your cards change. Let's say Ollie was dealt a shittier hand than you, Brandon. That doesn't mean he can't play his cards smarter than you and in ten years be sitting on a royal flush while you have eights and nines."

Ollie likes this, smiling as he puts the cake in the oven.

"Or maybe Ollie makes a bad call and wipes himself out and has to rebuild at twenty. That can happen too," I add. "The key to life is to play your cards smart. Don't take anyone else's and don't trick them into playing theirs by lying or cheating the system."

My mouth is dry as I look over my shoulder at Mariah. She's looking at the spot where my phone lays.

What cards do I play now?

"Okay," I tell the boys. "Get those dishes washed up and let's make the icing."

Chapter 26

Mariah

After drying off my hands from the dishwater, I check on the stir-fry finishing off on the stove. It smells spicy and delicious. I don't make it often because I hate cutting all the vegetables and chicken, but it seemed simple enough to make before Lance shows up for dinner yet complicated enough to be semi-impressive.

I'm not sure when he's coming. He said he had a few things to do before he could make his way over here, but I had some time and figured we could re-heat it. He seemed as surprised as I was that I invited him. I think I was so shaken from seeing the app still on his phone and listening to Ollie's story this afternoon that I just needed some comfort.

I haven't been able to shake Ollie from my mind all evening. There are kids worse off than him—I know that. I'm not oblivious to it. But to think a kid right under your nose, in the same school that you work in, has no parents. No one to love him. No one to make sure he doesn't starve to death or have a dry pair of socks once he hits eighteen is just heartbreaking.

There have been a lot of accomplishments I've achieved on my own. Applied and got accepted to college. Paid off my car loan.

228

Found a house to rent and got a job at a high school that was my first choice. Those all felt like huge burdens to bear at the time, but not compared to what Ollie faces.

As I flip off the burner, I think back to the discussion Lance and I had as we straightened the Family and Consumer Sciences Room after Ollie and Brandon left. He insisted his brothers would be able to help him find Ollie housing and a job. Apparently, they're connected around town. I promised to help with the deposit if needed.

Lance's face as we talked about this caused my heart to swell and sink at the same time. I love that he cares so genuinely about this kid. The way he was so gentle with Betsy this past weekend, yet so firm with Brandon makes him feel so ... sturdy. Like a man.

"What do I know about that?" I scoff, setting the spoon down. My phone blares from the living room and I jog that way to answer it. It's a number I don't recognize and having just told Ollie to call me if he needed anything, I worry it's him.

"Hello?" I say.

"Hey, Mariah. It's Chrissy."

I wanted to be more prepared in case this call ever happened. My stomach twists so hard it burns. Even though things went decently between us over brunch, I hadn't yet processed it all the way through.

"I know you weren't expecting to hear from me. I hope I'm not interrupting anything."

"Just making dinner," I say. "What's going on?"

I switch the phone between my hands, my palms sweaty. My sister clears her throat.

"Nothing, actually. I just, um ..." She clears her throat again. "I wanted to have a chance to talk to you without people around, you know?"

"I ... Chrissy, I really don't know what to say."

"You don't have to say anything. Just agree to meet me for coffee and I'll do all the talking."

Pacing a circle around my sofa, I wish Lance were here. He

couldn't make this decision for me, but he'd make me feel better about whatever decision I'd make. Just feeling his arm around me or seeing his crooked grin makes everything feel better.

"My schedule is pretty full," I tell her. "Why don't you just say what you need to say over the phone?"

"I deserve that."

"This isn't about who deserves what," I sigh.

"Mariah ... I'm sorry."

The words I've wanted to hear my entire life are there, out in the open. I still, waiting for the relief that I expect to follow but nothing happens. "What are you sorry for?" I ask.

She groans. "I've been pretty horrible to you our entire lives. Don't you agree?"

"Yes, I agree. I've agreed for the last twenty-seven years." Bowing my head, the muscles in the back of my neck stretch. It seems to pull up a sickness in my stomach, though, as floods of memories cascade around me. "Why now, Chris? Why all of a sudden are you so sorry? Do I have nothing left you want?"

I don't mean to spill such nastiness over the line, but it feels like a dam is broken. It's like I'm stepping out of a shell I've worn for so very long and now I'm me, the little girl who has been tempered inside who can now come into the sunshine.

My laughter isn't from joy or even amusement. It's more from a disbelief that this conversation is actually happening.

"I mean it," she insists. "This conversation should've happened a long time ago and I was too self-absorbed to see it."

"So, you woke up this morning and realized what an asshole you've been to me? And you grew a conscience? Why is that hard to believe?"

"Because that's not the way it happened," she counters. "I'll be honest, as terrible as this is going to sound, but the day I realized it—got an inkling of it—was the day I got married and you weren't there."

"Can you blame me? You were marrying the man I thought I would be marrying."

"No, I don't blame you," she scoffs. "And I'm not sorry I married Eric because I believe he's my soul mate. But I am sorry it hurt you and I want you to know, as unbelievable as this sounds, we didn't get together until you were broken up."

I had an entire little speech planned for this moment, one I didn't think would ever come to fruition. It consisted of a bunch of name calling and fact pointing and trying to humiliate her to a level from which she would never recover.

Now that the moment is here, none of it will come to mind. All I can think is *thank God*. Thank God that prayer went unanswered. Praise Jesus that Eric didn't ask to marry me. Where would that have landed me?

Glancing down at my shirt still wearing the signs of the flour from earlier, I feel a peace settle over me.

"You know what?" I ask, swallowing hard. "It doesn't matter."

"It does matter, Mariah."

"It doesn't." I wait for regret to hit me. "It doesn't. Eric and I not being together was the best thing that ever happened to me in retrospect."

"You really like Lance, huh?" she asks softly.

"Yeah," I grin. "I do."

The line rustles as she moves on the other end. "He seems like a great catch."

"I haven't quite caught him yet," I laugh, the words coming easier now that I'm on my turf. "But I wasn't really trying either."

"That's funny. I want you to catch him if you want to catch him. I want you to be happy."

"I want to be happy too."

I look at the tray of empty cupcakes from today. Lance makes me happy and I think I make him happy. But if I do, why does he still have the app updating on his phone?

I didn't mean to see it and I almost wish I hadn't. It's just enough to make my anxiety need a shot of whiskey to settle. It's probably nothing and he has every right to use the app. I just wish I knew for my own good.

My next statement is on the tip of my tongue and I try to taste it, work it around, before I say it. "I want you to be happy too, Chrissy."

"I am," she whispers. "I carry this burden around every day and I don't expect you to forgive me for being so awful to you. I just hope maybe one day we can start all over or start as the grown-ups we are now."

"Can I ask you something?" I ask, heading back into the kitchen. "Why were you so awful to me? Why did you always try to trump everything that meant anything to me?"

The line quiets as I get out plates and dip out some stir fry. I think she might've hung up when she finally speaks again.

"My room was by Mom and Dad's," she says, so softly I almost don't hear her. "I used to listen to them fight. Dad used to tell her he was leaving and they'd fight about us and he'd always say he was taking you. That you were the only one of us who had any sense."

My jaw drags the ground at her confession. *Is that true?*

"I was jealous," she says crisply. "He wrote off everything I liked as frivolous. He praised your grades. He loved your paintings and thought you were the next Monet and I couldn't do anything to get his attention."

"So you were a jerk to me?"

"I'm sorry, Mariah." She hesitates. "When I had Betsy, one of the first things I noticed about her was her birthmark. It felt like the universe was mocking me, that I was so horrible my sister wouldn't even be there with me. And then I imagined having another daughter and having one of them treat the other the way I treated you and I think I cried for two days."

"Probably post-partum," I say, taking a bite of chicken.

I hear Betsy cry in the background. Chrissy coos to her as the phone gets jolted all around. "Eric! Are you in here? Can you help me for a minute?"

"Hey, Chrissy," I say, setting down my fork. "Go take care of your baby girl."

The thought of that precious baby's face makes me soften.

"Are you sure?" she asks. "I, um ..."

"I'm sure. Thank you for calling me and for all the things you said."

"I meant them, Mariah."

I look at my reflection in the window over the sink. My little birthmark looks a little darker, a little more noticeable for some reason.

"I know you did. Just give me some time to think about things."

"Absolutely. Thank you for taking my call."

"Sure."

"Goodbye, Mariah."

Ending the call, food forgotten, I head into the living room and lay on the couch. The entire conversation, line-for-line rolls back through my mind as I dissect everything we both said.

I'm scared to believe her. I'm scared not to too.

———

Lance

"Hand me another box of nails," Peck shouts from overhead.

Machlan grabs the last box on the tailgate of his truck and climbs the two bottom rungs and hands them to Peck. There's a little patch of roofing on Nana's shed that she uses to store her Christmas decorations and yard ornaments that she needed fixed. My skill set usually has me coming by to check her taxes or deal with insurance, but when Machlan and Peck said they were coming over, I figured it was better than sitting around the house ruminating.

Cross flies down the driveway in his Jeep, kicking gravel all over the yard. We laugh, knowing Nana will have his ass when she sees him again.

"Typical," Machlan shouts. "Show up when the work is about done."

"I've been on the phone."

Machlan holds the ladder steady as Peck's boot hits the top rung. "I bet."

"Hadley called." Cross gives Machlan a 'you asked for it' kind of look.

"How is she?" I ask.

Machlan glares my way, disappearing to the other side of the shed so he doesn't have to hear. A part of me feels bad for asking knowing how hard it is for my brother to hear anything about her at all. Even though none of us are one-hundred-percent sure what actually transpired between them, it was enough to keep Machlan from settling down again.

"She's good," Cross says. "Had a question about the guy she's been seeing for a while. Can't say I like him much, but it seems like he's around for the long haul."

Peck's hammer taps against the roof before he whips around and sits on his behind. "Here I am, doin' all the work, and you guys will go inside and tell Nana what a great job you did. Such bullshit."

"Keep it up and that ladder just might give out on ya on the way down," Machlan says, coming back into view.

Peck grins, resting his arms on his knees. "So, Lance. With all this talk about Hadley, what's going on with Mariah?"

"I wish I knew," I say, feeling my stomach bottom out.

"She dump you already?" Machlan asks with a smirk.

"No, asshole, she didn't." Leaning back against Cross' Jeep, I sigh. "It's hard to explain."

"Women always are," Cross notes.

"*She's* not hard to explain. The situation is."

Cross looks at me funny. "If she's not hard to explain, marry her. Now. You've found a one in a million."

"No shit," Machlan adds.

I shove off the hood and start picking up stray nails. There's no way to tell them Mariah doesn't have a damn thing about her that makes her undesirable or off-limits or makes me not want to see her again. They won't understand.

"You're scared shitless, aren't you?" Cross cracks.

Peck just watches me from his perch, a hammer dangling from his hand. He raises a brow but chooses to remain silent.

"You're not getting any younger, you know," Machlan notes.

"Yeah, I know. Thanks for pointing that out."

He shrugs.

"Believe it or not," I say, dumping the nails in a discarded box, "this really has nothing to do with her."

"Oh, so this is one of those 'it's not you, it's me' kind of things?" Cross jokes. "You better get something better than that before you go fucking up all kinds of shit."

"Kind of."

"You're admitting you have flaws?" Machlan asks. "I didn't think we'd see the day."

"I've never said I didn't have flaws. I just said I didn't have as many as you fuckers."

They all laugh, Machlan holding the ladder as Peck climbs to the ground. "Tell you what," my youngest brother says. "I have a feeling there's a lot more to this conversation than you're letting on. But I'm not a pushy guy. When you're ready to get slammed and pour your heart out, I'll have an Old Fashioned ready for you at Crave."

"Gee, thanks."

We work together to clean up the mess. Nana calls from the house, ordering us inside for sandwiches before we leave.

"Hey," I say, pulling my thoughts away from Mariah. "Do any of you need someone to do some odd jobs or have an apartment for rent?"

Machlan looks up from the toolbox. "Maybe. Why?"

"There's a kid at school. He's a foster kid. Good boy. He's turning eighteen soon and apparently he'll be on his own as soon."

"No shit?" Cross flinches.

"I wanted to see if I could help him find something."

"If not, I could take a roommate," Peck offers. "And I bet if you call Sienna, she'd make Walker give him a job."

We all laugh, knowing that's true.

Machlan and Cross get in their cars and drive a few yards to Nana's back door. Peck and I load the rest of the tools and then stand next to the bed.

"If I can do anything to help that kid, let me know," Peck says, shaking his head. "That's gonna bother me all night now."

Laughing, I take off his hat and throw it at him as I walk by. "He'll be fine. We'll work it out."

"What about Mariah? You gonna work that out?"

My steps falter as I make it to my car. Head hanging, spirit deflating, I sigh. "I don't know, man."

"Did you even talk to her?"

"I talk to her every day."

"You're a dumbass," he says.

The sun begins to set, the evening air cooling. A heaviness settles around me, a sadness, almost, that I haven't felt since my parents died. It's not the same, not as tragic, but not entirely different either.

I'm on a precipice of losing something important to me and I don't really have a choice.

"You ever think of adopting?" Peck asks quietly. "I mean, there are ways to build a family without using sperm."

"I'm not against that. I think it's a damn good idea. But that's a choice for my life and I'm not at liberty to make that choice for her."

He grins. "I don't think that girl would let you make any decision she didn't want."

"Probably right," I laugh, thinking of how hard-headed she can be. The toe of my boot scrapes against the ground, sending a load of pebbles scattering off the driveway.

"I love her, Peck."

"I know you do."

"Why am I not terrified about that? How can you be so fucking sure and so fucking scared at the same time about the same thing?"

"Because you love her," he laughs. "I think it's only terrifying when you aren't sure. And if you aren't sure, you probably don't."

"How'd you get so wise?"

He takes his hat off and wipes his brow with the sleeve of his shirt. "Baby, I was born this way."

Shaking my head, I open the door to my car.

"She doesn't love your sperm count," Peck notes. "Remember that."

"So eloquent."

"You don't pay me enough to be eloquent."

"I don't pay you at all."

"Good point," he says, pulling a drink out of the cooler in the back of his truck. "Look, I feel invested in this relationship. I need you to tell her you love her."

"Not happening," I say. I climb into the driver's seat.

Peck just shakes his head. "You're a bastard, you know that?"

"I'm also a liar," I tell him, starting the car and revving up the engine. "This isn't only about her. It's also about me."

"What about you?"

"I'm a pussy who can't admit my weaknesses." A resolution slides over me. "Do me a favor and tell Nana I got sick or had to do something, okay?"

He gasps. "You want me to lie to Nana?"

"Just pretend it's you telling her you didn't sneak in here and eat all the leftover fried chicken last weekend."

"How'd you know about that?"

I tap the side of my head. "I know everything." Closing the door, I throw the transmission in reverse and head down the driveway.

Unfortunately, I do know things. Even the things I was happier not knowing. Now I just need the balls to pull the trigger.

Whipping out my phone, I search for Mariah's name.

> Me: Something came up I have to do tonight. I won't make dinner. I'm sorry.

Before I can change my mind, I turn my phone off. Tossing it in the back seat, I take off down the road, gravel crunching beneath my tires.

Chapter 27

Mariah

Whitney pushes her plate to the center of the table. It's streaked with stir fry sauce and a few pieces of cooked onion. "That was really good."

"Thanks." Whether she's lying to me or not, I don't have a clue. My taste buds are gone. That or my brain is too occupied at the moment to really taste anything. "How's work?"

"Eh, about the same. I think I might be moving floors though."

"We're happy about that?"

"Yes," she gushes. "My schedule would stabilize and I'd have more daylight hours." Taking a sip of her water, she watches me over the rim. "Jonah asked me out today."

My jaw drops. "He did not."

Her laugh floats easily through the air. Mine isn't as easy, nor is it as engaged. I just don't feel it.

"I turned him down. I mean, you dated him—"

"I so did not date him," I insist. "That wasn't even a date, let alone dating."

"Fine. But he's not my type either."

"But you thought he was mine?"

239

"I thought you were desperate," she laughs. "He was a good starter date."

My hand smacks my face. "Starter date? Men aren't objects, Whit."

"Nah, they kind of are." She runs a finger around the edge of her glass. "Speaking of men, I've refrained from asking about Lance so you could bring it up. But, you haven't and I'm tired of waiting."

"You're so kind," I groan.

"Not really. Spill it. What's going on?"

What *is* going on? Hell if I know, but something is because I can feel it. It's that sixth sense you get when something is awry. That niggle in your stomach that doesn't quite feel like you have to puke but makes you a little leery of getting too far away from the restroom.

It's in my scalp, that prickly sensation like my hair follicles are standing on end, waiting for me to process whatever unknown that's coming.

I've told myself over the past two hours that it's nothing. From the second Lance's text came through, I've passed this sinking feeling off as leftover stress from the day. The problem is, I can't work it out enough to believe myself.

"Nothing," I say, getting our plates together and carrying them to the sink. I busy myself with scraping leftover bits and pieces down the garbage disposal and rinsing off the rest. When I finish, she's still watching patiently like she's expecting more from me. I toss down a dishtowel. "What?"

"You don't cook like that just for you. And when I showed up, it was already done, which tells me you had plans. If that's true, then what happened to them? Because that would explain this 'my goldfish just jumped out of the bowl' thing you have going on."

"Really? Goldfish?"

"Yeah, goldfish. You aren't crying, so it's not one of your thousand fictional cats," she laughs. "People don't get as attached to goldfish unless they're like six."

"Fair enough," I sigh, collapsing back into my chair. "Dinner was for Lance. He was supposed to come over but I got this short text that he 'couldn't make it' and then my return message wasn't delivered."

"So, you think he shut his phone off."

"Yup. Or it died, I guess, but ..." I flex my neck, that half-cringe thing people do when they're working something out in their heads that I never understand. It's like the universal delivery, the same as opening your mouth to put on mascara.

The honest way of answering that question has me one step closer to needing the toilet. I've been in an anxiety spiral since seeing the app earlier today, but then with Chrissy calling and Lance calling and his phone dying, it's all adding up to more than I can handle and I'm clinging to reason to keep from toppling over the edge in a freak-out fest.

"What's the rest of it?" she asks.

"Probably nothing."

"But ..."

"Can't you let it be?" I laugh, a nervous energy in the words that Whitney doesn't miss.

"I wouldn't be your best friend if I let it be. Might as well spill so we can move on to dessert."

My eyes close and all I see is that little notification on his phone. The green square with the pink splash of color, the same icon I hit every night to talk to him for weeks.

"It's no big deal," I say, wiggling in my seat. "I just saw today that he still had the app where I met him. Well, where Nerdy Nurse met him."

She lifts a brow. "Do you still have it?"

"I deleted it after we went to my mom's. There was no agreement to delete it. I mean, we aren't even in a place where that's a conversation we're having, you know?"

"But you feel like maybe it was an unspoken agreement?" she asks guardedly.

Groaning into my hands, I try to settle myself. "Apparently, but I shouldn't."

"You aren't wrong to feel this way."

I hear her but I don't *hear* her.

"Maybe it's nothing, Whit. It's an app. It means nothing." Scraping my teeth over the inside of my bottom lip, the words echo in my brain. Like if I hear them enough, I'll believe them. "It means nothing."

My friend looks at me, her head tilted to the side. "What brought this on?"

"I saw it on his phone today. It was lying there. I wasn't snooping." I try to reason with myself, fighting a surge of bile in my stomach. "I'm just paranoid, I think."

"You think?" she asks, trying to override the laugh that wants to permeate the words.

"Insecure. Do you like that word better?"

"I don't like any of them, to be honest."

Me either.

My muscles pull tight across my back, my neck tensing as I struggle to stay even-keeled. I'm a ball of taut, twisted emotions on the inside and out and a good, loud scream is the only way I can think of to release some of the energy. But that's what crazy people do and I'm not going crazy. Not today, at least.

"I'm just struggling with being smart and being open at the same time," I explain. "I want to be open with Lance, give him all the benefit of the doubt. I don't want to burden him with Eric's sins."

"Sounds very reasonable of you," she grins.

"But, at the same time, I did that with Eric and look where it got me. That wound still stings and if I don't pay attention to that, I might get stung again."

Whitney chuckles. "It must be terrible to be so logical. You can't even have fun."

"I know," I whine. "This is the first time since Eric where I've felt like maybe I've put those rose-colored glasses back on. Like maybe I was seeing what I wanted to see and not what was real. I refuse to do that again, you know? I won't be that blind girl ever, ever again."

"You aren't blind. You're nervous and nervous is good. Nervous is smart. But you being nervous makes me want dessert." Whitney stands, slipping her sneakers back on.

"I think I have leftover brownies," I offer without a lot of initiative.

"Come on," she says, pulling me up. "Let's go buy overpriced slices of cheesecake at Peaches. We'll bring them here and binge watch a show."

I don't love television, but I also don't love sitting around sulking. Or worrying. Or lamenting over a man I'm not sure is mine.

"I don't even have a show," I note, shoving Lance out of my mind.

"Oh, girl, I'll fix that."

She gives me a complete list of all the offerings currently available on my subscription service as we get in her car and head through Linton. The streetlights are on, casting a pretty glow over the little town I've come to love.

"The one about royalty is my pick based off your fabulous descriptions," I add, watching Dr. Burns' office pass by.

"You'll love that."

"I don't want to watch it if you've already seen it," I protest.

"Only one episode," she insists. "Besides, I watch so many shows I can't remember what they're about. It's one of the fabulous things about being me—"

"Hey." I lean forward quickly, the seat belt snapping me back in my seat. I try to see down the side road leading to Crave but we've gone by it before I can get turned around. An eerie calm fills my veins as my brain clears out everything that's not absolutely necessary. "Take a right up here and go around the block."

"Why?" she asks as she hits the breaks to slow down for the turn.

"Just do it."

My breath steams up the window as I pant against it like a puppy. Using the sleeve of my shirt, I wipe off the fog so I can see.

The side streets are fairly empty except for a few cars sitting on the street in front of houses. There's a dog in the yard of the large

Victorian house I love on the corner as we turn and make our way back toward Beecher Street.

My breath is the only sound in the car as I pull oxygen in through my mouth. There's a burn in my chest, like the bitter fluids from my stomach have somehow escaped and now fill my entire cavity.

Whitney pushes the car slowly up the road. There, just a few slots back from the corner, is Lance's car.

"Son of a bitch," I whisper. My clothes feel too clingy, everything too tight, too itchy, as we pass the parked car. There's nothing around open this time of night in this part of town except Crave.

He did blow me off.

Mentally, I start linking things together, things I hope don't belong together. Things like a broken date with me, his car at the bar, the app I saw today.

Stop it.

My hand shakes as I toy with the necklace rising and falling with every harsh breath. I tell myself the gut instinct I had today that something was wrong was actually right and I should have some sense of comfort in that. But I don't. I don't when it's still churning, warning me there's more to come.

"You think he's in there?" Whitney asks, watching me out of the corner of her eye.

Gulping, I nod. "Yeah."

"It was rhetorical," she sighs, pulling through the stop sign as a car comes up behind us. "Where else would he be?"

"I don't know," I admit, picking at the corner of my fingernail. "Just head to Peaches and let me think about it."

"By thinking do you mean talking? Because I have opinions."

"I'm sure you do," I grumble. "His brother owns Crave," I note. "Maybe he's there talking about something with him."

"Maybe." She doesn't sound persuaded.

"Maybe." Neither do I.

Chapter 28

Lance

I'm not sure how the temperature dropped quickly enough to have me shaking. I'm also not one-hundred-percent sure how long I've stood on Mariah's doorstep, but it's been long enough that her neighbor has looked out the window twice.

The kitchen light is on and I can see through the opening in the curtains that her purse is sitting by the sofa. I ring the bell again. Rocking back and forth on my heels, I pray she answers. Then I turn around with a follow-up prayer that she doesn't.

If I fail to come out hitting hard tonight, and I'm not even in a place to appreciate the pun, I won't have the balls to do it tomorrow. There's a chance I don't have the balls to pull this off now either but the fact I'm standing on her porch, fortified with a little tequila thanks to Nora at Crave, I'm as close as I'll ever be.

It would seem I have two choices: to tell her I love her or to tell her it's over. That, however, is not the case. There is only one possible answer and it's the one ripping my insides apart.

I love this girl, so it has to be over. It's some fucked-up mathematical equation that reminds me why I went into history and not algebra. Then again, history says the best offense is a strong defense, so here we are either way.

I'll miss the quiet times with Mariah as much as the loud ones, the moments where we're in the car and not saying a word. Those times almost soothe me somehow. I'll crave for the rest of my life the look she gets when she sees me for more than what I present to the world. She sees the good in me, the potential, the man who's capable of more than a quick, amazing fuck. There won't be a way to replace the privilege of being the guy she chooses to spend an evening with.

Blaire says there's always hope, but I'm not sure if I even want to go there. What can I hope for at this point? That she moves on from me? That I don't miss her so much I lose my mind? That she doesn't feel half the pain I'm going to feel if I manage to go through with this?

I turn toward my car when a set of headlights comes down the road. It slows as it nears, pulling up the driveway at a crawl.

Scratching the side of my neck, the feel of my nails digging into my flesh is barely discernible in relation to the tight pain stretching across my chest. It's hard to even take in enough oxygen to stay standing as Mariah gets out of the car. She gives a quick goodbye to whomever is driving, not even looking my way until the car has backed out onto the road.

She fiddles with a take-out bag in her hand as she makes her way toward me. Her steps are methodical, one in front of the other. Each one ratchets tighter on my nerves.

"Hey," I say as she draws near. The frog in my throat is obvious and I swallow to press it down. "I hope it's okay I'm here."

"Sure." She plays with a lock of her hair. "I, um, went with Whitney over to Peaches to get dessert."

"What'd you get?"

"Cheesecake." She flips her gaze to mine, her baby blues filled with unease. "We were going to bring it back here and watch some show about the royals, but we ran into Coach Collins and the new guy the school board hired for soccer."

His name alone creates a storm inside me. My hands ball into fists at my sides as I try to remind myself I can't be jealous. *She's not mine.* And that right there is the most frustrating part of this whole damn dilemma.

"What'd he want today, anyway?" I ask, unable to help myself.

She pops the key in the lock and swings the door open. "Just to see about the delivery of some books and manuals I ordered for the football program."

"Oh."

"Why?" She steps inside the house, taking her shoes off by the door.

"It just seemed like a lot of talk and laughter over football manuals."

Her shoulders lift and fall. "He's nice."

There's more to it than that but she's not going to give it to me.

My body burns from the tension in my muscles as I watch her busy herself with a hundred things besides looking at me. Each tick of the clock that goes by reduces my frustration over the fucking coach and moves it more toward a hollow sensation that tells me something is wrong.

"Are you going to come in or not?" A look is cast over her shoulder, one that can only be defined as on guard.

Before I step inside, I rethink what Nora told me at Crave: how you only come across true love once in your life, the kind of love that sets your world on fire. Love that makes you happily lose yourself in the smoke because you'd rather die from the fumes than live without it.

That's Mariah for me.

For the first time in my adult life, a relationship is not just about the sex. With her, it's more than the conversations we have, or the way she looks at me, or the way she makes me want to consider what impact my actions have on the world. She doesn't just make me want to be better for her. She makes me better in every way.

Nora said coming over here and breaking it off with her was the stupidest move I could make. She's seen me do some seriously stupid shit too.

I agree. This is *so* fucking stupid. It's stupid in the same way chemotherapy makes you sick but you have to undergo it to rid yourself of cancer. But, just like chemo, this is best choice I can make under the circumstances.

I cross the threshold and shut the door behind me. She stands in the little hallway that leads to the kitchen, the light illuminating her from behind.

There's a suspicion, a leeriness to her gaze that seems so utterly unfair. It's the most cutting thing I've felt in a very long time. I want to whisk her up into my arms and kiss the hell out of her. I want to tell her to stop looking at me like that. I want to tell her I'm standing here wondering what she would look like under the kitchen light at three in the morning when she comes down for a glass of water and I follow her because I can't stand to be in bed without her. That I wonder what she'd look like in this position in the middle of the night prepping a bottle while I lie in bed with a baby awaiting her return. What she would look like coming in after a concert she'd always wanted to see.

All of this confession is on the tip of my tongue, ready to be screamed from the deepest recesses of my consciousness.

"How was your evening?" she asks, choosing each word with the care of a surgeon.

"Good. Helped Machlan and Peck fix Nana's shed."

She arches a brow. "Really?"

"Yeah."

Exhaling a hasty breath, she turns away. Her hand plants on the refrigerator door. "What's wrong, Lance?"

I take a step back. I'm not ready for this conversation. I thought I was in control, still figuring out how to bring it up, and I'm sure as hell not ready to go there yet. There was supposed to be time to figure this out first, to get a game plan, to maybe hold her one last time.

"Lance?" She turns on her heel and leans against the counter. "What's the matter?"

"Why do you think something is the matter?"

Her arms cross her chest. "I don't know what all of this is, but it's not us."

This is the opening I need, handed to me on a silver platter—one I'm trying to shove right back her way instead of just accepting.

My heart clenches as I read all the messages her eyes are telling me. "What is us, Mariah?"

"I don't know. You tell me."

Goddamnit.

Not yet.

I'm not ready.

"Can I ask you a question?" I ask, wrapping my hands around the posts of a chair.

"You just did."

Cracking a smile, I can't find it in my heart to fire back at her with some innuendo-filled response. "What do you want?"

"You mean like pizza?" she gulps.

"I know you like pizza."

"And sushi," she adds, her bottom lip starting to quiver.

"And tacos, right?"

She nods, sitting at the table with her hands in her lap. I don't trust myself to move because I know exactly what I'll do—It'll end with her in my lap, putting off this conversation.

"I meant more like ..." I think about how to phrase it. "What are the most important things you want out of life?"

Pretending I'm just waiting on her reply, I send her a silent plea that tells her to answer in a way I can feel good about. I want her to talk me out of this.

Her features soften, letting go of the fear that had crept into the lines of her face. She pulls her knees to her chest. "Night kisses," she says just loud enough for me to hear.

I look at the ceiling as her words slice open a wound across my heart I'm certain will never heal.

"I don't want anything fancy," she says softly. "Loyalty from those I love. Feeling safe, like I don't have to compete with anyone for anything."

"You deserve all of that."

"I think I do." She puts her feet back on the floor as I look down at her. "What do you want, Lance?"

I pace a circle around her kitchen, my hands in my hair, tugging at the roots. I wish I could tell her what it is I really want.

Her.

Just her.

"I don't know what I want," I lie, unable to even look at her as I say it. My teeth clench, trying not to let the words by.

"I see."

No, you don't see!

Panic gathers in my core, melting everything in its path as it spreads through me like a virus. I pivot on my heel and look at my girl.

There's a steeliness there. It's cold and guarded and not at all the way she should look. I hate that I put it there. Me. I put that look of distrust on the woman I just want to protect and love and shower with kisses day and night.

I imagine the war that would be waged in those beautiful baby blues when she had to pick between the experience of a lifetime, of carrying a child, and of loving a man who is, by all accounts, unworthy of that love. The truth is, I know she loves me. Maybe even as much as I love her and the fact I've let this happen is heartbreaking.

She deserves so much more than me, a broken version of a teenage boy who's gone to bed after eating everyone's cookies.

"You know I don't expect anything from you, right?" she asks.

"Mariah, wait ..."

She gets to her feet, pushing in her chair. "Lance, it's fine. I—"

"You have no idea what you're talking about." My chest rises and falls like I've ran a marathon, the air rushing out of my body in sharp, painful bursts. "It's not you, Mariah."

She smiles, but not at me. It's directed inwardly, I think, like she predicted this.

I can predict too. I know she'd choose me over children. And my fear is too fucking deep that one day she'd turn forty and realize she'd given up something she could never get back just because I wrecked a car at eighteen and fucked up my life.

It's unfair for someone's tragedies to bleed onto another. I won't do that to her, even if this kills me.

"Look," I say, fighting the blaze in my ribs, "this isn't about you."

"It never is." She shakes her head, turning away from me. "You've been kind and—"

"Mariah, stop it," I say, barely able to utter the words past the lump in my throat.

"You don't owe me an explanation. You don't owe me an excuse."

"It's not an excuse."

She pulls her hair to the top of her head, letting a tendril fall to her right temple. I want to tuck it behind her ear, kiss her just below the lobe, and feel her lean against me. But I can't. Ever again.

"I think, um ..." I say, clearing my throat. "I think things were getting too complicated."

The stinging in my eyes appears for the first time since my parents funeral as I realize the death of my dreams. I've fought so hard never to find her, although I didn't know she was the one I was trying to run from.

I've used dating apps, blown off calls, purposefully ended communication with women, done everything I could to never get to this point in a relationship. And here she sits, at the very apex without me ever having seen it coming. I was head over heels for this crazy girl before I even realized what love felt like. Now I have to break my own heart so that I won't ever have to break hers.

God, I love you, I want to tell her. *I'm so sorry it has to be this way.*

"Yeah," she says, her voice raw. "Complicated. That's true."

The air around us twists and turns, seeping through the entangled lies we're both telling. She steps to the left. I step to the right. She looks at me. I look away. I look at her and she turns to the sink and becomes fascinated with a dishrag.

"I have some things to do ..." Her voice trails off and she doesn't even try to finish the sentence.

Still, I can't go. "Mariah ..."

"Lance." She clears her throat and turns back around. Her shoulders are back. Her eyes clouded with tears. Her face more beautiful than I've ever seen it. "Please go."

My voice shouts inside me, tries to be heard outside my head. My mouth moves, but I don't know what I say, only that she nods and looks down as she walks around me.

I find myself following her to the front door and stepping through it as she opens it. I'm on the porch, the cool night air whipping at my skin when I get myself together enough to realize ... *this is it.*

"If you need anything—" I start, but she cuts me off.

"I know where to find you. Goodnight, Lance."

And the door shuts.

Chapter 29

Mariah

"Thank you, Joe," I say. The maintenance man puts the few tools he needed for this task back in his little metal container. "I'm sure installing a lock on my door at six in the morning wasn't your idea of an emergency, but I really do appreciate it."

"It was this or go clean out a toilet in the boys' bathroom," he chuckles.

"Glad I could help you."

He tips a beat-up Dodgers cap, before moseying out of the library. I round my desk and try the lock. It snaps with the crispness of not having been used before.

It breaks my heart.

I just stare at the brass latch, like somehow if I look at it long enough, everything will be different.

I won't get on the app. I won't humor Lance when he comes in here every afternoon. I won't cry.

I lie to myself over and over again, making promises I know I'm going to turn around and break.

The sun hovers at the horizon, rays of orange sunshine spraying up from the tree line across the soccer fields. All night I lay in my bed and wondered how I'd feel when the sun came up. Daylight has a way of making prospects look different. Somehow it didn't seem like the sun, moon, or stars would make the words Lance spoke last night seem any better.

Tears dot the corners of my eyes as I look at the corner of my desk. The absence of baked goods just drives home the certainty that my life isn't the same. The pang in my chest is a guarantee that I will never rebound. Not fully.

I dated Eric for years. I thought I would marry the guy. He ended up marrying my sister, which was the most painful experience I've ever been through and it doesn't hold a candle to this.

Eric said he loved me and that felt good. It was nice having a companion, someone to build something with. I would tell him I loved him all the time, so much so that it would annoy him. I thought it was a habit back then, but now I think maybe I needed to hear it out loud. I needed to remind myself, which is how I know I didn't really love him.

I've never said out loud that I'm in love with Lance. I never needed to. He's my first thought when I wake up and what I'm smiling about when my eyes shut at night. He's who I consider when I'm baking brownies and the person I want to tell when my sister decides to finally call me. It's Lance I wait for at lunchtime and who I'm reminded of when I hear a song on the radio.

I never knew this definition of love. It's not a thing, a word, a piece of paper, or a joint bank account. It's not a last name or a mortgage.

It's a tingly feeling in the pit of your stomach when you hear their name. It's a grin stretched so hard across your face when you get a whiff of their cologne. It's the touch of his hand when you need it most, a silly laugh when you're ready to cry. It's standing up for you when you feel weak and letting you fall when you can no longer be strong.

You don't love because you're required to, like my mother does with me. You don't love out of guilt, like Chrissy. You don't love because it's the right thing to do and what's expected of you, like Eric. Love is a choice. It's a connection with someone else that can't be explained, a relationship with someone who both helps you feel your best and reciprocates the good you have to give.

I love Lance Gibson and locking him out of my heart will be the hardest thing I've ever had to do. There's a vacancy in my chest, an ache that hurts just as much mentally as it does physically. How he managed to dig his way in my psyche despite my best efforts to keep him out, I'll never know. Why I was stupid enough to let my guard down—I'll never know that either.

Taking my seat, I sort through emails from the staff. The list of books they requested is enough to distract me for a few minutes, at least until there's a knock on the door.

My heart beats me to the doorway and falls as spectacularly as my spirits when it's Tish who's looking back at me.

"Don't look so happy to see me," she chirps, sauntering in. "Why you here so early?"

"Lots of emails," I say, nodding towards my computer. "What about you?"

"Science projects." She makes a face. "I've seen every possible experiment in my teaching career. I get that it's not about me, it's about the kids, but is it wrong for me to just give them all the solutions and take a field trip instead?"

I try to smile. I really, truly do.

"Did you run over a puppy this morning?" she asks.

"No. Why would you ask me that?"

"Because the look on your face is the one I'd wear if I had."

"Yeah. About that ..."

"What happened? And why are there no browniessss ..." Her eyes go wide. "Oh."

Sighing, I find a spot on the opposite wall. "That about sums it up."

"Okay, I knew you were all flirty with each other. But was it more than that?"

Yeah. No?

Dragging my gaze to hers, I just shrug.

"Do I need to make his life hell?" she asks. "'Cause I can. I have connections. I can even get him on Homecoming Committee and that's just about equivalent to ordering him into the pit of Hades."

"Don't do that," I sigh again. "It's fine. We had a little fling. I guess. I don't know but it's over now so let's try to be as normal as possible."

She sits where the cupcakes usually go. "Either he's a terrible lay, which I'm inclined to toss out based on looks alone, or he's a dick. I feel like that's probably not true either."

"Guess you're as confused as I am."

"You honestly don't know what happened?"

I mull this over for the eighty-ninth time. At least it's a little numb now, a little gift from above that I expect to wane by the time I leave school today. Or, more likely, as soon as I see him.

"I know this," I offer. "I knew better than to do this with a guy like him. In his defense, he never treated me badly. In mine, he made it way too easy."

My lashes flutter in a desperate attempt to hide the tears that surge at my lash line. I can't look at Tish. I can't look at the computer. I just sit like a bump on a log, saying a quiet prayer that I can manage myself like the grown woman I am.

"Honey, it would be easy for anyone to lose themselves in that man." She gets situated on my desktop. "And he's so cute with you. I've seen it myself."

"Yeah, well, it doesn't feel so cute this morning."

"I bet not," she frowns. "I have a meeting with Principal Kelly in ten. I might just suggest Mr. Gibson to help with the floats for the parade."

"You do that."

"I will." She lifts up, the wood creaking as she moves. "I'm here if you need me, Mariah."

"Thanks."

I wait for her to leave, until I hear the main library doors shut, before shutting the door to my office and crying my eyes out.

————

Lance

My pen hits the desk.

Tap.

Tap.

Tap.

Tap.

It's been the longest morning of all time, partly because I didn't even make it to bed last night, let alone sleep. Partly because I know she's just a floor above me and there's not a damn thing I can do about it.

Around four o'clock this morning, I was in my car, engine started, a spiel sitting on the tip of my tongue. I sat there for fifteen minutes, trying to talk myself out of going to her house and just spilling my guts.

I brought my lunch in a little brown bag, figuring I could keep myself busy and not be tempted to go to the library. No such luck. I look at the clock, watching each minute click by. With each number that rolls over, my heart gets a little crazier. With each second that ticks, my feet become a little more desperate to move. Not until ten minutes after the normal time I head upstairs do I spy a book that doesn't belong to me on the table under the window.

Jumping up so fast I crack my knee on the desk, I hold it in my hands like a prize. Stamped on the bottom of the title page is LINTON UNION HIGH SCHOOL. *Bingo*.

I take the stairs two at a time, berating myself for wasting time by thinking I was capable of not coming up here. We're still friends.

This is what we do. It would be abnormal if I didn't go check on her today. I'd be a dick not to make sure she's okay.

The main library doors swing open. I'm across the burgundy carpet in half the time it usually takes.

How I'll keep my hands off her, how I won't just break down and end this insanity is beyond me, but it's a risk I have to take.

Her door is closed as I approach, which isn't unusual. The little apple cutout that hangs near the window is cockeyed and I make a note to fix it for her when I leave. Grabbing the handle, I push forward and take a step with it ... and run right into the wood.

I flick the handle again.

It's locked.

Glancing over my shoulder, I confirm I'm alone. I test the handle again, peeking in the blinds to see if I can see her. It takes three different angles to confirm: she's gone.

My back hits the wall, a poster of the new hit young adult novel comes unattached on the top and falls partially to the floor.

This must be what it feels like to have your heart sliced into little pieces and fed to you. The tinge of bitterness in my mouth is enough to make my stomach recoil.

I asked for this. Every motherfucking day I walked up those stairs in the afternoon to see her, I asked for this. I knew. Deep down, I knew I was getting too close to the edge of not just being acquaintances *before* I found out she was Nerdy Nurse. Back then, what feels like forever ago, I'd wonder on the weekends what she was doing or if she'd like the book I was reading. *We're friends*, I thought, even though I knew where I was headed wasn't a place you go with a friend.

Allowing my head to fall against the wall, a sense of hopelessness envelops me. This is all too new to process. *Do people survive this?*

I look at the door, the cool drywall at my back only adding to the frigidity of the moment. There's nothing warm about this moment, nothing warm about my life.

Everything I used to enjoy all seems lackluster now as I consider going back to the way things were before. I could pull out the app, make some arrangements for the weekend, humor myself until work is over. But ... why?

My body trembles with a shiver. It's not the external cold that's causing me to move; it's the thought of never being with Mariah again that makes me feel like I'm freezing.

This can't be it. This can't be where our story ends, our jokes stop, our lunches completely halt because I was stupid enough to fall in love.

No. Fuck that.

This can't be it. There has to be a way around it.

Do I wait? Do I pick the lock and wait inside her office? Do I call the main office and have her paged?

It all seems logical, completely rational, and I'm one step from picking the lock when the library doors open.

My hand goes into the air to tell her not to turn around when I realize it's Ollie. He sees me and stutter-steps, a puzzled look on his ruddy cheeks.

"You okay, Mr. Gibson?"

"Yeah. Fine. Just wasn't expecting you, that's all."

"I can come back later ..." He thumbs over his shoulder toward the doors. "It's no problem."

"No, no," I sigh. "It's fine, Ollie. What can I do for you?"

His grin could light up the entire city. "I wanted to say thank you to you and Ms. Malarkey. I'm going to pass Family and Consumer Sciences. Ms. Holden was impressed."

"I'm happy for you."

"Me too."

Pulling my head out of my ass, I remember I'm a professional and an educator. Also, that I have news for my favorite student. "I have something to tell you too."

"Okay," he says.

"I talked to my brothers and it turns out they have rooms available. Maybe even some jobs, if you're interested."

His eyes match the sparkle of his smile. "You're serious?"

"As a heart attack." *And as I am about Mariah.* I glance towards the doors again, wondering if she went home sick or something. Her car was here when I got in at seven, hoping it was early enough to run into her in the parking lot.

"Well," Ollie says, pressing his lips together in thought. "I might take you up on that. I, um, this is really weird and all, but I stayed at Brandon's last night. His parents are really cool and, um, I'm not sure if anything will come out of it or if they meant it, but they used to have foster kids. They know how the system works and said maybe they could help me work some stuff out for college or something. At least put me in contact with the right people."

For the first time in a couple of days, I feel hope. "Ollie," I say, my voice rough, "that's seriously great."

"It is. I'm trying not to get my hopes up, but I think maybe ..." He smiles again. "So, thank you, Mr. Gibson."

"Anytime, Ollie. And my offer stands. No pressure," I say, holding my hands up. "But if you need anything, come to me."

"Will do." He turns and heads back to the door, pausing before he shoves them open. "And Mr. Gibson?"

"Yeah?"

"You and Ms. Malarkey will be great parents some day."

"Oh, Ollie," I say, my throat raw. "That's not, you know, probably in the cards."

He sends me a knowing look, one only a kid like him can decipher. With a small nod of his head, he sighs. "I thought I'd never find people who gave a shit about me—sorry for the language," he adds. "I used to go to people's houses and try to be what I thought they wanted to see thinking that would make them accept me." He takes a step back my way, his voice growing stronger. "There was a family that was super religious once. I read the Bible every night. I can almost quote it for you," he chuckles.

"That's not entirely a bad thing," I laugh.

"I guess not. But there was another family who thought they were mobsters and I promptly wiped all that religious stuff from my brain and filled it with ... a lot of things a kid should never know." His lips turn down. "You and Ms. Malarkey make me feel good just for being me, you know?"

"You're a great kid, Ollie. You just do you."

He tilts his head to the side. "You just do you too, Mr. Gibson. It's all you can do."

I'm left standing, poring over his curious words, as he exits the room.

Chapter 30

Mariah

"Thank you." I take the change, three dollars and thirty-three cents, and want to toss the cashier a penny back just to get away from all the threes.

It's been three days since I talked to Lance. Each day gets a little easier and a little harder.

I'm not the same person I was when I logged onto the app for the first time and found History Hunk in my matches. Even though he doesn't want me the way I want him, as someone I'd like to test out forever with, I feel confident that someone great will someday. That my love of books and desire to curl away from the population isn't a complete turnoff. My pooched belly isn't as horrendous as I've believed my whole life. How could I believe that when Lance Gibson has kissed every inch of it?

But it's more than that. It's something deep inside me that knows I can handle shit. I can handle life. I can handle my mom and Chrissy. I can call the shots with them for the first time in my life with no hunkering down and no caving to their wants or exploding with rage. Lance not wanting me is not breaking me—bending me until the point I can hear the straps creaking, but not breaking.

Maybe he doesn't love me, but I do. I love me again. I'll always be thankful that he showed me how.

It's the wee hours of the night when I wonder if I'll ever fall in love again. They say it happens once and it wasn't with Eric. I know that now. I fell in love with Lance. I'm *in love* with Lance. And if I never feel this way about another man, that's a soul-crushing realization to consider.

With Eric, I thought we'd go through the motions of life—engagement complete with photos that would make me cringe in ten years, marriage with overpriced wedding hors d'oeuvres, honeymoon, kids, blah, blah, blah. The blahs though were filled with enough excitement to make me think I wanted it. Maybe I really even did. But with Lance, if I let myself consider what life would be like with him, there were no blahs. With him, it wouldn't have been about the milestones and checking off each box that adults are supposed to check. It would've honestly been about the journey—the cuddles on the couch and arguing over what movie to watch, the snowy afternoons in front of the fireplace spent reading books and discussing thoughtful passages. It would've been a life filled with fountain Cokes and Bluebird Hills and maybe some of Nana's Pyrex dishes brimming with leftovers. Maybe I could've made Sunday dinner with her and gossiped about her grandsons and really have become a part of that family.

"Ma'am?"

I jolt back to the present, stuffing the change in my pocket. "I'm sorry. I dazed off," I tell the cashier.

"No problem. Have a great day."

The sun shines happily through the door and I have to squint as I approach. When it opens, the glare goes down just enough for me to focus my vision. Then I stop.

Peck with his floppy blond hair and adorable grin stands in front of me. Beside him is a darker, stockier version of Lance on one side and a slightly shorter, huskier version on the other.

My throat goes dry, my drink almost falling from my hands. "Shit," I mutter, getting it right side up.

"I have that effect on women," the stockier one smirks.

"Shut up, Machlan," Peck laughs. "How are you, Mariah?"

"Oh," Machlan nods, a look of approval shifting over his rugged features. "You're Mariah."

"I am," I say, looking back at Peck. "It's nice to see you."

"It's nice to see you. This is Machlan Gibson," he says, pointing to the darker man. "And that is Walker Gibson. Lance's brothers."

Walker twists a toothpick around his lips. "This explains a lot."

"No shit," Machlan laughs. "It's nice to meet you and I'm sorry for whatever idiotic thing my brother has done."

"What makes you think he's done something?" I ask.

"Because you don't look crazy." Walker shrugs.

"I'm not following you …"

"Look," Machlan says, waving at someone across the store, "Lance is all kinds of fucked up right now. Your boy is drinking more tequila than I've ever seen and I can't even add it to his tab because he's so pathetic."

Peck winces. "Pathetic, Machlan? Let him keep his balls."

"Fuck his balls," Walker snorts. "He's driving me nuts. Whatever he's done, Mariah, just forgive him. Make him grovel and buy you something nice but just get on with it."

"Before I go broke," Machlan adds.

I can't help but laugh at their camaraderie, the easy way in which they play off each other. Being with them seems like the best family vacation ever, filled with lots of ribbing and jokes and overall shenanigans. I also can't help but notice how every woman who walks into this place immediately looks our way.

Individually, they're all incredibly good-looking. Together? Together it's hard to take.

"I hate to break it to you guys," I say, gathering my pride, "but I don't know why he's being an asshole."

Walker looks at Machlan. It's Peck who looks at me.

There's a kindness resting there that gives me something to latch onto for a moment. I have no idea if he knows Lance broke things off with me, but something tells me he does. Maybe he even knows why. But there's no pity in the pools of his irises and I appreciate that.

"I need to get going," I tell them. "I have a bunch of cupcakes in the back of my car to deliver to the nursing home over by the church."

"Lance is outside," Walker says, twisting that toothpick again. "He's especially irritating today, so be warned."

My heart clamors around my ribs, pattering so loud I struggle to block it out. I look out the windows, shielding my eyes with my hand, but I don't see him.

"He's in that truck over there," Peck tells me, pointing to a silver truck.

"Feel free to take him with you," Machlan jokes.

I suck in a breath to steady myself, keeping my eyes peeled on the truck. "I might just wait in here until you leave."

"I'd say you have a minute before he comes busting in here looking for you," Walker notes. "Might be easier having a conversation outside."

Naturally, my car is parked right beside the truck so I can't even sneak out a side door. Besides, I feel his gaze on me through the glass and it only makes me miss him more.

"It was nice meeting you all," I say. With a quick smile at the Gibson Boys, I step into the sun.

Keeping my head down, I make a beeline for my car. I can't hear anything over the steps of my shoes against the asphalt—that is, until Lance says my name.

Despite my brain saying, *'Don't look up,'* I look straight up into his eyes.

They're the same beautiful green I remember, and the ones I see every time I close my own. There are bags underneath them, lines creasing from the corners announcing that he hasn't been sleeping well. Or at all.

I hate seeing him like that. I hate him making me feel like this. I hate this whole damn thing.

"Hey," I say as evenly as I can manage. It's not even at all. It's a shaky mess of a voice that I'm half embarrassed about. "How are you?"

He leans against my car as I unlock the door. "Shitty. How are you?"

"Fine." My cup goes into the cup holder. The little buzzing sound that drives me crazy starts chirping, reminding me I just stuck my keys into the ignition. I want to ask him about the tequila, ask him if he lost his comb, but I don't because those things are none of my business. "I need to go."

"Where you going?" he roughs out.

"I baked for the nursing home. I need to get them over there before their dinner time." I look at the blacktop beneath my feet. I've given him more information than he deserves, even though none of it really matters. Still, I need to stop this and get on with my day. "I really do need to go, Lance."

He shoves off my car and stands just a few feet from me. "Talk to me."

"Why?"

"Why not?" he sighs. "Why'd you put a lock on your door?"

"To keep you out." I lift my chin and look at his five o'clock shadow. "I need some space, okay?"

"Mariah, I—"

"No." My answer is firm, my tone strong. It's a good launching point. "I'm not mad at you. I don't hate you. But I'm very tender right now and I need to shore myself up some before you come back in. Okay?"

I put my hands behind me just so I don't reach for him as he skirts his fingers over his face. He lets out a low, frustrated groan and I want to kiss his cheek and make him laugh, but I don't because it's not my place.

"This is the best thing for you." He blows out a breath as I wonder if he meant that for me or for him. "I know you don't under-stand that, but it's true."

"You know what I don't understand?" I ask. "I don't get why you let me in so much, knowing you didn't want to keep me there."

He looks at the sky, stretching his neck all the way back.

"You knew my reservations," I tell him. "And if I didn't know you better, I'd think you drug me in just to see if you could."

His eyes fly wide. "That's bullshit."

"I know it is," I say, biting back a lump in my throat. "But pardon me for feeling like you made me fall in love with you and then slammed that door shut."

The words are into the universe with no way to reel them back in. His mouth hangs open like it's some kind of epiphany and that just annoys me more.

There's a bubble threatening to burst, one I've held back from exploding since he broke things off with me. But standing here in this parking lot, looking at him like he's the hurt one, makes me want to scream.

"I have to go," I say, climbing in my car with a hurried frenzy.

"What did you just say?"

I turn over the engine. "You heard me."

"Mariah ..."

With a final look his way, I smile sadly. "Goodbye, Lance."

The door shuts as he continues his protest and I pull out with only a quick glance in the rearview mirror.

Chapter 31

Lance

I hate this fucking place. It's no place to spend a Saturday morning.

My shoes sink into the soil. It's never solid. For whatever reason, the ground is always soft here and I don't even want to imagine why that is.

Machlan comes here a lot. He makes sure the stone is decorated for each holiday and that the crew that mows the cemetery doesn't damage the headstone my siblings and I had designed when our parents died. Machlan says he finds peace here. Well, he doesn't say it like that, but it's what he means. It doesn't do that for me.

My steps fall with trepidation at seeing the black stone sitting near the back. There are purple flowers in the urns. It was Mom's favorite color and although Machlan acts like a badass, and is one, really, he's the one of us who remembers things like that.

"Hey," I say to the stone, a flock of birds taking flight at the sound of my voice. "I know you aren't here and that I'm talking to an inanimate object. Yes, Dad, that worries me too."

There's a bench Mom's bowling league asked to place on their grave perched right next to the stone on the slab. I sit, feeling the sun on my face.

Despite the warmth, I haven't felt alive in days. It's funny, really. I've always been a guy who springs out of bed in the morning fairly excited about my day. But since Mariah and I stopped talking, since she goes out of her way to avoid me, none of that is true.

"You always taught us to be a blessing to others," I say out loud, wishing my parents were here to answer me. "Told us we had so many advantages, so much to offer that was given to us by no work of our own, and we had to share that." I stroke my chin, trying to get my thoughts together. "How do you decide what's a blessing to someone and what's a curse?"

"Depends how you figure." The voice rings out behind me, making me jump. I spin around to see Machlan standing a few feet back. "Didn't mean to scare ya."

"What are you doing here?"

"The landscaping crew left a bunch of trash the mowers cut up around the cemetery, so I picked it up and threw it in the garbage over there," he says, motioning over his shoulder.

"Where's your truck?"

"I walked down here. Not too far from my house."

"Yeah. Guess not," I say, getting to my feet.

"What were you talking about?" he asks. "Yeah, being nosy, but you have a lot of shit going on and I'm starting to worry a little. You haven't told us one fuck story in weeks." He looks at our parents' stone. "Sorry, Mom."

Shrugging, I look at my little brother. "I've been thinking a lot."

"That spells trouble."

"Right?" I sigh. "Mom always preached about blessings and all that, but ..."

"Look," Machlan says. "If you take one thing away from our parents' lives, take this." He bends down and circles the date of their death. "Take that."

The numbers are etched into the stone, a stark reminder that the end of their lives was marked on a certain day, month, and year. Still, his point is lost on me.

"I don't get it," I tell him, still looking at the etchings.

"Did any of us expect them to die that day? Hell, no. If you would've gone with them, you would've been right beside them in the ground and I'd be sticking flowers on your grave too."

The thought makes my skin crawl. We were all supposed to be with them that July afternoon on the boat. We all opted out, choosing instead to do our own thing. When the news reached us, it was devastating to a degree I didn't know existed. Every time I think it could've been me sends a shock wave up my spine.

I look at Machlan. He doesn't flinch.

"How different do you think things would've been if they'd lived?" I toss the question out there, not sure if he'll answer. It's all a guess anyway.

"Who knows? I think it's safe to say it's changed us all in one way or another."

"I've been thinking about Mom a lot," I admit. "I wonder what she'd have to say about the choices we've made in our lives."

"She'd be pretty happy more or less. More about Blaire's successes and Walker settling down, less about my arrest record and your fighting this thing with Mariah." He gives me a look, begging me to argue with him. I don't. He sucks in a breath and blows it out slowly. "We can keep pussyfooting around whatever the reason is you're here or you can just tell me. But I do have shit to do today."

"I didn't come here to see you. Let's remember that."

"Guess it's your lucky day I showed up then, huh?" He sits beside me, his elbows resting on his knees. "What'd she do?"

"Nothing."

"Nothing as in you aren't telling me or nothing as in it was you that fucked up?"

I hang my head. "Nothing as in it was me who lied to her."

He works his head in a circle, realizing this is a little deeper than some one-night stand I have to figure out. "What'd you lie about?"

"Listen, if I tell her the truth, it'll put her in an impossible situation."

"Fair enough," he says. "Answer me this: did you cheat on her?"

"Nope."

He seems shocked but continues on without commenting. "Did you hurt her in some way?"

"Nah, but I'm trying not to. If I tell her the truth, she might get hurt eventually."

"Lord, you're such a girl."

"I am not," I say, tossing him a dirty look.

"We're in the twenty-first century, bud. Women can make choices. They like them. And, quite frankly, they get a little pissy if you try to take them away. Just throwing that out there."

My stomach knots up as I consider what he's saying. Mariah is an intelligent woman. She's capable of handling her own business. Should I have just laid it all out there, no matter how embarrassing to me it is?

"I don't know," I groan, still unsure.

"Even if it means not getting her back?"

I hate the way he put that. It feels ... final. I'm considering that when he taunts me more.

"Even if it means never feeling her—"

"Our mother is right there," I say, motioning towards the ground. "Have a little couth."

"Fine. Even if it means never feeling her in your arms again," he says with a mock-sweetness. "I don't know what you lied about. But I know you're in love with that girl and you're going to feel this way for the rest of your life if you don't grow a pair and at least come clean. Maybe she loves you too."

I'm zapped right back to a couple of days ago at Goodman's when she said she loved me. She glossed right over it, but it's the only thing I remember hearing her say.

I've replayed that single line over and over and held onto it like a life raft.

Women have said they loved me before. Lots of them, really. But even when they were looking me in the eye and professing their undying devotion, it didn't register like Mariah's words did. It didn't feel the same. Not even Britt, the woman I thought I loved. The woman I'm sure now I didn't. Not even close.

"You're overcomplicating this," Machlan tells me. He ponders this for a second. "Let's go back to the blessings, okay?"

"Yeah."

"Mom didn't say all blessings were pretty. She just said to find them, identify them, and use them. That they were given to us so we could do something with them, right?"

"I guess ..." I try to follow him, but the surge of adrenaline in my veins starts to make it difficult.

"Take Britt, for example. If you hadn't had that accident, you'd be married to her sure as shit. If that happened, we wouldn't be here right now all pussy-whipped over Mariah."

I turn my head to react to that, to smash him in the arm, but the weight of his words stops me.

Oh.

My.

God.

He's right.

"What if Mom and Dad had lived? Yes, we'd all make that happen if we could, but we can't," he continues. "Let's look for the blessings. Well, Blaire is a hotshot at her law firm in Chicago. Walker happened to be at my bar the night Sienna rolled into town. Us kids are really fucking close, something that might not have happened had we not had to rely on each other." He looks at me. "You feel me, Lance?"

"Yeah," I say slowly, trying to keep up with the thoughts pouring through my head. "I think I do."

"Good." He stands and stretches his arms over his head. "I got shit to do. Come by and see me at Crave if you need more professional opinions."

He cackles to himself as he walks away, leaving me on the bench alone.

I consider everything that's happened over the last few weeks, the things that have really affected me. Getting to know Mariah, hearing Ollie's story, seeing Brandon start to turn around—all of those are blessings. But what if my story took a turn the day I had the accident? What if the one thing I considered a stain on my manhood is actually a blessing in disguise?

I plant a kiss on top of the tombstone and let my gaze linger on that date for a long moment. Then I turn and head to my car, my shoes sinking into the ground once more.

Chapter 32

Mariah

"The three most popular answers are on the board. Name a place you go where you can't touch anything."

"Work," I deadpan, popping the rest of a brownie into my mouth. Flipping off the television before I can hear the answers, I toss the remote onto the couch.

Whitney called earlier to see if I wanted to go to the movies and I told her maybe later. I'm probably going to have to pass altogether. The sun coming up this morning didn't bring me the relief I'd hoped.

Last night was the worst night yet. I'm sure the fact it coincided with seeing him at the gas station isn't ironic. Or that Gretchen gave me the best hug at the nursing home when I told her what was going on. Or that I was really bored and loneliness is the biggest bitch I know.

Dressed in sweatpants riddled with holes, ones I can't make myself throw away because they're so perfectly soft, and a t-shirt with a logo from Ruma, a restaurant I loved in California, I get off the couch and look for my phone. I find it where I left it last night, sitting on top of a book about finding inner peace. I've never read a book that made me so hateful.

Leave nothing unresolved. Accept what is.

It can fuck right off.

I switch to a playlist that aligns with my mood and am ready to hit play on some girl power jams when the doorbells rings.

Working my hair into a makeshift ponytail, which is harder than usual because I haven't even brushed it today, I pull the door open with one hand without even looking through the peephole. If someone wants to try to kill me on the other side, bring it. Today's their day.

Or maybe it's mine.

Lance stands on the stoop, his hands tucked into the pockets of his jeans. A plain black Henley hangs from his frame; his hair is a mussed-up mess.

The look on his face is somber, pained, almost, and as my hand falls to my side, my brain issues orders for it not to reach for him. *And don't invite him inside.*

"What are you doing here?" I ask.

"I want to talk to you."

"I'm busy," I lie, bouncing on my toes to the lyrics in my head.

"Doing what?"

"Feeding my fish."

The corners of his lip quip up. "You have fish?"

"No," I shrug, narrowing my eyes. "Get the picture?"

"Give me ten minutes." There's a smirk hidden in those full, delectable lips and I want to kiss it and smack it at the same time.

Damn him.

"Nope," I say, pulling the door closer to me so he can't see inside. I have no idea why I do this. It just feels like the right thing to do.

"Mariah."

"Will you stop?" I bark, losing my grip on the door. I ignore the way he melts me with his gaze, how my knees wobble as he makes no secret of sliding his eyes down my body and up again. "You're driving me absolutely insane. Is that what you want? I have never in my entire life met a man as frustrating as you are, Lance Gibson, and it's so mean for you to show up here and want to talk to me after breaking my heart—"

My words are stolen as his lips crush mine. I'd fall on my ass if his hands weren't holding my face, cupping my cheeks like he might not ever let them go.

I raise my hand to smack his chest, but my arms fail to take commands. Instead, like the loser I am, I give in and kiss him back.

His lips take control, leading mine in a motion that feels like a lot more than a kiss. Lucky for me I'm still riding the tail-end of my all-nighter and don't have the clarity to listen to whatever it is he's trying to convey.

His grip loosens just a bit on my face and my eyes pop up.

Stop doing this.

My palm connects to his shoulder and I shove him away. It's certainly not the punch I'd like to deliver, but it's enough to make him step away. But, when he does it, his eyes are on fire.

"Feel better?" he asks.

"No. You're still here." My voice is wobbly now, his stupid kiss throwing me off my game. "Please leave."

"Just talk to me. Or let me talk to you. You don't even have to say anything."

"Can I ever not say anything?"

He laughs, his hand moving through his silky locks. "Good point." He tucks his fingers back in his pocket, his smile starting to fade. "Please let me come in. Ten minutes. Tops."

With every decrease in his smile, my willpower goes with it. "Fine. But you aren't coming in. I'll come outside."

His eyes spring open. "Fine. I won't come inside. Let's go for a drive instead."

"I'm not going anywhere with you."

"It's chilly out here and I need to have your undivided attention for a couple of minutes, okay?" He looks at me without a trace of humor in his eyes. "Give me this and if you insist I don't come back again, I won't. You have my word."

The thought of that twists my insides into a bundle, but I have to hold firm. "Not even to my office?"

"You installed a lock." He raises a brow.

"Yes," I say, reaching inside and grabbing my keys and a jacket. "I did."

He waits as I lock the door, his proximity messing with my head. I can feel his energy swirling around me, teasing me, luring me in like the tempo of a Marvin Gaye song.

I start down the sidewalk but shoot him a look when I sense his hand nearing the small of my back. As badly as I want that contact, I know I can't have it. Boundaries and all that.

He does open the door and I let him, climbing in and settling into the seat. I grin as he nearly runs around the front and jumps in, pulling the car onto the street as if I might change my mind before he gets us gone.

"I want to tell you I only came with you because I'm weak," I say, looking straight ahead. "I won't always be weak, but I will always hold it against you for doing this to me."

"Doing what to you?"

"This." I look at him out of the corner of my eye. "I'm taking some of this blame. I knew this wouldn't end well. But I do feel like you pursued me, knowing I would fall in love with you and you would break my heart. So, at the end of the day, you, Lance Gibson, are a cocksucker."

One hand releases the wheel, resting on the console between us as he laughs. "I'm happy to know how you feel."

"Yup."

"I am, in fact, a bigger cocksucker than you know." The laugh falls from his voice, his hand going back to the wheel. He takes a turn at Carlson's towards Goodman's Gas Station as my heart falls to my feet.

This is going to be bad, worse than I thought. Not that I knew what to expect. I honestly didn't think about it enough.

Damn it, Mariah.

"Why don't you take me home?" I ask. "This conversation isn't necessary if that's what you have to tell me."

He turns the opposite way of my house, heading towards Bluebird.

"I dated a girl once," he says, his eyes trained out the windshield. "She—"

"I don't want to hear about your app girls." I grip the door handle to steady myself. I'm weak to him, even though I don't feel it, and I'll be damned if I sit here and listen to him talk about some girl I've already decided I hate.

I think he's going to smile, but he doesn't. "She's not an app girl."

He looks at me, the emotion in his irises bombing my soul. It shreds me, rips me apart, and I don't even know what it's about. My heart just hurts for him because I know he's hurting and I'm pissed at myself for that, but what can I do?

I love him.

"I've been with two girls who weren't app girls in my life," he says, his voice barely audible over the roar of the engine. "One was the reason I started using apps, the other was the reason I quit."

My breath stalls in my chest, the burn from not breathing only acceptable because I'm not thinking about it.

The other was the reason I quit ...

"It's not fair to do this to me," I say on an exhale. "Do you hate me? Is that why you won't just leave me alone?"

The car slows down as we hit a gravel road, the sun filtering through the trees. It's gorgeous here, a lake to our right and a cow pasture to our left. We ride a few minutes in silence as I fight tears.

I won't look at him. If this is what he's doing, he doesn't deserve to see me cry. Then again, maybe it would be good for him to see my pain.

"See that hill over there?" he asks, bringing the car to a crawl. He points to the other side of the lake. "This road used to go right through there. That lake was really two lakes until a few years ago.

We had a flood and they joined, the road went underwater, and they never separated."

"I didn't even know that could happen," I offer.

"One night, when I was younger," he gulps, clearly fighting with the words to this story, "I was out here screwing around with a friend. We'd been to this campfire at a barn out that way and were racing to see who could get to town first."

The car stops along the side of the road. He turns the top of his body to me, but his eyes are glued to the hill.

I look from where he's looking and back to him. "What happened?"

"I was going too fast. My tires hit the gravel the wrong way and I caught air." He cringes, balling one hand in a fist. "It rolled, almost going into the water right down there." He points again to a little spot dotted with tall grasses.

"You're lucky to be alive," I gasp.

He nods, forcing a swallow. "I am. It's one of those blessings Mom used to talk about. Out of a really ugly situation came one positive. I survived."

Reaching out, not sure who needs the contact more, I place my hand on his arm. I feel him relax beneath my touch, but he doesn't say a word about it.

Instead, he takes a deep breath. "I ... um .. I was dating a girl then. Britt was her name. And she broke up with me right after that."

"Good for you," I tell him. "She sounds like a jerk."

The car fills with a silence that comes right before a shoe drops. The air is heavy, pregnant, even, and I can barely breathe through the weight of it all.

I drop my hand as he puts the car in park and flips off the ignition. I consider getting out and walking back to town because I'm not sure if I want to hear whatever it is he's going to say.

"Lance—"

"A couple more minutes. *Please*," he chokes out. He waits for me to indicate my willingness to hear him out before continuing. "You don't deserve to think that me telling you this won't work out between us has anything to do with you."

"Lance, stop it."

"I should've been completely honest with you. I thought ... I thought I was protecting us both by just walking away. I'd keep you from having to make a hard choice and me from having to hurt my ego a little."

"What are you talking about?" I ask, my heart threatening to beat so hard it sends me into cardiac arrest. The uncertainty about where he's going with this is killing me and my hand is on the door to get out of the car. It feels too cramped in here, too small, not nearly big enough for whatever this bomb is that's going to fall.

"Britt left me because I couldn't meet the conditions she had for her life. She, like you," he says, eyeing me carefully, "wanted the entire thing—marriage, a little house ... a family."

"I don't understand ..."

The gorgeous green eyes I love blur with unshed tears. It causes mine to react the same way, even though I don't know why.

I grab his hand, holding it in my own, even though I shouldn't. Even though I know better than to get any more tangled up with this man who's already broken my heart once.

"Mariah ..." He looks at me completely unguarded. Completely broken. "I can't have kids."

I feel myself flinch, hear the rush of a swallow drop into my stomach. "What?"

"The accident fucked me up." He hesitates. "I'm sterile."

Sterile.

I sort through my mental dictionary and make sure I'm not confusing that word with another. This is not a word you mistake and react to incorrectly.

As it dawns on me what he's saying, his features smoothen into an emotionless mask, it breaks my heart. This is why he lied to me by omission.

"Oh, Lance," I say, the words bound up together as I force them by my lips.

He works a finger around the inside corner of his eye and then around his nose. He sniffles, like he's just clearing out his nostrils, but I hear the fear, the sadness.

I reach across the console, my arms going around his neck. Right or wrong, I can't stop myself from hugging this beautiful, broken man as a tear slips down his cheek. He squeezes me so tight I can barely breathe, but I'm positive I don't need air to survive right now. I just need him and for him to know I'm here.

We sit for a long time wrapped in each other's arms. A truck goes by all too fast, rocking Lance's car back and forth. We just sway along with it, unable, or unwilling, to pull apart.

With a kiss to the spot just below his earlobe, I finally lean back. My heart is so swollen it puts pressure on every other organ in my chest. Brushing a strand of hair off his forehead, I search his eyes.

"Fuck her," I say, trying to get him to smile. "There are so many ways to build a family. Fuck her for not seeing that."

His forehead creases as he now leans away from me. "I can't blame anyone for wanting kids."

"Then she didn't love you." I fall back into my seat, my eyes blinking back tears. This time, they're for me.

I wouldn't have left him after the accident. I wouldn't have left him if it left him in a wheelchair and I had to take care of him every day for the rest of my life. Because even if that were my day, it would still be a day with him.

Tears slip down my cheeks, burning hot as they fall to my shirt.

Why can't he love me as much as he loved her?

"I'm sorry," he whispers. "Now you see why I didn't tell you."

"Well, I'll hate her for the rest of my life." I dab my eyes with the neck line of my shirt. "She gets to walk away with your heart and—"

"Woah," he says, shifting in his seat. "Hold up."

"No. It doesn't seem fair."

He presses his lips together. "What doesn't seem fair, Mariah?"

"That you still love her." My words are woven in the emotion pouring from my heart, the tears flooding my lips as I try to speak. "That she gets to break your heart and ..."

I stop talking when he starts laughing. It's not one of his belly laughs like I'm ridiculous. It's more like he's in disbelief.

"What?" I ask, sniffling.

"Mariah, this isn't about her."

"No, it's about you," I acknowledge.

"No. This is about *you*." He looks at me, puzzled. "You are the blessing in all of this, even if I didn't see it like that before." He shakes his head, like his thoughts aren't coming together right. "I didn't tell you this before because, for one, it's kind of humiliating in a way."

I watch him bite his lip, flex his fingers and wonder what it felt like to tell me that. If the roles were reversed, I think I'd be terrified. I'd feel ... like something was wrong with me, even though logically that's just ridiculous.

"Why?" I ask, dumbfounded. "It's like me being embarrassed because I have small boobs. I can't help it."

He shakes his head, almost laughing. "It's not the same, crazy lady, but okay. We'll go with that for now."

I shrug.

"I ..." He looks down. "I love you. And I thought if you loved me too, you'd have to pick between me and having a baby someday."

I don't move. I don't even blink. I'm not sure I even breathe.

He loves me?

He loves me.

It's a few seconds before I realize he's still talking and I've heard none of it.

"Hey, Lance," I interrupt, waving my hand in the air. "I'm still back there on the *you love me* part."

"Yeah? What about it?" He stares at me. "You didn't hear anything I said after that, did you?"

"Nope." I crawl across the console, wedging myself between him and the steering wheel.

He laughs, moving the seat backwards so I'm not hitting the horn with my butt. I get settled, his hands locked at my waist. We're eye-to-eye with no place to go.

"There," I say. "Now let's go back to that part."

"I love you."

I must beam or do something similar because he laughs.

"This conversation was me explaining to you how I can't ask you to choose between me and your conditions."

I brush his hair back with my palm, searching his eyes for something to make me resist. Or hesitate. Or not trust him. All I see is a man who's asking to be loved despite his imperfections.

It seems silly that he'd think I'd hold his imperfections against him. Lord knows I have my own. I have terrible bedhead in the morning, I fall in love too fast, and I need to hold his hand whenever he's remotely close.

It all makes sense why he didn't tell me and although it frustrates me and we'll definitely have a conversation about it later, it's not what I want to focus on now. Right now? He needs me. And I need him.

"Good. Don't ask. I'll choose on my own." I kiss the top of his nose. "I pick you. We'll craft our life together."

"You need to think about this, Mariah."

"Are you telling me that if I were to develop ovarian cancer and couldn't have babies, you'd leave me?"

"No." His answer is quick. Sharp. Decided.

"Then why would you think I'm so shallow that I would basically do the same to you. That hurts."

He pulls me to him, closing the half an inch that separates us, until there's no air left between our bodies.

"This hurts a little too," I grumble.

He pops open the door with one hand. I climb off him and into the afternoon breeze. He never lets go of my hand.

The air smells of water and dirt and my hair is going haywire in the wind. He takes both of my hands in his and pulls me close.

"I love you," I tell him. "In case I haven't said that."

"I've known that for a long time. I mean, how could you not?"

Snorting, I let him bend me backwards in a long, leisurely kiss. Once I'm upright again, I take a deep breath.

"If Britt comes back, you're done with her, right?" I tease.

"Who is she?"

Laughing, I snuggle against his chest. His heartbeat is steady, predictable, as we sway back and forth in the middle of the road.

"Are you sure you're okay with this?" he asks.

"I'm sure if you ask me that again, I'm going to throat punch you." His chest shakes under my cheek. "If this works out between us, think of all the kids we could adopt. Kids like Ollie. We could have a house full of them."

He kisses the top of my head.

"I do have one condition though," I say, looking up at him.

"Good. Me too."

"You first."

"The lock on your door has got to go," he growls. "I've never been so pissed off in my life."

Laughing, I watch as our fingers lace together. "Fine. Joe won't be happy he has to take it right back off, but I'll make it happen."

"I'll take it off. It'll make my day."

"Fine. Done. Now my turn." A nervous wiggle spirals through me. "I don't want to be the kind of woman who tells you what to do. And I'm not sneaky and snoopy because if I have to do that, I don't want to be with you anyway."

"Just tell me what it is," he chuckles.

My cheeks heat. "I want you to delete the app."

"I already did."

"Really?" I ask, not sure I believe him. "I didn't mean to see it on your phone when we were baking with Ollie, but it was sitting there and an update came on and ..."

"And that's when I deleted it. I hadn't used it since you messaged me there last and the update notification reminded me I still had it."

Swinging our hands back and forth, I breathe in the clean,

country air. I'm not sure if it's that, or Lance's cologne, or the way he presses a kiss up the side of my neck, but I tug him back toward the car.

"What are you doing?" he laughs, following me.

"You need to take me home. Your ten minutes are up."

He spins me around and pins me against the side of his car. "If I wasn't completely clear, I want you. Only you. For as long as you'll have me." ·

I don't respond because I can't. My throat is too tight, my eyes too watery, my mind too buzzed by the look in his eyes.

This man, Lance Gibson, the man I've wanted and fantasized about since the first day I met him, the man who promised me he'd never settle down with one woman, loves me.

Me.

How this is even happening, I don't know. The last few months feel like a blur but the only thing that matters is he's standing in front of me, imploring me to listen.

I'll listen. I'll listen as long as he'll speak.

"Nana told me to search for happiness in the right places. I've never been happier than when I'm with you," he whispers.

As I take in the two of us, I realize how sometimes the most complicated relationships really aren't all that complicated. At the core, Lance and I love each other. Everything else is just noise.

"There have been a lot of dark times in my life," he says. "I prayed for a lot of things and didn't get many of them. Now I see why."

"Why is that?"

"They were all a path to get me to you, so I'd be the right man for you when I met you. Without the accident and Britt leaving and even my parents' death in a lot of ways, I wouldn't be the same person I am today." A slow grin slides across his lips. "I wouldn't be nearly as smart."

"Is that so?"

"Or as handsome," he adds.

"Right."

"Or as charming." He takes my hand and guides me around the car. "I'm about to say something I never thought I'd say."

"Oh, I can't wait for this," I say, looking at him.

"We're in a word ending in ship, right?"

"A relationship?" I tease. "If you'd like to ensure I don't call the coach back and take him up on his offer of dinner ..."

"I'll kill him," he growls.

My giggle pierces the air. "Then I guess we are."

"I guess we are ..." His voice trails off as he goes to the front. He pauses by the hood and looks at the hill that changed his life. Then he looks at me and grins. It's that look, one filled with a soft strength, that changed mine.

Chapter 33

Mariah

The door to my house swings open. Lance is behind me, his hand on the small of my back. I don't think he's broken contact since he got back in the car.

We step inside and he closes the door behind us; the Mandarin orange candle I burned last night scents the air.

"Two things," Lance says, taking a moment to take in my living room. "Make it three."

"Okay."

"First, let's reiterate we're exclusive. No apps, no coaches, no random men or women in the grocery store that ask for our numbers. Cool?"

I grin. "Does that happen to you often?"

"Look at me. Of course, it does," he winks. "It's actually never happened to me there, but I wanted to cover all our bases."

"I can agree to that."

"Good. Number two," he says, sauntering over to the window. His muscles work under his shirt, the light hits it just perfectly so I can see every ripple in the fabric. "We have to be honest. Maybe that's a normal requirement in a relationship," he cringes, "but with the divorce rate as high as it is in this country, I'm not sure."

"I've been honest with you. It's you who's been the little omitter."

"No omissions," he says, turning around. The sincerity on his face slays me. "We have to make this work and ground rules at the beginning seem the smartest way to go."

"What's number three?" I ask.

"That I can touch you any time I want," he grins, stalking towards me.

He lugs me against him, his body as solid as a rock. His kiss is slow, methodical, his breath hot against my mouth. He works his tongue across my bottom lip and I melt in his arms.

"Hey," I giggle, as he presses kisses across my jaw. "I have a thing too."

"What's that?" he asks against my throat.

I pause to release a moan as his hands grip the globes of my ass. "I'm not sure you're going to like this one," I tease.

He jolts me forward, pressing a wet, loud kiss to my lips. When he pulls back, his eyes are wild, just a few seconds from losing control.

"What is it?" he asks.

Stepping back, feeling his gaze scald my skin, I lift the hem of my shirt over my head. His eyes get darker, broodier, as I get wetter. I'm tempted to stop all of this and just race into my bedroom, knowing he'd follow, but I enjoy this feeling a little too much. Besides, the rest will come soon enough.

"Well," I say, slipping off my shoes and hooking my thumbs under the waistband of my sweatpants. "Since we've been honest with each other and we're firmly in a word ending in -ship," I say, "I'd like an agreement we don't use condoms."

He closes the distance between us in a half a second, picking me up before my pants are even off my feet.

"Lance!" I giggle, my legs thrown across his arms. "Stop it."

"You're driving me crazy on purpose." He kisses me as he heads down the hall, my feet knocking a sconce off the wall on the way. He doesn't care. Neither do I.

I'm tossed on the bed. The pillows bounce along with me as I look up at him. He stands next to the bed, his clothes coming off as quickly as he can possibly shed them.

"Is that okay?" I ask, working the latch of my bra free. "I really like the feeling of your cock sliding into me."

He crawls across the bed, his shoulders flexing. My mouth goes dry as I part my legs so he can hover over me.

"I hope you like it," he whispers. "I'm going to be sliding into you for a long fucking time."

Raising my hips, I lock my heels at the small of his sculpted back. "What are you waiting for?"

He presses into me, filling me inch-by-inch. This time it's different.

It's not simply a give and take of pleasure, an exchange of satisfying sensations like it was before. It's not a kiss here, a stroke there, a lick for good measure—a "I need you right now" type of thing that has a start and an end.

As he touches me, and not just on my skin but rather in places untouchable by the hand, he reaffirms the things he's told me, the things he's all but promised me.

He shows me he thinks I'm beautiful, tells me I'm worthy. Not just of him, but of the one part of yourself you can give to only one person—his love. He caresses me tenderly and slams into me without mercy, owning me and building me and giving me the freedom to explore who I am in the safe bounds of his arms.

This is different. A prelude to something else.

And when he looks at me and gives me that cocky smirk, I laugh.

"This is nothing to laugh at," he warns as he shoves himself completely inside my body.

"I wasn't laughing at you. Or at this," I add, raising up and kissing his shoulder.

"Then what were you laughing at?"

I don't know how to explain, especially in this moment, that it was a laugh of joy. Of pleasure. Of feeling this comfortable in my skin.

Instead, I look at the vaguely purple circle on his shoulder. "I was thinking of biting you in my mother's pantry."

He rolls over, bringing me with him and positioning me so I'm straddling him. "You know what?" he asks, his voice gravely.

"What's that?"

"I think I loved you then."

I capture his lips with mine. He sinks back into me.

The sun sets long before we're finished. My stomach growls, the only part of me not satiated, as I curl up under his arm and close my eyes.

His breathing behind me is steady, his heart beating at my back in a gentle, continuous strum. I look out the window at the stars sparkling in the sky and fall into a peaceful, easy sleep.

Epilogue

L^{ance}

"Peck! Come on," Nana hollers out the door.

The rest of the family settles at the kitchen table, ready to dig in to a Sunday dinner of fried chicken. Machlan grabs a drumstick, bringing it to his mouth as discreetly as he can.

"Don't you think about it," Nana warns him, swatting the back of his head as she walks by. "We haven't said grace."

Machlan posts an argument, mostly for Nana's benefit. She loves that Machlan loves her fried chicken—she told everyone at church today she'd have a hard time keeping him out of it until dinner was ready. This is his way of humoring her, making her feel good.

I look to my right, at the beautiful woman moving Nana's water glass so she doesn't spill it as she sits down.

It's been a few weeks since the start of our relationship and the fact that the word almost makes me happy is still so weird. But if that's what it takes to keep Mariah in my bed, in my bathtub, in my car for quick make-out sessions during lunch breaks, then so be it.

Sometimes I look at her while she's sleeping or reading a book and wonder how in the hell I got so lucky. That she, a smart, kind, classy woman would take an animal like me as her own. An animal like me just the way I am.

I grab her hand as she sits back down and pull it to my lap. She smiles, used to it by now, because I can't help myself but to touch her when she's near. It's not always a sexual thing, which surprises me as much as anyone. Just the feel of her skin reminds me she's real, she's mine, and she wants me. It's like the best Christmas present ever every time it happens.

Peck comes in, Cross at his side.

"I didn't know you were coming," Nana says, pointing towards a chair by the window. "Get a chair."

"I'll get you a plate, Cross," Sienna offers.

"Let him get his own damn plate," Walker says.

"If he goes in there, he'll make a mess and Nana will end up going after him and then Machlan will eat the chicken and Lance will pop something off to Peck and they'll go at it," Sienna says, making us all laugh. "I'm saving everyone time, babe."

She gets to her feet and disappears into the kitchen, returning with a yellow plate for Cross.

"Thanks," he says, smiling sheepishly, knowing he'll get the raw end of this later from Walker.

Peck removes his hat and says grace as is customary on Sunday afternoons. Mariah leans close, her head on my shoulder, as I trace a little heart with the pad of my thumb on the top of her hand.

"Did you make these rolls?" Walker asks, looking at Mariah as we pass the plates of food around the table.

"I did," she beams. "It was my grandmother's recipe."

"They're great." He stuffs a half a roll in his mouth, much to Sienna's chagrin.

"I got the recipe, but I'm not making them if you're going to eat like a barbarian."

Walker chuckles. "I thought you liked when I ate like a barbarian."

I choke on my potato as Machlan bursts into laughter.

"Ha," he says, covering his mouth with a napkin. "Getting a little risqué there, aren't you Walk?"

Sienna's beet red as she tries desperately to change the subject. "Want to go to the lake with me this weekend?" she asks Mariah.

"Sure," Mariah replies, looking at me. "We have dinner with my sister and her husband on Saturday night. I could try to get out of that."

I flash her a huge, annoying smile. "No. We are having dinner with Chrissy and Eric."

Sienna laughs. "I don't want to know what that's about."

"It's about me trying to reconcile with my sister," Mariah says, rolling her eyes at me. "Lance's idea."

"Lance's great idea," I insist, sitting back in my seat so she can see Sienna again.

"We could leave in the morning and be back by late afternoon, if that works?" Sienna asks.

"I'd love to," Mariah says. "Maybe Lance can get Walker to come over and help put up our new bed."

"Break it already?" Cross asks, picking out a chicken thigh. "You work fast, Lance."

"No comment," Machlan says, stuffing his mouth full of potatoes as I glare his way.

Peck signals my attention and winks when I look at him. "Hey, Cross. I heard at the gas station Hadley is coming to town."

All eyes go to Machlan. He takes a slow, deliberate sip of water and does not look at Peck or Cross.

Cross clears his throat. "Well, she called this morning and said she'd be coming to town next weekend for Homecoming. I just, uh, hadn't had time to tell y'all, really."

Machlan shoves away from the table.

"Machlan, where are you going?" Nana shouts after him.

"Let him go," Walker tells her "Better he break shit outside than do it in here."

"Watch your mouth, Walker," she chastises him. "Maybe you should go check on him."

"I'm not." Cross shakes his head. "I'm always the bad guy when it comes to those two. Sick and tired of it."

Peck rolls his eyes as he gets to his feet. He searches for the plate of fried chicken only to find it empty. So, he takes a chicken leg off Machlan's plate. "I'll go find him."

"You're a good boy, Peck," Nana tells him.

"Sienna, you know who to call if I need medical attention," Peck sighs before disappearing around the corner.

I settle back in my chair and take in my family. Walker and Cross are explaining the Hadley situation the best they can to Sienna and Mariah while Nana talks about antique china.

This is a situation I never thought I'd be in, one I didn't really know I wanted to be in. I was always the observer, always the one not quite participating.

My arm lays across the back of Mariah's chair, her hair brushing against my arm. As I watch her laugh at a lame joke Nana made about banana bread, I think of all the things I'll tell her tonight when we get home. How I noticed the swell of her breasts as she passed out pamphlets at church. How I heard old man Dave talking about her to the farmers in the parking lot of the gas station. How I read somewhere that you can't understand the word unconditional if you don't understand conditions. How you can't truly fall in love with someone if you don't love yourself first.

It took me being me—the real me, the flawed version I thought no one would ever want—to be open enough to love.

Maybe there's something to that.

Mariah turns in her chair, her hand cupping my cock under the tablecloth.

I look at her like it's hard to believe she's my girl. Because it is and she will be until the day I die.

I'll tell her all those things after I fuck her. Because, after all, I'm still me.

THE END

CRAVE, Machlan Gibson's story, is live now on Amazon, Audible, and free with Kindle Unlimited. Keep reading for Chapter One ...

Chapter One
Hadley

"This is the best idea I've ever had," I say to myself. "Or it might be the worst."

I park my car along the curb a few spaces down from Crave. The bar sits in front of me with its crooked 'a' hanging sideways on the sign. Some of the red tube lights used to form the letters are bright, while others are dim, and I wonder if I should just re-start my car and go back home.

"No," I say aloud. "You have to do this."

The sun hovers over the horizon. The sky is spectacular with bright oranges and deep purples. Sunsets are one of my favorite things in the world, but I can't enjoy this one. There are too many distractions.

Like how I didn't tell my brother, Cross, I was coming to visit a night early.

And how I forgot my toothbrush and cell phone charger back at my apartment.

And how the underwire in the push-up bra that's supposed to make me confident is actually poking a hole in the side of my boob.

Distractions abound, and I haven't even made it to the biggest distraction of all—the one with deep chocolate brown eyes and a smirk I usually want to punch off his handsome face.

Machlan Gibson. The man I'm here to convince myself I can live without.

He might tie up my insides without trying. He might've been my first kiss and my first unofficial date—the first boy I snuck out of the house to meet in the middle of the night. He might know more about me than anyone in the world and be the one person with whom I hold the most secrets.

But it doesn't matter. Not to him. And it can't to me anymore.

Every time I come back to Linton, Illinois, I hope it's the visit I stay for good. That Machlan will see what we can be, wrap me up in his arms, and ask me to work things out.

I've had that hope for years. That ends now.

This time, I'm over him. Or I will be before I leave. Somehow.

Taking a deep breath, I look back at the sign hanging askew. "You can do this," I prep myself. "Just go in, lay some groundwork, and get out before you get in over your head."

My sneakers hit the asphalt before I can rethink this entire thing. My stomach squeezes so hard I think I might have to sit back down.

Straightening my shirt, I pull a deep, steadying breath. The only indication of how wobbly I am on the inside is the way the little four-leaf clover necklace vibrates on my chest. "I've got this."

"You got what?"

I spin around, hand covering my heart, and find Peck leaning on the hood of my car. My friend since the day I met him, he's also Machlan's cousin. Ridiculously charming with his blond hair poking out the sides of his baseball cap, he has a smile that could end a world war.

"I got your number, that's what I got," I say with a laugh. "What are you doing, troublemaker?"

"Oh, just seeing what this cute little redhead was doing talking to herself. Then I realized it was you and I was like, 'Eh, I don't really need a trip to the ER tonight.'"

I know what he's getting at. Machlan *is* at Crave.

I pop him in the shoulder. He winces, humoring me, before shoving off the car and following me as I head down the sidewalk.

"What brought you back to town?" Peck asks. "Haven't seen you in a while."

I gaze at the horizon and the way the sun is barely visible over the tree line. I wish I were on Bluebird Hill watching it go down.

"Do you remember that tire swing we put up on Bluebird Hill?" I ignore his question and ask one of my own. "Is it still there?"

"I think so." He takes off his hat emblazoned with a machinery company's logo and runs a hand over his head. "I haven't been up there in a while. The last time ended up with my truck being buried up to the axle in mud and me having to call Machlan to come get it out at two in the morning." He grins sheepishly. "I'll let you guess how that call went."

My feet stop moving, so Peck halts too. We stand a few feet from the doors to Crave. His eyes search mine in a way only capable someone you've known for a long time can.

"He's in there," he says, motioning toward the door with his head.

"I hope so."

Peck's brow furrows. "Not the answer I was expecting."

"Why else would I show up here?"

"Don't you guys usually try to do this behind closed doors?" Peck asks.

"Do what?"

He runs his tongue along his bottom lip before biting down to withhold a grin. It doesn't work. I roll my eyes at both his question and reaction and head toward the door.

Whatever happens once I'm inside Crave will be fine. Either he'll serve me a drink or he'll be a major ass—either option I can work with in my plan to get over Machlan Gibson.

"Are you ignoring me?" Peck asks.

"I just want a drink," I lie.

"And what do you drink these days?" he prods, seeing through my lie. I've never been much of a drinker, and I'm definitely not the kind of girl to just stop by a bar for a drink—this bar, no less.

My mind races to come up with a drink I've heard my friends order, all the while trying not to let Peck see how hard my heart is racing and the sweat glistening on my palms. "I'm drinking a tequila and Coke."

Peck chuckles behind me. "Can I give you one quick tip?"

"No."

With a deep breath, I step into the building. Antique lanterns on the ceilings and various Christmas lights strung around the building illuminate the bar. I hold my breath before allowing the scent to hit me. It's the smell of desperation and sweat, of a thousand spilled beers and even more bad decisions. It's like perfume on your man that isn't yours: repulsive.

"Fine then," Peck says. "But when Machlan laughs his ass off because no one has ever, in the history of the universe, ordered a tequila and Coke, don't say I didn't warn you."

My cheeks burn. "Oh."

"Rum and Coke or tequila shots. Not tequila and Coke, Had." He shoves his hands in the pockets of his worn jeans as he eyes me with amusement. "But do the rum and Coke. You'd be a mess on tequila, and while I'd pay a lot of money to watch Machlan lose his shit over that, I'm not sure he'll even serve it to you."

"He has to if I order it," I say.

Peck leans back and releases a full-belly laugh. "You tell him that."

"I will." Looking him in his bright, blue eyes, I almost lose my courage and tell him to get me the hell out of here. He would. He'd take me to Goodman's, buy me a sweet tea, and drive me around as I spilled my guts. But I can't do that to him. Or me.

This wasn't a spur-of-the-moment decision. It's been a long time coming, and I finally broke down last week and realized it had to be done. I have to figure out how to move on with my life. I can't put roots down somewhere else and allow myself to fall in love or really start a life when my heart is still here. With Machlan.

Peck's face breaks into a sympathetic smile. "Take my advice and order the rum and Coke. You have a shot at getting that. Though it's a small one, it's better than your tequila chances, which are negative sixteen hundred."

"I don't understand why you don't think he'll serve me."

"Rhubarb moonshine mean anything to you?" He makes a face reminiscent of someone dying before heading toward the bar.

I stand next to the bulletin boards lining the front wall, thinking about the night with the moonshine. How Mach and I got into a huge fight and I didn't realize what moonshine was. And how he picked me up and took me home and stayed with me all night to make sure I didn't pass out in my own vomit.

Besides the people playing pool in the back, the only other patrons drinking are seated near the old jukebox. As my gaze runs across a pair of pink panties pinned to the top of one of the bulletin boards, it settles on Peck. He waves at me to join him.

His merriment at my situation is written all over his face. I hope confidence masks the fear on mine. No matter how I get to the end result, this is going to hurt.

No, this is going to be hell.

I make my way over the cement floors. A man wearing a sleeve of tattoos and an undeniable invitation tickling his lips passes me. He turns around and whistles as he walks backward to the door.

This helps.

My confidence slightly bolstered, I look back at the bar.

This *doesn't* help.

My feet shuffle, nearly tripping over an invisible boulder in my way as Machlan's lips form a thin, hard line. His arms cross his thick chest.

Even with the cool reception, my cheeks still heat.

Machlan sure knows how to make hell feel like home.

Crave is now available on Amazon, in Kindle Unlimited, and Audible!

About the Author

Adriana Locke is a USA Today and Amazon Charts Bestselling author with a knack for writing swoony, unforgettable contemporary romances. At nineteen, she traded her small-town roots for big-city life, only to realize her heart beats for quiet mornings and cozy chaos. These days, she's living her happily-ever-after in Ohio with Mr. Locke—her high school sweetheart—four lively sons, and two hilariously hyper Jack Russell terriers.

When she's not penning love stories that will leave you laughing and sighing, Adriana is battling the epic quest of missing silverware, "gardening" (a.k.a. chatting with her plants), or leaving her grocery list on the counter as she heads to the store. Grab a cup of coffee, settle in, and let her books whisk you away to a world of heartwarming romance and irresistible heroes.

Join her reader group and talk all the bookish things by clicking here.

www.adrianalocke.com

Acknowledgments

As always, first and foremost, thank you to the Creator for all my blessings. Sometimes I forget that they aren't always the "pretties" of my life, but I've been keeping an open mind. I'm grateful for them all.

A huge hug to Mr. Locke and our four Little Lockes. You are the real champions. You fill me with love and light and laughs, enough to write sixteen books (so far). Our family is my greatest accomplishment. I love you all.

It's hard writing about a mother like Mariah's when you have a mother like me. Mama, you're the best. No matter what you're going through, I always come first ... even now when I've been twenty-nine for a number of years. I thank God that you're my mom.

I lucked out hard when I married my husband. He's great and all, but so is his family. Massive hugs to Peggy and Rob for their endless support and patience as I forget to return calls and respond to texts. I love you guys.

My team makes this all possible. Kari March, Tiffany Remy, Jen Costa, Susan Rayner, Carleen Riffle, Kara Hildebrand, Michele Ficht — thank you for your dedication to everything I do. You are all brilliant in your own way and I'm eternally blessed to not only call you teammates, but friends in every sense of the word.

Mandi Beck is awesome. Read her books.

Mara White didn't quite know what she was getting when she signed on for this project. God love her soul. Thank you, sweet lady, for ploughing through this with the patience and grace of a saint. I'm in awe of you in so many ways.

Becca Mysoor is sunshine through and through. She also leaves the funniest notes in my documents and tells me when she's not "feeling" it. Thank you for helping me deal with Lance. The bastard.

Ebbie Moresco keeps Books by Adriana Locke moving and Kaitie Reister is the admin-in-chief of All Locked UP. Thank you ladies for your time, your sweet dispositions, and your dedication to making our groups feel like home to so many.

Working with Give Me Books again was a treat. Thank you for treating this project the way you do with each one: with great courtesy, commitment, and kindness.

Bloggers are the link that brings books from authors to readers. Thank you for all you do. Thank you for your passion for these stories and the time you spend reading and reviewing. I appreciate you.

Books by Adriana Locke is my Facebook group and also my happy place. Filled with the most amazing women (and a few men), it's a concentration of laughs, support, and love. Thank you for being just as an important member of my team as anyone.

And you, the person reading this—thank you. I appreciate your willingness to try Craft. I hope you enjoyed it.

Xo, Adriana